PEEP SHOW

VOLUME 2

NOV 11, 2012

PEEP SHOW
VOLUME 2

EDITED BY PAUL FRY

SST

Short, Scary Tales Publications
Birmingham, England

- 2012 -

ISBN: 978-0-9542523-6-6

2012 SST Publications Trade Paperback Edition

Published by Short, Scary Tales Publications
15 North Roundhay, Stechford, Birmingham, B33 9PE, England

sstpublications.co.uk

Typeset by Paul Fry
Printed in the United Kingdom, United States of America and Australia
First Edition: November 2012
10 9 8 7 6 5 4 3 2 1

Dedicated to
the memory of Richard Laymon,
a true master of erotic horror fiction

Table of Contents

The Farm House   11
Jeremy Terry

The Silkworm Moth Effect   22
Gene O'Neill

Under Nighttime Rainbows   37
Savannah

Pixie Cut   45
Allen Dusk

The Misfits of Mayhem Meet Their Match   60
John Claude Smith

Curfew   69
Eric Red

Blood, Sex and Eternity   84
Florence Ann Marlowe

Little Miss Sanguine   119
Terry "Horns" Erwin

The Line-Up at Buddy Milam's Trailer   126
Walter Jarvis

Legacy of the Bokor   140
Walt Hicks

The Eye of the Devil is Brown   157
Owen Z. Burnett

The House of Pain   168
Wayne C. Rogers

For the Love of Death   190
Deb Eskie

A Head Full of Hell   197
Mark Zirbel

Imitation is the Sincerest Form of Flattery   205
Vi Reaper

Biographies   228

PEEP SHOW
VOLUME 2

The Farm House

Jeremy Terry

The rain fell in sheets, blanketing the world. Each drop that struck the roof of the small car was like a small bomb going off right over Scott and Tara's heads. A bolt of lightning flashed across the sky, turning the night into day, illuminating the interior of the vehicle. Scott looked over at his wife and frowned. She was running a shaky hand through her long, dirty-blonde hair and using the other to push her glasses back into their accustomed place on the bridge of her nose. The eyes that peered from behind the lenses were dark with worry, but still beautiful for all of that. Scott turned his eyes back to the rain-soaked blacktop, scratching the two day old stubble that looked at home on his tanned cheeks. Thunder crashed a moment later, rattling the windows with its might. "Shit!" cried Tara, jumping against her seatbelt. Scott had to bite his lower lip to stop himself from laughing.

"Scott?" she asked.

"Hmm?"

"We need to stop."

"If we stop now, we'll be late for the rehearsal."

"But, it's not safe," she said. "You can barely see the road as it is and the storm is getting worse."

"Tara, it's fine."

Tara stared at her husband a moment longer, feeling the sting of hot tears in the corners of her eyes, and then turned away. She looked out the rain-streaked window into the night, seeing scenes from earlier in the day play out in the mud and wet. They had had another fight, a bad one, and now they were both being stubborn, neither wanting to take the first step towards making things right again.

Scott leaned forward in his seat, willing his eyes to see through the wall of rain falling in front of him. Why did he snap at her? It was stupid and mean and she didn't deserve it. Hell, she was probably right anyway. They should stop and wait for the storm to pass or at least let up a bit. If he kept going like this there was a good chance they would end up in the ditch or wrapped around a tree on the side of the road. He smiled to himself, remembering a time, not too long ago, when he would have been more than happy to be stranded on the side of a deserted road with her. They could have crawled into the backseat and got up to no good. It would have been even better if a cop had pulled up and caught them in the buff. That would have been exciting, an adventure in the middle of a normal, mundane day. What happened to those times? Is it my fault? Hers? Both of ours?

The wind gusted, rocking the little car on its springs. Scott shook his head to clear it and turned on the radio. He pressed the scan button and let it cycle through the channels until he found a weather report.

". . . to repeat, the National Weather Service in Tallahassee has issued a Tornado Warning for Jackson County . . ."

Tara whirled away from the window, panic shining in her eyes, "Scott!"

"Shhh," he said.

". . . is ten miles southeast of Marianna, Florida and is moving north at twenty miles per hour . . ."

"Scott! That's right on top of us!"

"We're okay, we're—"

A fierce gust of wind struck the car, the strongest yet, and pushed them towards the center of the road. Scott jerked the wheel to the right and felt the tires lose traction and begin to hydroplane. He watched in horror, helpless, as the car slid into the ditch, burying the front end in three feet of water.

"Oww!" moaned Tara, her hand going to her forehead where she could feel the beginnings of a large lump forming where the dashboard had met her face. Hesitantly, she pulled her hand away and looked for blood. Seeing none, she turned to check on her husband.

"Scott? You okay?"

He lifted his head off of the steering wheel and smiled at her, "Yeah, I think so. You?"

"My head hurts, but I'm okay. You sure you're okay?"

"Yeah," said Scott, looking himself over once, "I'm sure."

"Good," said Tara, balling up her fist and punching him hard on the arm.

"Hey!" shouted Scott, leaning away from her against the door, "Knock it off!"

"If you had pulled over when I told you too, we wouldn't be in this mess!"

"Do you really want to sit here and play the blame game right now?"

Tara looked out into the dark, stormy night and shook her head, "What are we going to do?"

"Call your brother," said Scott, "see if he can come pick us up."

Tara dug through her purse and pulled out her cell phone. She flicked it open and stared in dismay at the tiny screen which read "No Service."

"That's just great!" she said, "Now what?"

"We find a phone," said Scott, undoing his safety belt and opening his door.

"Find a phone? We are in the middle of the fucking woods!"

Lightning flashed, a brilliant purple arc that connected sky to ground, and they both saw the house. It was fifty yards up the road, a two story farm house with peeling white paint and dark windows. There was a huge oak tree growing in the front yard with an old tire swing swaying back and forth in the strong wind.

"See?" said Scott, a smug smile on his face, "I bet they have a phone." He reached under the driver's seat and pulled out a small flashlight. "Come on," he said.

Tara sighed and opened her door, getting drenched to the bone the instant she stepped out into the frigid downpour. They ran up the road, side by side, the rain drops stinging their skin with each impact, and came to a skidding halt on the front porch of the house, out of breath and cold.

"Hello?" called Scott, knocking on the door.

There was no answer.

"The grass hasn't been mowed in a long time, Scott. I don't think anybody lives here."

Scott tried the doorknob, it twisted easily. He pushed the door open and peered into the dark interior of the house. Nothing moved. He turned on the flashlight and stepped inside, followed reluctantly by Tara. They were standing in a long, damp hallway with rough wooden floors and wallpaper that was faded to a non-color, its original design lost to the ravages of time. There were wide archways to their left and right, each opening onto spacious rooms, and a hallway straight ahead that ran alongside the narrow stairs to the second floor and led to the back of the old house.

"Hello!" called Scott, his voice reverberating back to them from the empty rooms, "Is anyone there?"

"Just stop it, Scott. There's nobody here."

"I had to try," he said, turning to her.

"Whatever. So what do we do now?"

He shrugged, "We wait for the storm to pass and hope that the tornado doesn't come our way."

"Oh, joy," said Tara, shivering in the gloom. She turned away from Scott, fighting the depression and anger that was trying to take hold inside her. Looking out into the still blackness of the deserted house didn't help ease her mood.

Something moved near the top of the stairs.

Tara froze, starring into the shadows, but there was nothing to see, the landing on the second floor was empty. *Wonderful,* she thought, *now I'm seeing things. Can this night get any worse?*

There was a scratching noise to her left. She turned to see Scott kneeling in front of a fireplace, coaxing a small pile of wood into flames with an ancient book of matches. She stepped into the room and picked the flashlight up, cradling it in her arms. "Where did you find the matches?"

"They were sitting on the mantle," said Scott, not taking his attention off of the burning wood.

"And the wood?"

He shrugged, "It was already here."

"Doesn't that seem a little odd to you? You just happen to find a book of matches and a pile of wood in a fireplace that hasn't been used in years."

"Not really. I'm happy to have the fire so I can get dry. Don't look a gift horse in the mouth as the saying goes. Come on, baby, sit down and warm up."

"Fine," said Tara, sitting down beside her husband. Minutes passed by with the two sitting shoulder to shoulder, neither one speaking. Finally, Scott cleared his throat, breaking the silence, "Well, this is cozy."

Tara laughed, "Cozy? You're having fun, aren't you?"

"Yeah, a little," he replied. "Why? Aren't you?"

"No, I'm not."

"Oh, come on, Tara," said Scott, putting his arm around her shoulders. "This could be just what we need. All alone in a deserted farmhouse, rain falling on the roof, and us cuddled up in front of a roaring fire. You gotta admit it's kind of romantic."

"If you say so," she said, turning her back to him.

"Don't be like that, babe," he said, wrapping his arms around her body, one hand lightly brushing her left breast. "I'm sorry for hurting you. I'm sorry for the hurtful things that I said and for being stupid and not listening to you. I'm really sorry for wrecking the car and getting us into this mess in the first place."

"Apology accepted," said Tara, standing to her feet. "But, I'm still mad at you and I'm definitely not in the mood to fool around right now."

"Tara, wait."

She shook her head and walked out of the room, taking the flashlight with her. She paused in the hallway, shining the light along the landing at the top of the stairs. There was nothing to see. She glanced behind her to see Scott kneeling before the fire, his back to her, poking the embers in the fireplace. As angry as she was with him, she couldn't help but smile. He might be an idiot sometimes, but he was her idiot. She turned back around and crossed the hallway into another room, which appeared to have once been a sitting room of some sort. There were several smashed bookshelves along the walls, a few broken chairs, and an antique couch that sat below a set of double windows that looked out onto the front yard. She thought that it would have been a nice room once upon a time, a comfortable place to sit and read a good book.

She heard the sound of footsteps in the hallway, coming towards her. She stood still, her back to him, rigid and unforgiving. The footsteps stopped behind her and she felt his warm breath on her neck.

"Scott, I said no and I meant it."

She felt hands on her body, gentle, but firm, setting her

skin on fire wherever they touched. They found their way down the neck of her blouse, cupping her full breasts and teasing her sensitive nipples. She moaned as the fingers tweaked and pulled and squeezed, sending chills down her spine. The hands drifted up and out of her blouse, traveling down her firm stomach and pausing to toy with her bellybutton before plunging down the front of her pants.

"Oh, Scott!"

"Did you say something?"

Tara spun around, backing into the couch and falling onto it. Scott was standing across the hall, looking at her with concern; there was no one else in the room.

"Babe," said Scott, rushing to her side, "Are you okay?"

"No, I'm not," she said, her voice shrill and much too loud. There was a smell in the air, light and flowery, that reminded her of the way her grandmother smelled on Sunday mornings before church. She looked up into Scott's eyes and whispered, "There's somebody here with us."

"Tara, the house is deserted. There's nobody here but us."

"Someone touched me, Scott."

"What! Who touched you?"

"I think that it was a young woman. I smelled her perfume."

"Tara, I didn't see anyone."

"Really?" she asked, glancing around the room.

"Really," he said, taking her hand and helping her to her feet. "Come on. Come back to the fire with me. It's cold in here."

Tara nodded and followed him back across the hallway, sitting down in front of the fire. They sat like that for what seemed like hours, both silent and deep in thought. Occasionally, a shiver would crawl its way up Tara's spine as she remembered the touch of the strange hands as they explored her body. How powerful the pull of those sensations. How wanton they made her feel. Lust kindled inside of her, radiating warmth from her stomach outwards; a powerful lust, but not for her husband.

Tara stood up, once again grabbing the flashlight.

"Where you off to now?" asked Scott, concerned.

"I've got to use the bathroom."

"You want me to come with you?"

Tara frowned down at him, "No, I'm fine."

"Okay," said Scott, turning back to the fire. "Just be careful. Yell if you need me."

"Sure," she said, walking out into the hallway. She played the flashlight beam around the sitting room, not surprised to find it empty and cold.

Where are you?

She remembered the shadow that had moved at the top of the stairs. She cast one quick glance back to see if Scott was watching, then she climbed the stairs to the second floor landing and looked around. She was standing in another hallway that ran the width of the house. She stood at the top of the stairs for a moment, unsure of where to go next, then her eyes fell upon two open doors down the hall to her right. She walked towards the first, her heart like thunder inside her chest. She reached the door and pushed it open. The room beyond was a small bathroom with a shattered toilet and an antique claw-foot tub. There were dirty towels draped over the edge and cobwebs hanging from the ceiling.

She isn't in here, she thought and turned away.

The second door creaked open on rusty hinges, revealing a small bedroom. A large wooden wardrobe stood against one wall and a tiny writing desk sat beneath the lone window. Nestled against the far wall was a sleigh bed made of cherry or some other dark wood.

"Hello?" whispered Tara.

There was no answer.

Tara stepped into the room, glancing into the corners, behind the desk, and under the big bed. Nothing. Sighing, she turned towards the door.

There was a naked woman standing in the doorway, a candle in her slender hand.

Tara barely heard the flashlight hit the floor as it dropped from her numb fingers. The woman was an angel, a picture of perfection. She was young, no more than eighteen or nineteen years old, with long blonde hair that fell down her back like water and eyes as gray as a stormy sea. Her lips were full and red, her breasts small and firm. Her hips were broad, supported by long, toned legs.

"W-who are you?" asked Tara.

"Shhh," said the woman. She stepped inside and shut the door behind her. "He'll hear you."

"Who? Scott?"

The woman walked forward and placed a slender finger on Tara's lips, "Shhh."

Tara moaned at her touch and fell back onto the bed. Instantly, the woman's hands were exploring her body again, pulling her shirt up and freeing her breasts. The woman's breath was hot on her skin, her lips soft as they kissed Tara's stomach, the swell of her breasts, her erect nipples. She felt the quick flick of her tongue as it traced a soft line down her abdomen and lingered in her belly button. The skilled hands unbuttoned Tara's slacks and slid them off, dropping them to the floor and beginning a slow track along the inside of her thighs to her most intimate place. Her tongue left Tara's belly button and joined the hands, flicking as lightly as the wings of a butterfly. She felt fingers inside her, pressing deep into her wetness. Tara arched her back, running her fingers through the woman's golden hair and pulling her closer as the urgency grew. A cry escaped her lips and suddenly there were sticky fingers pushing into her mouth and another whispered warning that they must be quiet. Tara closed her eyes and sucked on the digits, becoming more aroused by the taste of herself. The orgasm began in her womb and spread throughout her body and she cried out again, unable to quiet herself in the extremity of her ecstasy.

There was a creaking noise and Tara looked up to see a large man standing in the open doorway with his hands hidden behind his back.

"No!" breathed the woman, her eyes shiny with terror. "Please, Frank!"

He was silent as the grave as he stared, unmoving, at the two naked women.

"Um, Sir," said Tara, pulling her legs under her in case she needed to make a spring for the door, "I'm sorry. If you will move, I'll just leave."

He didn't seem to hear her. His gaze remained fixed on the woman.

"I told you what would happen," he said, his voice low and menacing.

The woman stood to her feet and backed into the corner by the desk, shaking her head as tears began to flow down her pale cheeks. "Please, Frank. Don't, I'm sorry."

"I told you!" he screamed, bringing his shaking hands out from behind his back. He held a large butcher knife in his right hand.

"No!" shouted Tara, reaching out to grab the man. He ran by her and pinned the woman to the wall with his free hand, thrusting the knife forward. There were brutal ripping noises and something heavy and wet splattered to the bedroom floor. Tara leapt from the bed, screaming, and fled from the room. She ran down the stairs and out the front door, naked as the day she was born.

The police searched the house the following day. They found cobwebs, broken furniture, and footprints left in the heavy layer of dust by Scott and Tara. There was no blood, no man, and no body. Back at the police station, Tara and Scott sat in silence.

"Excuse me?"

Scott and Tara looked up to see an elderly woman standing in front of them with a thin folder clutched to her chest.

"Yes?" asked Scott.

"Here," she said, handing the file to Tara. "You should see this." She gave them a sad smile and walked away. Tara opened the folder and read. The couple's name had been Williams. They were married in August of 1954. Frank was twenty eight and Anne was nineteen. The local Sheriff had been called to their house in December of the same year when the neighbors heard shouting inside the house. When they arrived, they found Anne huddled in a corner, badly beaten. The Sheriff conducted a short investigation and let things go. After all, things were different in those days. A man had to take care of things. Two months later, on February 7, 1955, the Sheriff returned to the farm to find Frank hanging by the neck from the oak tree in the front yard. He found the bodies of Anne and one Leslie Godwin in the upstairs bedroom. Frank's diary was found during a search of the house. In it, he wrote of catching Anne in bed with Mrs. Godwin, "writhing in sin." The first time had been in August. He had beaten her and told her that if he ever caught her at it again he would kill her. The second time he had made good on his promise.

Tara closed the file and looked into Scott's eyes.

"What happened here?" he asked.

Tara leaned into his chest and wrapped her arms around him. She didn't know how to answer his question.

The Silkworm Moth Effect

Gene O'Neill

Dr. Seamus Chacon surveyed the night crowd moving up and down O'Farrell Street just off busy Van Ness.

Kind of wrinkled and seedy, mostly street people just ambling about, he thought. Not too surprising this close to the Tenderloin. Actually, if he traded his sport coat for a faded army field jacket and grew a ponytail, he would fit right in with the appearance of many of the passersby. He was thin and stooped, almost gaunt, wore a droopy bandito mustache, his face slightly pockmarked, his features and demeanor bearing a slight resemblance to the James Edward Olmos character in the movie, *Zoot Suit*: A kind of streetwise Chicano hustler. Funny, because he was half-Irish and a PhD in bioneurology.

A fog had slowly drifted in from the Bay, cooling the evening air, typical San Francisco weather for late summer, making Chacon shiver. He turned up the collar of his brown herringbone sport jacket and eyed the neon-blue sign in a nearby blackened window front: THE SHADY LADY.

Cool name, he thought, kind of 50s retro. But apparently not the trendy in spot like some of the new South of Market clubs. In the several minutes he'd been standing out front, watching street people, not one person had gone in or come out of the ebony door. Still, he felt compelled to check the club out. It was after eleven-thirty on a weeknight, he was running out of research opportunities.

Tense with nervous anticipation, Chacon sucked in a deep breath and entered THE SHADY LADY. Inside he found it dark and pleasantly warm. As his eyes adjusted, he glanced around and let his breath out slowly. The decor was retro, predominately black and white art deco, including the square tiled floor and hardwood bar with chrome fittings; and playing softly in the background was the classic jazz piece, "Take Five," with Dave Brubeck's distinctive piano riff. No typical stale beer smell in here, no loud laughing, pool balls clicking, or other disturbing noise. Nice, classy, stylish—

Except the place was dead, nearly empty.

Only two stools were occupied at the far end of the bar near the jukebox—a pair of men in business suits, ties loosened, drinking wine and talking quietly. No women, except for the bartender working behind the highly polished bar.

With a practiced eye, Chacon quickly looked her over as a potential research subject. He dropped his head slightly and whispered out of the corner of his mouth the date, time, and location into the mini-recorder hidden in the breast pocket of his jacket, then he added, "White subject, ah . . . late thirties." She appeared to be at least ten years his senior. He checked the men at the bar, insuring he wasn't being observed, and continued, "Tall, modest curves contouring a muscular, athletic figure, obviously a gym rat, and dressed simply in a white blouse, black satin skirt, no jewelry except for silver dangling loop earrings, her auburn hair in a neat bun, high cheekbones, full sensuous lips, only a light touch of make-up—"

He clicked off the recorder after the bartender glanced his

way and flashed a quick fake smile—pretty teeth. "Be with you in a sec," she said, a hint of tired disinterest detectable in her tone. Looking back down, the woman placed two wine glasses into a nearly empty dishwasher tray. As she stooped over to load the tray into the washer, he caught a glimpse of modest cleavage and a nametag that read: *Cilia*. Well, Chacon admitted to himself, she did fit in with the elegant, stylish decor of the place, no question about that, an attractive lady. But not his usual subject, too prim and proper; he liked younger, bustier, sleazier subjects, women who did not mind getting down, dirty, and scuffed-up. But Cilia, old girl, he thought wryly after checking his watch, afraid you will just have to do. Hell, maybe she'd surprise him, not be the type that whines: *Please, don't mess up my hair*.

Chacon smiled charmingly, sliding onto the nearest high-back ebony and chrome stool. Nonchalantly, he unbuttoned his sport coat; then, with a practiced flick of his wrist, he fanned one of his jacket lapels a couple of times, as if the temperature in the club was a little too warm . . . and he waited, one ear tuned to the drum riff in "Take Five."

Suddenly, the attractive bartender popped up from the dishwasher and looked curiously at Chacon, a slight crease etched between her eyebrows. At first she appeared concerned, a little sheepish, at a loss for words, as if she'd suddenly realized she'd rudely neglected a customer. But it was much more than trying to be professionally polite; she'd shaken off her late evening tired look, her eyes shining now, giving away her keen personal interest. Chacon could almost detect the minute flaring of her nostrils and the olfactory processing of his special scent, knowing that the classy bartender was giving him her full attention now. Yes, indeed.

"Sorry to keep you waiting," Cilia said after clearing her throat, moving closer, nervously wiping the already immaculate shiny countertop. Oh, yeah, attentive, eager to please, a 180-degree change in attitude. For an awkward few moments the bartender just froze and peered silently into Chacon's eyes. Her pupils were slightly dilated, her eyelids drooping noticeably, her neck bearing a deep blush. She eventually broke eye contact and asked in a husky, sexy voice, "What can I do for you, sweetie?"

Of course he understood her enticing question. But he closed his eyes, put a forefinger to his lips, as if considering thoughtfully. He could just make out her faint scent, a mix of spice and tingling citrus. After a long silence, Chacon blinked, nodded, and with a slightly lascivious grin that matched the tone of her question, he leaned across the bar, covered her hand with his, and whispered in her ear, "Cilia, are you wet already?"

"Yes," she admitted without a moment's hesitation or embarrassment, staring unflinchingly back into his eyes.

Patting her hand, as if she were a child who had answered the teacher's question correctly, Chacon suggested in a matter-of-fact tone, "Well, maybe we should do something about that right now?"

Cilia nodded enthusiastically without a trace of reluctance, a look of almost grateful relief, like a kid accepting an adult's permission to take a cooling swim on a sweltering day. She did glance down the bar at her two other customers for a moment, then shook her head dismissively and untied her white apron, drying her hands before discarding the wrinkled linen in the sink well.

"Where?" he asked, his grin fading, his expression serious. Game time, folks, he thought, deal closed.

She pointed tentatively beyond the opposite end of the bar, toward the darkened hallway leading to the restrooms. "In the office?" she suggested in a higher-pitched voice.

"Okay, fine."

Chacon slid off his stool, and met Cilia as she ducked under the end flap of the bar. She reached out and took his hand, eagerly leading him down the hallway past the MENS and LADIES to a door labeled: PRIVATE. Abruptly, the shapely bartender spun around, grasped the slightly shorter Chacon by his jacket lapels, jerked him close, and kissed him wetly on the lips. Then her tongue was darting into his mouth, exploring. She broke apart, gasping for breath, and cooed into his ear, "Oh, you sweet devil."

He reacted in kind, pulling her closer, flattening her breasts against his chest, kissing her roughly, nipping her earlobe and neck, his hands slowly sliding down her back until they were resting on her firm butt. Rhythmically, he began to rock side-to-side—

Cilia responded with a deep-throated moan, squirmed in his arms, and leaned back, as if to gain her bearings. "Wait." Sucking in a breath, she broke completely away from his embrace, fumbled for a key in her skirt pocket, clumsily unlocked the office door, and pushed Chacon into the darkened room, whispering hoarsely, "Take off your clothes."

She flicked on an indirect light on the wall above a big walnut desk, and frantically abandoned her blouse and skirt, flinging them in the direction of a brown leather chair beside the desk. In another second or two, she had discarded her black panties and bra in the pile and was completely nude, standing in front of Chacon, unabashed, breathing loudly, not trying to conceal her eager readiness.

Almost casually, he folded his coat, trousers, and polo shirt, draping them carefully over the chair, before turning his attention to the panting woman. Her breasts were indeed smallish as he'd first thought, but tipped with large dark aureoles, her nipples standing erect in the cool air of the small office. Body perfectly tanned. A peek at the woman's dark, thick, pubic triangle quickened his lackadaisical movements. Chacon tugged off his T-shirt and boxer shorts, matching Celia's nakedness except for his socks.

He was short, skinny, stooped, with a pale body, and his partial state of arousal was modest by any standards.

But the attractive bartender, blind to his lack of physical

endowments and good looks, growled with an animal-like admiration, as if he were a rock star, and she a common groupie, eager to rut. She swooped Chacon into her arms and molded her well-defined body against his thin frame. Skin-on-skin, slightly damp with perspiration. Balancing on her right foot, she hooked her left leg around him, her heel digging into the small of his back, locking their bodies together. Her wet sex radiated heat.

He felt himself stiffening.

She kissed him again, her tongue thrusting in and out of his mouth lewdly. After biting his bottom lip, she announced loudly, "I'm ready." Without waiting for a response, Celia pushed him backwards. Chacon's thighs hit the desk edge, and he dropped into a seated position on the desk top, partially stunned by her roughness.

The enraptured woman kneeled, took his member in hand, and in a few seconds teased him to full erection with her mouth. Then, pushing against his chest, she scooted him backwards several feet, and joined him atop the desk. She clasped both her legs around him in a scissor lock, and with her hand she deftly guided him into her slippery sex.

In a moment her pelvic movements soon became unpredictable, jerky, rough, accompanied by a series of unrestrained grunts, gasps, and groans. Rocking, slamming, thudding. A snarling, scratching, biting, bumping, wet and wild, animal-like copulation. Not a moment devoted to any aspect of tenderness.

But it soon ended explosively for Cilia. She suddenly shuddered violently as if experiencing a seizure, then cried out joyfully, "Ohhhh, yes, yes, yes, ahhh . . . you sweet devil!" Drenched with sweat, Cilia collapsed against Chacon's chest, panting heavily, like a great she-cat in heat, after encountering a male suddenly in the humid jungle and mating violently. And, not unexpectedly, she had a slightly scraped cheek and puffy eye, injured during the frantic sex.

Good, Chacon thought, but the party wasn't over yet. Uh-uh.

Different drummer, different position . . .

Abruptly, Celia, on her hands and knees, gasped loudly, arched her back like a cat, and shuddered again not quite so violently. "Oh, yeah."

But he didn't stop.

Sweaty now himself, nearing completion, Chacon continued, picking up the beat, growing more excited as the minutes passed, grinding into her rapidly drying sex, until she finally cried out in pain, and tried to straighten up and pull away. But he pushed her back down in place. "Hold still," he ordered, Cilia remaining a passive partner as he finally reached orgasm. Drenched, Chacon groaned and fell forward, plastering himself against her back and flattening her against the desktop.

In half a minute, after he'd caught his breath, he roused himself and withdrew from the bartender, who remained prone where she rested. "Okay, Cilia, time to get up now," Chacon said. She didn't respond. "C'mon, get up."

He rolled her over, and Cilia moaned weakly, apparently only partially conscious, her nose bleeding profusely. Had he pushed her down that hard? Ah, shit, he thought, working up a little righteous indignation. Serves her right for only thinking about herself. He quickly pulled on his clothes, and did not even say goodbye to the groggy, bleeding bartender, as he left the office and hurried down the darkened hall.

The businessmen were still at the far end of the bar, in about the same position as earlier, but the number on the jukebox had changed. Now, The Ramsey Lewis Trio was playing, "Hang On Sloopy." Chacon walked toward the door, managing to draw only disinterested glances from the two men before he made his exit.

Back on O'Farrell Street in front of THE SHADY LADY, he paused, took out his mini-recorder and carefully again noted the time, date, and name of bar. Then he added: "Positive encounter, with previously described white subject in late thirties." Makes three tonight, he thought, smiling, with a sense of exhausted satisfaction.

On the Muni ride home to the Mission area, Chacon thought about the last two months of research—over a hundred positive encounters—and grinned to himself. Women had not always been so cooperative. No indeed. He laughed aloud, making an older black woman seated nearby frown, get up, and take another place on the bus, three rows away.

From his earliest undergraduate days at Cal, Chacon had been intrigued by the possible neurological effect of odorants on human behavior, especially after he'd first read about female silkworm moths sexually attracting males by secreting overpowering odorants called pheromones. No one had identified a human pheromone at that time or how they might even be detected, but there was speculation. Eventually, he went on to get his doctorate from Cal in neurobiology, his thesis strongly supporting the existence of a Vomeronasal System (VNS), an accessory olfactory nerve network in the upper nasal passage near the sinus cavity, which he believed was capable of detecting human pheromones.

Right after hooking up with the specialty pharmaceutical company *Irresistible.Com* in 1998, he read the ground shaking article in *Nature* by the two University of Chicago researchers, Stern and McClintock, that identified the first two human pheromones in women's axiliary secretions—one accelerating the menstrual cycle and ovulation, the other delaying it. Of course this discovery finally explained the 1971 report that female college roommates' menstrual cycles tended to become synchronized. But most importantly, it clearly demonstrated that pheromones existed in humans.

I.Com developed herbal/organic sexual performance

enhancers, stimulators, and attractants. But soon after being hired, Chacon talked the CEO into establishing the Charisma Project, exploring why certain men are so successful sexually regardless of their physical appearance. He was convinced that these special males gave off pheromones that females subconsciously detected with their VNS and found overwhelmingly seductive. His team gathered data at San Francisco State, CCSF, and USF, eventually identifying and cross-verifying twelve male subjects as being valid Don Juans, and collecting a number of axiliary secretion samples.

But *I.Com*, during the San Francisco dot com collapse, shut down the project and eventually laid Chacon off six months ago.

Nevertheless, he continued work at home, with his computer in a make-shift lab, eventually isolating, analyzing, and chemically classifying the hypothesized odorants—a cluster of three pheromones in the underarm secretions of the college romeos. Two months ago, he'd managed to synthesize the pheromone cluster at industrial grade strength and experimented, using himself as the sole subject. Oh, it worked like a charm; and he playfully dubbed his discovery, *Love Potion #9*, like in the song. The results to date had actually been quite remarkable, Chacon finding he had a one hundred percent success ratio—a string of only positive sexual encounters—the absolute power to seduce any woman he chose to expose to a close-up whiff of LP #9.

But as Lord Acton warned over a hundred years ago: *Power tends to corrupt and absolute power corrupts absolutely.* Instead of immediately publishing the amazing results of his successful experimentation as initially planned, Dr. Seamus Chacon became a ruthless sexual predator, selfishly exploiting his discovery, casually discarding each of his entranced partners . . . except for one.

*

Later that night after taking the bus home from THE SHADY LADY, the front door intercom buzzed in Chacon's SoMa apartment.

"Hey, it's Etta—"

Jesus. Etta St. John was Chacon's first subject, a hanger-on, his only blunder since initiating the experimental use of LP #9. "Etta, you can't come up, now—"

"Why?"

"I-I'm sick . . . the flu or something, you know," he lied. "Throwing up, diarrhea, the place trashed."

"Hey, mon, I can help, clean up, maybe shop for you, pick up medicine," Etta suggested, her sing-song Caribbean-Brit accent more pronounced when she was nervous or under stress.

She'd never go away tonight if he didn't cut this off.

"I really don't need anything, right now, Babe," he replied. "But maybe we can get together soon, you know—"

"When?"

"I don't know . . . when I'm better?"

"Tomorrow, Seamus, *tomorrow*," Etta insisted. "Last chance."

A pause; then: "Okay, tomorrow night," Chacon agreed.

"How 'bout over on Noe just off Market, a new place, THE O.K. CORRAL?"

"Sounds good, Babe."

"Eight-thirty?"

"I'll be there."

"Doan fuck me over, again, mon," she warned.

"Yeah, I won't, Babe," he said, leaning against the wall, waiting . . . After a few minutes he decided that she'd been satisfied by his promise to meet tomorrow and left. He sighed with relief.

Etta St. John was a drop-dead gorgeous black woman from Barbados, short corn-rowed mahogany hair with a reddish tint, exotic gray eyes, broad-shouldered and tall, the long legs of a New York model, intelligent, a senior program analyst at

I.Com, one of its first employees and still on the job. All the males at work, even a few females—this was San Francisco after all—hopelessly smitten with her. Of course, Etta hadn't given Chacon the time of day, when he first went to work at the lab over a year ago. The sex-goddess of *I.Com* and the newbie klutz? No way, Jose.

But after Chacon synthesized LP #9, he first tried it out at LOONY TUNES, the local watering hole next to the *I.Com* labs on Harrison Street.

It'd been an unusually warm fog-free evening for the City, Chacon wearing only a tank top and shorts. He'd taken a stool next to Etta, whose eyes had instantly lit up after getting a strong whiff of the LP #9 that he'd dabbed heavily in his armpits.

"Sea-moos," she cooed, her accent thickening as she used his first name for the first time, "how you doin'?"

He smiled. "Fine, just fine."

"Mon, you are lookin' *good*," the shapely beauty said, her hand sliding along Chacon's bare inner thigh. "Yeah," she purred in his ear, rubbing her ample breasts against his shoulder, the beauty all over him now like a strawberry rash. Her long fingers extended into his boxers, brushed his testicles . . . Then she lightly stroked his growing erection. "Oh, my, Sea-moos," she rasped hoarsely. "Is there a private place close where we can go?"

He hadn't planned on being so instantly successful and was taken aback by her aggressiveness. "Ah, ah, m-my place, I guess?" he stammered huskily. "Shotwell Street in the Mission, about twelve blocks away. We can take a bus or grab a taxi—"

"C'mon," she said, tugging him roughly off the barstool and clasping his hand tightly in hers. "We doan need a taxi, mon, let's run!"

Startled pedestrians parted and turned to watch as the tall, beautiful black woman thundered by, a shorter, pale white guy in tow but barely keeping up, like an irate mother dragging her recalcitrant youngster home for a good whipping.

And Chacon was about to experience the whipping of his

life.

They were both sweating heavily and out of breath when he fumbled at the lock and finally let them into his downstairs apartment.

Inside the front door, they embraced and kissed open-mouthed in the dark, then gasped for breath, and quickly shucked out of their clothes, making it only as far as the hallway to the bedroom, before Etta grabbed him from behind and tugged Chacon down to the hardwood floor. She rolled him over onto his back and fondled him momentarily; then she reached under his buttocks with one arm, her sweaty breasts clinging to his chest and making a wet, squishing sound as she lifted him up and guided his partial erection into her with her free hand. She growled lewdly, "Oh, yeah, the short yo-yo," their slippery bellies making a sharp splatting sound, as she pumped madly.

It was over briefly, both breathless and perspiring heavily, like wrestlers after a hard-fought but quick pin.

Chacon extricated himself, struggled to his feet, and stumbled weak-kneed off to the bathroom, returning with two towels, only then getting a good look at the naked Etta who was standing now. She was indeed a statuesque beauty, her unblemished skin a glistening creamed coffee color in the dim light, her up-tilted breasts highlighted with large purple aureoles and thick nipples, her pubic triangle matching her mahogany hair. He handed her one of the towels—

Etta knocked it away. "Uh-uh," she uttered, grabbing him roughly by the shoulders, towering over him almost six inches. "We are just beginning, Sea-moos, best two out of three," she said, with a thin smile, then tripping and easing him carefully back to the floor.

"Wait a minute, Etta, give me a chance to catch—"

"Hush," she ordered, cutting off his protest, by smothering his mouth with an open, wet kiss, her tongue probing. He soon forgot what he wanted to say. After a minute, she slipped down his chest, kissing and nipping with her sharp teeth, lingering for a second at his bellybutton . . . And a few moments later, he moaned with delight as she orally coaxed another erection.

Even lying on her back, her pelvic thrusts had the combative force of a series of blows . . . She finished with a shudder that traveled the length of her body. "Oh, yes, Sea-moos!"

"God," he murmured, finally back on his feet, but feeling battered and vulnerable, staring at the wild-eyed woman circling him, indeed resembling a stalking opponent in an ultimate fighting bout. Involuntarily, he shivered. Jesus, maybe I used too heavy a dosage of LP #9, he thought, just before Etta pounced on him again.

So it went for the rest of the evening—a night wilder and exceeding all of Chacon's sex-starved, violent masturbation fantasies.

In the morning his body was scratched, poked, bitten, bruised, and exhausted, feeling like he'd been captured in a net by Etta, and beaten severely with a cudgel seven . . . no eight times. He'd been a gladiator—oh, yeah, a losing gladiator.

But he'd made two mistakes that night. He'd used triple the proper dosage of LP #9. And Etta had been an acquaintance, knew exactly where he lived, and after that night of extreme sex, he'd stupidly told her about his discovery. At first, Etta didn't care that she'd been exploited. She was madly in love, the overdose of LP #9 permanently affecting her judgment. She phoned constantly, showed up unannounced at his door, and bugged him unmercifully. But he soon developed a number of clever dodges, managing to successfully evade her for the most part.

Chacon never made those two mistakes again. He carefully corrected the strength and proper application of the pheromones. And after that night in his apartment with Etta, his conquests were always with strangers, consummated on the spot in nightclub restrooms, a number of times in the back seats of cabs, several times in alleys on cardboard, once standing up in a well-lighted phone booth, but usually in nearby hotels or motels. Always afterward, he was immediately gone—love 'em and leave 'em his modus operandi.

But regardless of his shoddy treatment and obvious infidelities, he could not completely shake Etta. She hung on like a bad cold.

The next morning after his agreement to meet Etta, Chacon resigned himself to working on the paper he planned on submitting to *Nature* about identifying and synthesizing the three pheromone cluster. He could not delay reporting his research much longer. Any one of a number of research neurobiologists working on pheromones might easily duplicate his discovery. After Chacon called up his rough draft, his fingers froze on the keyboard of his computer—

A red light flashed on the screen. His special security program, ICY (internal computer integrity), was flashing him a warning.

He'd been hacked! Someone had got past ICY and read his partially completed paper that included the synthetic formula for LP #9.

But who? Who even suspected the paper existed . . . and had the necessary computer expertise to hack him? *Jesus.*

The answer was obvious. It had to be Etta. She'd threatened to get even with him a number of times, babbling about exposing the project, ruining him. She probably figured on blackmailing him tonight at the club, forcing him to let her move into his apartment.

"No, I don't think so," Chacon muttered to himself, knowing he had to do something drastic. He thought for a moment. He'd bring her home, talk sense to her. Offer to make her a co-author of the paper . . . whatever. And, if all else failed, he thought, walking into the bathroom and taking his straight razor out of the case, he'd threaten her life.

Well, he probably didn't have the balls to use the razor, but maybe he could scare the shit out of her, if he had to.

Noe Street was on the fringe of the Castro district.

Inside the O.K. CORRAL, Chacon glanced around not spotting Etta.

And nothing but country music blaring loudly.

Chacon frowned, looking at the bartender, who asked, "What can I get you, bro?" The young guy was really buff, filling out a white T-shirt with blue letters that read: *Wanna Ride, Cowboy?*

"Uh, beer," Chacon replied, looking away quickly and swallowing dryly.

Anxiously, he began to check around more carefully, hoping to spot Etta. But she wasn't in the place. Unlike her to be late, especially after setting up the meeting. Maybe the restroom?

That's when it dawned on him that there were only men in here, dancing, hugging, and doing other stuff quite openly.

Jesus, Etta had picked a gay bar. Why—?

But before he could finish the thought, *it* slammed him, like an invisible blow right between his eyes . . . And suddenly, his nose was twitching out of control, his nostrils were flaring, and he felt a tingling itch deep, up near his sinus cavities. His attention was drawn overpoweringly back to the bar.

Several empty stools away, sat a huge individual dressed in a gaudy purple western shirt, faded blue jeans, a greasy dark Stetson, and scuffed-up cowboy boots. His right cheek bulged slightly with a tobacco chew, his face covered with a shadowy, bristly three-day growth. He was fanning the lapel of his black vest, looking directly at Chacon and smiling . . . knowingly.

Chacon forgot all about Etta stealing his research paper and who she might've revealed it to, the straight razor at home and his plan, or Etta's odd absence. Because the cowboy's gap-toothed smile was absolutely irresistible.

Under Nighttime Rainbows

Savannah

Late afternoon, two officers had found a body in the vacant apartment house. After they ran a quick check, they radioed back. "We've got another. It don't look right. Get the Examiner over here."

The dispatcher grumbled something about an overload of victims from a shooting across town. "We'll send O'Connor to pick up the bodies and process them at the morgue."

"No," the incoming caller insisted. "Something's weird. We're not touching them. Send over a team, now. We'll wait out front."

Rookie Wilson arrived to secure the place and was told, "Don't leave until the investigators show up."

Heavy workloads had delayed the men. Detective Moreno had been the first to arrive.

He stepped into the dark lobby and glanced towards the vacant guard desk. "Wilson! Where are you?" His words echoed through the hollow building. "Hey Rookie! Shake a leg."

He ignored the sounds of rats scurrying through scattered debris. "Typical damn rookie-style. Scheduling falls behind—and they can't wait around. Just can't spend the extra damn time."

Moreno stormed through the lobby, his heavy boot heels thudded as he headed down the corridor, flashing his light along graffiti streaked walls. The glaring beam startled pigeons that fluttered overhead like bats. Moreno shuddered. Focus was hard in the confining darkness and for a moment, he hesitated. The eerie silence had a bad feel. "Wilson!"

A noise rustled in the lobby. A paper bag, Moreno questioned and stared back at the desk expecting to see the rookie. Maybe, he brought some coffee. But no one was there. Rookies! You'd think they'd eat up that overtime pay. He tried his handheld: only static. A low disconcerting hiss like a huge rat came from behind the guard's desk. A chill shot through him. It was hard to see so he flashed his light toward the sound. More noises, then glowing red eyes reflected back. He strained to focus. "Is . . . Is that you, Wilson?"

A large black cat leaped onto the desk, hunched its back and glared at him.

"Get outta here!" Moreno yelled as he pounded on the desktop.

The black feline leaped to the floor. Papers scattered.

Moreno groaned as he crouched to pick them up. "Must be from the rookie." He read the handwritten note: *You are the velvet fog consuming the night.* "What?" With a crumple, he tossed it aside and skimmed the next one. *Contours pressed into endless rhythms, desires permeate with passions of fiery lust.*

"What the fuck?" He stared at the paper. The precinct logo was in the upper right-hand corner. Had to have been from the rookie, he thought and shook his head. "He must've sat here writing romantic poetry to . . . to yeah, to the cat." He smirked, then hollered, "Wilson!"

Something rubbed against his leg.

"Damn thing."

Its soft fur felt sensual: its motion seductive. The cat's movement bunched up his pant leg and stroked against Moreno's bare skin.

About to kick it away, he hesitated. The movements of soft fur eased his tension. He glanced down at the cat. Its form wavered in the dull light. A mesmerizing glow drifted from its red eyes capturing Moreno's thoughts. He gasped at what he thought he saw. The shape of the cat's face changed. It drifted from that of a feline to an alluring woman curled at his feet.

His hands fumbled as he grabbed for his flashlight. Moreno tried to shove the cat off. A distant moan broke the odd spell.

"Wilson?"

The cat darted down the dark corridor.

Moreno watched it. The cat stopped and turned back, as if coaxing him to follow. "Get outta here!" he hollered. It sauntered off. "Gotta find the bodies," he mumbled. "Where's that backup?"

Another soft purr rolled toward the desk. Moreno's flashlight washed down the hallway and stopped on what seemed to be a woman's wavering figure. She stood seductively, motioning for him to follow. He rubbed his crotch and shrugged his shoulders. A pussy or . . . a pussy, he laughed at himself, then followed. She lured him into the darkness, then like the cat, faded away.

Moreno stood puzzled, his bearings tangled.

Something brushed past and touched his arm.

He dropped his light. It rolled for a moment and then clanked down what sounded like a metal staircase. Barely able to see, he worked his hands along the walls and felt a cold steel doorframe. She must've gone through here, he thought.

He eased through. A metal mesh grate sounded underfoot. "Must be the stairwell landing." His fingers grasped an iron railing. He stepped carefully down the staircase. Sounds of the woman seemed to be just ahead, as if leading him through the dark.

"This don't feel right." Whiffs of moldy air stopped him. I'm going back to the lobby and wait for the guys, he told himself.

He turned and headed back up the staircase, but soft enticing purrs bewitched him and he turned back to follow the illusive woman. "Okay, sweetheart. You're on."

Another chill breeze whisked past like icy fingers stroking his skin. Then a warm breeze whirled changing the air to a steamy mist that smelled of wet soil and rotting leaves. Am I outside, he wondered. It sure smells that way. But how? He stumbled along moist ground stepping on tangles of vines and roots. "Cripes what a stink."

Moreno cringed. He recognized that old familiar stench of rotting flesh. In a flash, the odor pulled him back to his tour in Vietnam: to the humid jungles where he searched though steamy vegetation for dying men. "What the fuck? Where the hell am I?" Past memories drew from his mind flooding through his feverish body. (It was if his past memories were being drawn from his mind and he was reliving them.)

The smell of death whirled. His senses aroused from the bizarre thrill that old war memories stirred. Sensations tinged with traces of panic.

Rookie Wilson's poetic words, the ones Moreno had read earlier, came to mind. An odd excitement of sensuality grew. He eased into a strange dreamy stupor. A hand reached out and gently touched his arm. He pulled away, but there was nowhere to turn in the dark. Whiffs of strong incense drifted, pulling his thoughts back to 'Nam's bars and whorehouses.

He heard a voice.

"Who are you?" he said. "What's going on?"

Soft red eyes glowed. A woman materialized. She stepped forward and pressed her voluptuous naked body into him. She pushed him down onto the soft moist ground.

Am I dreaming, Moreno thought.

Silently, she lay on top of him, moving like those seductress whores. Moreno's thoughts spun into a whirl of sexual fantasies. He thought of his service furloughs and the faceless women he'd fucked in those smoky incense-riddled dens. Breathlessly, he moved, groping her full breasts and fingering her growing wetness. Building lusty tension pushed him to relive those old sexual encounters flooding through his mind, and then his body fatigued.

But the faceless woman teased him on, creating lusty wants and satisfying new desires. Each time his cock exploded, she'd arouse him again until he'd come so many times that he'd collapse, but with no fulfillment. Was she entertaining herself, not him? Like an incubus, she left him wanting more. And, then the surface desires of sex parted and she skillfully drew ones from deeper avenues of Moreno's mind. Desires he'd tried to bury away—ones that no one knew.

Old repressed thoughts surfaced: how the men in his fighting unit openly masturbated in the dark steamy jungle. Their breathy crescendos turned to muffled moans. He remembered how some satisfied the others under the cover of night: hands fondled cocks and fingers stroked them, tongues flickered around ridges, men's heads disappeared into each other's laps. Soldiers hid in the foliage on their knees and sucked each other off; others mounted partners from behind and moaned pleasurably as they came.

Moreno was often approached but Catholic upbringing stopped him short: forbidden desires. He obediently withdrew from the sinful temptations and secretly stroked himself, but thinking his hand was that of a male companion, not an encounter with a woman. Something about the forbidden temptations drove him more pleasurably.

After his tour, he took a civilian job working with the police officers on the Lower East Side. But lingering thoughts from those lusty escapades in the dark jungle taunted. I should have tried it, he told himself.

In the precinct showers, he watched others lather their cocks with light soapy strokes. His eyes traced along their asses. His dick grew into soft hard-ons as he pictured the men from his old fighting unit. He took stolen glances at the bulges in his companions' pants when they straddled benches and chairs pulling on shoes and boots.

Now, he enjoyed his boiling passion as his seducer continued to arouse his desires. This time she eased him to his feet. Darkness veiled her: Moreno only felt her soft body. His fingers moved along her sensual soft shoulders and down her long graceful back. He spread open his trembling hands to cinch her waist trying to slow her advances and rest for a moment. She grasped his hands and pulled them forcefully across her firm inviting buttocks. She somehow managed to rekindle his desires. His cock swelled.

He slid his hands down her belly to reach for her pussy. But in an instant, she spun turning her back to him. She wants it from behind, he thought. Her eyes and wriggling tongue inflamed his fiery lust from over her shoulder. Moreno clutched at her hips. She pushed her buttocks in tight against his throbbing cock. Her ass pumped against him, hard then soft.

All the while, his inner voice tried to stop him but she always managed to rekindle his lust. He inched his hands forward to her belly then down, anticipating her mounting wetness.

A low moan, like the one he'd heard earlier, whispered, "Moreno." He snapped back to reality. "Who's here?"

Something moved.

"Who's here?"

"Moreno?" a weak voice moaned.

"Rookie?"

Wilson's voice groaned, "Stop. She's not what you . . ."

Soft cat-like purrs rolled and drew Moreno back to the woman. She bent forward pressing her ass onto his cock. His hands moved to her navel, then lower to circlets of soft hair.

Her ass pumped as Moreno's hands lowered. He touched a large swelling between her legs. He felt the taut contours of a huge cock, its firm long shaft, and smooth head that throbbed in Moreno's grasp. He shoved his seducer away.

Seductive cat purrs turned into shrill hollow cackles. A powerful surge lifted Moreno up and spun him down across a wooden tabletop. Strong hands pressed against his back, his face pushed into a smothering pile of fabric. He pushed back struggling to get up, but was pinned motionless. Fingers snapped his stiffened legs apart, then tore open his pants, exposing his fleshy ass.

Moreno fought to move, struggled to holler, "Get away!" Strong hands traced teasingly over the swell of Moreno's taut ass. Wartime desires resurfaced as skillful fingers parted his cheeks. He moaned with carnality. A firm throbbing dick lay against him. Its swollen head dribbled lubricating cum as it brushed across his opening.

"What the hell?" Moreno choked out.

The throbbing penis thrust into him.

Moreno moaned. Red-hot sensations shot through his body and his muscles tensed. The pursuer slapped Moreno's cheeks easing the constriction. Moreno pictured himself back in the jungle. Repressed wants of other men released. Erotic expectations exploded.

Strong masculine hands clenched his waist, warm massive balls pressed firm against his legs. Cool breath traced down his neck and along his back as masterful strokes drove him to a sexual frenzy.

The seducer bent forward and nestled into the contours of Moreno's back leaving his long, hard cock inside. His fingers tightened around Moreno's dick stroking it until he came. Moreno lay in a pool of warm sensual cum. The seducer's moist tongue slithered across Moreno's neck with a strange coolness that raised tingling sensations. Cat-like purrs rolled, relaxing Moreno, like that after sex drag of weed.

Suddenly, a swift passionate bite of cold sharp teeth punctured deep through the fragile skin of Moreno's neck. He gasped and shrieked like captured prey. The erotic strike burned like wild fire. The seducer stroked from behind while nursing his fill of warm pulsing blood. The bizarre sensations of his encounter turned Moreno on. Then his seducer released his hold, shoved him aside and cackled, "Now, you are mine."

New desires flooded through Moreno. The commanding creature that had beguiled him with feminine wiles had fulfilled Moreno's desires of masculine union.

Pleasurably, Moreno turned and faced his new companion knowing he had eased into the realm of the undead. He openly embraced his male consort, tracing his hands over his firm muscular body, enjoying realized desires.

Sounds of approaching squad cars echoed down the hallway. Moreno and his partner moved out into the night. Together they joined the others whose remains had lain in waiting within the abandoned building. Now, Moreno and his new clansmen hunt more recruits with their sexual prowess under the smoldering shadows of nighttime rainbows. And only Wilson, if he survived, knows of their existence.

Pixie Cut

Allen Dusk

Justin handed his driver's license to the fat-ass bouncer perched on a stool outside the bar. He rested it on his sloppy gut and clicked on a flashlight so he could better scrutinize its contents under the neon sign buzzing above their heads.

It's not hard, stupid. Justin kept his thoughts to himself while he brushed his dark hair away from his horn-rimmed glasses. *It's just a series of numbers and letters that have significance, unlike those atrocious tats scribbled across your pig knuckles.* He noticed his impatient foot tapping away precisely at the same time the bouncer did.

"Five bucks." His greasy brow rippled.

"What?" Justin rolled his eyes. "When did this place start charging a cover?"

"New owners, new rules."

His first impulse was to grab his ID and storm off down the street, but he could already taste the frothy Guinness sliding down his throat. "Fine." He paid the man and stepped through the door. Shotgun shell Christmas lights scalloped along the walls and punk music raged from the tarnished jukebox in the corner. Rows of antique railroad lanterns cast flickering beams along the pub's extensive tap collection. He fell in love with the Fireback a few months ago while pub crawling to celebrate his big jump to Silicon Valley. He wanted to get his finger on the pulse of the latest tech news, and this proved to be the place. Practically everybody inside the place was fellow techies looking for an escape from their mundane jobs inside the corporate megaliths which consumed the skyline.

His buddy Nic would be been joining him at any moment, so Justin grabbed two perfect seats at the edge of the bar. The vantage point allowed plenty of crowd watching and offered a superb view of the pool table. They enjoyed chuckling over comments about the crowd of women wearing miniskirts who seemed to flock around the scarred green felt when the average blood alcohol level in the room hovered just past the legal limit.

His smartphone buzzed inside in his hoodie pocket. He scowled when he read Nic's text. *Gotta cancel bro. Kim and I just got into a big fight :-(*

Justin didn't even bother replying. He knew typing, *just dump the bitch already*, would only start another fight he didn't need right now.

The bartender tipped his straw fedora. "What can I get you pal?"

"Hit me with a Mandarin Press, and make it a double." Screw the beer. Plunging into vodka drinks would help him forgive his friend quicker.

"You got it."

Justin became entranced by the long pours of liquor that assembled his drink. His spell was broken when somebody suddenly bumped into him. He spun defensively toward the blow and found a blushing smile twisted across a beautiful face.

"Shit, sorry," she said, nervously twisting a black pigtail on the back of her short shag. Emerald green circles glimmered inside her darling eyes.

"Oh, that's all right."

"Is that seat taken?" She stroked blue fingernails over the empty chair beside him.

"No, not at all," he stuttered. He never did well with girls, especially the pretty ones. "I mean, I was saving it for a friend, but now he's not coming, so you can have it."

"Thanks." Her dark red lips smiled.

Her short, black skirt rose up when she slid onto the bar stool, revealing nearly every inch of her firm, smooth thighs. Just another inch, and he would have known what color of underwear she was wearing, if she was wearing any at all.

"That'll be six bucks." The bartender set his drink on a black napkin.

Justin tore his eyes from the dreamy sight and set his cash on the bar. Soft lavender perfume drifted past. He could feel her alluring gaze before he turned to meet it. "Um, can I get you something?"

"Sure, thanks." A thin eyebrow rose over her right eye. "I'll have a Purple Haze," she told the bartender before setting her small, black purse on the bar.

"You got it." He grabbed a glass and started mixing.

"Where are my manners?" She spun towards him and grabbed his hand. "I'm Claret. It's nice to meet you."

"Um, Justin." His heart fluttered from her velvet-smooth touch. "Do you come here often?" He hated the cliché, but her allure sent the rest of his vocabulary running.

"Actually, this is my first time here. Cute place." Her eyes flickered between the lanterns hanging over the bar before their focus returned to him.

"Yeah, it's pretty cool." His lips flared their signature awkward smile. "I come here a lot."

"So, Justin, what's your day job?" She leaned closer to talk over the music pounding through the speakers. Her perfume intoxicated his blood with all the euphoria of morphine.

"Um, I run a tech blog. It's called Tech Junkeez. Um, maybe you heard of it, CNN mentioned it a few months ago."

"Sorry." Her head shook slowly. "Never heard of it. But, this is a great area for that type of thing. Do you make a lot of money doing that?"

"It's not much, but it's enough to buy a girl a drink once in a while."

As if on cue, the bartender slid Claret's drink across the bar. "That'll be eight bucks."

Justin slapped down a ten spot. "Keep it," he winked. The bartender tipped his hat and promptly confiscated the cash.

She slowly wrapped her lips around the straw and sipped the swirling lavender fluids from the tall glass. "Mmm, that's good. Thanks again."

"My pleasure." Indeed it was; women like her never bothered to glance twice at a guy like him. "So what's your line of work?"

"I'm in acquisitions." She fondled the straw between her fingers. "Wanna sip? You bought it."

"Oh, no thanks." He realized he hadn't blinked since she first touched the straw. "It looks good, though. What's in it?"

"It's like, vodka and some raspberry liquor, and something else, I think. My girlfriend bought me one when we partied at this place over in Soma, and I was instantly hooked on them." Her purse rattled across the bar. "Excuse me for a moment."

"Certainly." He finally tasted his own drink. It was a perfect blend of citrus and spirits.

Claret slipped a silver smartphone from her purse. A thin blue light flashed around the sides while it buzzed in her hand. She zigged her finger across the screen to accept the call. "Hello? Yeah, it's me."

Justin pulled a double take and stared at the sleek design. *No way.* He watched the phone kiss her ear and wished he could touch them both. The micro buttons down the side and the illuminated bumble bee on the back could only mean one thing. *There was just no way. It had to be fake.*

"No, I'm at the bar." She suddenly frowned. "The one you gave me the address to. One two four East Freemont." Her head jerked back. "West Freemont? Shit. But there's this cute geek here." Her perky breasts rose and fell with her deep sigh. "All right, I'll be there as soon as I can." She ended the call.

"Is there a problem?" He felt stupid questioning what he already knew.

"Yeah, I guess I'm at the wrong place. I gotta get going, sorry."

"Is there anyway your friend or friends can come here?"

"No, I wish. She has reservations for a late dinner and the bar is just around the corner from where we're going." She grabbed her glass and poured the drink down her throat.

"Impressive."

She giggled while she patted a napkin against her lips. "I know, right? Look, I'm sorry, but I have to go. Thanks for the drink."

"Wait," he lurched forward. "Before you go, I have to ask you something."

"Sure." She eagerly leaned her ear towards him. "But make it quick."

"Is that the new Buzz 3K?"

"What, this?" She scoffed at her phone.

"Yeah, that's a Buzz 3K, right. I'm sure of it!" His eyes opened wide with all the excitement of a child in a toyshop. "How on earth did you get your hands on one?"

"What are you talking about? It's just a phone."

"Only *the* most anticipated phone of the decade," he scoffed. "That's not supposed to be on the market until this fall. Is that a beta unit?"

"I don't know. My girlfriend gave it to me."

"I would love to get my hands on that so I can review it for my blog." *I'd have all the other tech sites and news agencies green with envy. It could be my big break; we're talking millions of hits a day*. His energy neared its boiling point.

"Well, maybe another time. I have to go." She turned to leave.

"Can I get your number?" He reached out to grab her shoulder.

"You asshole!" She whipped around before his fingers ever touched her. "A hot girl practically throws herself at your dick and you're more interested in her fucking phone." She slapped his hand away before vanishing into the crowd.

"What the fuck?" He mumbled to himself. He looked around his immediate area and was relieved nobody seemed to have noticed the incident. *This is why you don't get involved with the pretty ones. They're all bitches.*

He swallowed his drink and waved down the bartender. "Another round, please."

"You got it bud." Moments later, he presented another perfect drink.

Justin whipped out his phone and fired up the web browser. *Buzz 3K photos*, he typed. His 3G connection slowly spit back several grainy images.

That certainly looks like it . . . but maybe it was a Korean knock-off? Oh well, now you'll never know since you just graduated to dick of the year. He chugged his second drink.

The bartender walked over to collect the tab and stared with amazement. "Jesus buddy, did you drink that already?"

"Yup. Give me another."

"Are you driving tonight?"

"Nope. Walked down here from the Triple Pines up the street."

The bartender weighed the odds of serving him. "All right, I'll give you another, but then I have to cut you off."

"Fair enough." He steered his hand through the alcoholic haze closing around his vision and dropped his cash on the bar. "In advance and keep the change."

"Thanks." The bartender grabbed the mandarin vodka and

worked his magic.

By the time the third Mandarin Press kissed the napkin, Justin realized he had just downed four shots of vodka. That was at the very least because he knew the bartender was pouring heavy tonight. His heavy eyes studied the tiny seltzer bubbles dancing up the sides of his glass. *Maybe I shouldn't have ordered another.*

His phone buzzed. It slipped through his butterfingers and bounced off the bar. Somehow, he managed to catch it before it shattered across the floor. He was surprised to see the new message from Nic. *U still @ bar? Need to get away from this bitch.*

Justin stared at the screen while the culmination of his binge drinking furnished apathy through his senses. He was tired of Nic always canceling at the last moment. *Nope,* he replied. *Called it an early night.*

He took a deep breath before downing his third drink. His hand slowly drifted through the ether and startled him when it slammed the glass against the bar. Every breath became a slow, orchestrated effort to push back against the dense, smoky air bearing against his chest. He pulled himself off the stool and watched his feet touch the floor to know when he could stand. When he stepped away from the bar, gravity's tricky fingers sank into his shoulders. He grabbed the stool and steadied himself. *This hangover is going to suck.*

He focused his attention toward balancing and staggered toward the door. "Hey buddy!" The bartender yelled, "Don't forget your phone."

"Oh shit." Even he could smell the booze on his breath. He swayed over and grabbed the phone sitting on the bar. "Thanks!" He waved to the bartender.

His phone was always attached to him, just like his dick. He stored everything dear to him and his business within the confines of its flash memory. Even drunk off his ass, he knew losing his phone would completely fuck him over.

Justin dragged his heavy feet outside to discover the street consumed by thick sheets of rolling fog. He zipped up his hoodie to defend himself from the cold breeze blowing in from the bay and started his search for the crosswalk. He could barely see the spectral glow of the *WALK* light when it blinked to life amidst the milky haze. He lingered and listened for cars before stepping into the street.

His phone buzzed halfway through the intersection. He resisted the compulsion to check the message while he walked. He figured Nic sent him another message but it wasn't worth being struck by a car just to read it.

The moment his sneaker safely touched the curb, he fished the vibrating pest from his pocket, and stared at the screen. Disbelief bathed his senses with warm awe.

No fucking way. He flipped the phone over and grinned when the glowing bee on the back drifted into focus. *How did I get her phone?*

Justin spun towards the noisy bar, its usual brilliant neon sign reduced to an orange smear in the murk. His drunken memory replayed his events of the evening. He distinctly remembered watching her slide the phone inside her purse before she left.

There's no way she forgot it, was there? Maybe a remote chance existed in some strange alternative dimension. *How did it sit there that long and I never noticed it? Am I really that fucked up?*

His droopy eyes lingered on the flashing *New Message* icon. Excitement swelled through his rising pulse as his dreams of dominating the blogosphere resurrected themselves from the ashes of missed opportunity. All he needed were a few hours to explore the operating system and snap a few photos to authenticate his find. As long as she never set a pass code, he would be golden. He swiped his finger across the screen and nearly pissed himself with glee when the home screen popped up. *1 New Message from Sage*, a message box appeared which contained the photo of a sultry Asian coed smiling behind a glass of red wine.

Justin tapped the icon. Strange characters resembling some form of Asian language appeared. He was thrilled and let down at the same time. *Is that Japanese? Fuck if I know. I can't read this.*

He backed out of the message and searched through the other apps, all of which were labeled with the same foreign symbols. He had been blogging about tech long enough to recognize basic functions in any device. A calculator app typically had a calculator for an icon, a settings menu was usually represented by tiny gears, and a schedule app was often indicated by something resembling a calendar.

He walked in the direction of his home and continued searching through the phone. He glanced up once in a while to make sure he didn't walk into something. He made his way through another page of icons when he found the icon for the photo album. He didn't resist the desire to peek. *It's all in the name of research, right?*

A surge of blood tickled Justin's balls when a batch of photo thumbnails filled the screen. Sage's stunning thin body occupied the first frame. She had snapped a photo of herself standing in the mirror of some grungy motel bathroom. Thin violet rings illuminated the dark pupils in her almond-shaped eyes. Red streaks frosted the tips of her dark pixie cut locks. One crossed arm concealed her small, firm breasts while she held the camera with the other. A thin black thong hugged her bony hips. A palm tree adorned the scratched key fob sitting beside the rust-stained sink.

Are those contacts or a lens flare? He pinched his fingers over the image to enlarge the detail of her mystical eyes. *They must buy their contacts at the same place.*

He swiped the screen to view the next photo. Claret's green eyes begged for a fucking beneath her shiny wet hair. She clutched a white towel against her chest while she posed for an impromptu *Psycho* impression in the dingy motel shower. His cock swelled against his zipper while he ogled her image a moment longer.

The next photo was better. Both women stood completely nude with dripping hair and wet breasts pressed together during a passionate embrace. Intricate tattoos with Asian accents flowed up their knobby spines before spiraling over their shoulder blades.

Goddamn! Justin adjusted the angle of his stiff cock. *They could both suck my dick.*

He scrolled through the photos faster, searching for more revealing images. Those which followed were both titillating and frustrating at once. The girls continued posing for the camera but always managed to twist their bodies just enough so he could never get a full look at all of their alluring nudity.

Let me at least see some nipple here . . . He slid his finger and grinned at what came next. Claret lifted her nude breasts toward her open mouth. A thin strand of saliva glistened between her bottom lip and the puddle of spit dripping around barbell pierced through her nipple. Justin's balls churned inside his jeans.

Expecting more raunchy antics, he quickly advanced to the next photo and stopped in his tracks. The image seemed oddly out of sequence from the others. Sage's violet contacts flared with rage in the bright flash. An angry sneer twisted her face while she reached out to block her photo from being captured. Her bloody fingers blurred through most of the image. Dark red smears trailed from the black trash bag she clutched in the other hand. She stood next to a dumpster in an alley awash with pink light from a towering motel sign.

What the fuck? The urge to glance behind crept down Justin's neck. He slowly spun on his heels. Dense fog glided past. An elephant could have been standing ten feet from him and he would have never seen it. He studied the image closer. *That's got to be fake blood.* He shrugged off his sudden onset of paranoia and advanced to the next picture.

A chunky Asian man squeezed inside a shirt and tie sat

within a cluttered cubicle and flashed a dorky grin full of coffee-stained teeth. Another photo focused on a small green plant sprouting from a ceramic Lucky Cat perched amidst a jumbled desk. He flipped through several photos of office equipment before coming across the image of a humble Asian woman staring blank-faced without so much as a smile beneath her empty glare. The ID badge clipped to her lapel stated her name in both English and Chinese. *Yan Mei, Quality Control.*

Justin instantly recognized the orange logo on her badge. Forbes recently declared Júzi Technologies the premier consumer electronics manufacturer in the world. Empowered by shady trade practices, cheap resources and labor rates compared to slavery, the company easily leapfrogged past its competitors when their social networking buzz triggered global stampedes lining up for their trendy products.

Every bone in his foot cracked as he kicked something and his momentum toppled him forward. The phone slipped from his grasp and skipped across the ground.

"Shit!" He found himself doubled over a bus stop bench. Alcohol spun his balance around as if he'd stepped onto a carnival ride. *There's a reason people die texting, you stupid asshole.*

He promptly regained his balance and started searching around for the phone. Luckily for him, the backlit screen's aura made it easy for a drunk to spot it down in the gutter. He plucked the phone from a pile of rotting leaves, worried to death that the tumble could have cracked it. To his amazement it seemed to survive the fall unscathed. *Nice to see they engineered these better. That damn 2K scratched easier than a stick of butter.*

A light blue arrow hovered in the middle of the media player. His spastic mistake must have triggered the app. The gallery contained a single video labeled with yesterday's date. *Fuck it, why not.* He tapped the file with his numb finger. An animated film reel spun while the file buffered into memory.

Pitch black filled the screen. Stiletto heels clicked against concrete. Sonorous echoes carried a woman's moan. Light slowly filled the screen.

The camera flipped up quickly and caught a glimpse of tarnished beams supporting a cavernous warehouse roof. Thick black cords strapped a nude woman to a rusted office chair. Her nostrils were the only piece flesh allowed to escape the mask of duct tape encircling her head. Black scraps of hair fell over her bare breasts. Her chubby torso jiggled with every sob. Sage was naked and knelt between her legs, tracing tiny circles with a finger through her wiry pubes.

"Look what I found in her bag." He recognized Claret's soft voice the moment she spoke. "It's a fucking 3K! Can you believe it?"

Sage's brow curled. "Fuck, really? Can't you leave those toys alone?"

"You know I love posing." She turned the camera on her own naked body and used her free hand to twist the silver piercing gleaming in her nipple. Her areola puckered beneath her hard nipple. She softly sucked her bottom lip into her mouth and chewed softly. "Oh, it hurts so good."

"Quit fucking around and put that thing down."

"Yes mother," Claret's voice cackled with a whiney tone. The video jerked when she set the phone down on something.

"Is that thing off? I'm starving."

"Yeah, it's off." She leaned over and winked into the camera. The green halo around her iris flickered in the dark.

What the? Justin watched her firm, bare ass while she swayed toward the others. The tattoos etched in her back twinkled with the same green light. She walked behind the chair and leaned over the woman's shoulder. Sage lifted to meet her halfway for a kiss.

Sweat glistened across the masked woman's quivering flesh. Justin suspected Yan Mei's face could have been buried beneath the layers of gray tape, but there was no way to know for sure. His attention snapped back to the kissing women when he noticed the slimy, black tongue slip between Claret's lips and flick its forked tip around Sage's mouth.

Justin held the phone closer for a better analysis. High definition didn't lie. The young women's snakelike tongues flirted and danced in the air before they pressed their mouths together and moaned. Violet light twinkled through Sage's tattoos. Their glowing eyes rolled with ecstasy beneath their shuttered eyelids.

The lovers broke their kiss and ran their hands over each other's breasts. Claret dipped down and flicked her tongue across cables biting into the woman's breasts. The chair creaked against her fraught writhing. Buried whimpers squeaked through flaring nostrils. Sage leaned forward and slipped her tongue between the woman's legs. Justin couldn't see the details from the angle, but his brain overflowed with imagery of her forked tongue probing the innermost crevices of the helpless woman's cunt.

Black talons sprouted from Claret's hands which she raked over the woman's tits. She pinched her nipples and twisted them in violent opposite directions. Muffled screams ripened into shrieks as her nipples were carved away and flicked into Sage's eager mouth. Sage slid her sprouting claws along the woman's pale thighs before leaning in to suckle the warm crimson oozing from her slashed flesh.

"Do you like that, lover?" Claret reached down and shoved Sage's face against a bleeding breast. "There's plenty more where that came from."

Ravenous bloodlust trembled within Sage's bones. She stroked her claws over her hard nipples and moaned. "Fuck yeah, give it to me." Shimmering light danced through her tattoos. Her glowing eyes stroked the woman's bleeding chest with beams of purple light.

An ancient language rattled across Claret's thin tongue. "Oi nila olani nop nis shal hoath!" She wrapped her fingers tight around the woman's throat and squeezed. Bright red blood surged past sharp talons dissecting virgin flesh. The woman frantically rocked against the chair and jerked her arms against the cables holding her captive. Ragged breaths screamed beneath suffocating adhesives. The pixie threw back her head and a lustful growl filled her throat.

Blood spurted from the woman's nose when her head popped away from the tissues meant to secure it in place. Bloody mist discharged from liberated vessels. A spasm shuddered through her body and her hands wildly slapped against armrests. Sage grabbed her by the shoulders and showered her face with the arterial fountain erupting from shredded neck carnage. Orgasmic coos filled the abrupt silence trailing behind the woman's painful squeals. Claret leaned her head back and slurped at tattered fleshy ribbons dangling from the severed head.

"No fucking way!" Justin's heart galloped again his chest. He jerked away from the horror and found himself standing safe beside the bench. His stubbed toes throbbed to remind him he was still alive. Whatever he just watched, even though it had been played on a phone, seemed just as visceral as if he had been standing beside the woman when she died.

There's no way this shit is real. He had seen his fair share of "tentacle porn" on the web, he knew the sick shit those *Japs* were into. He pored over the phone just in time to watch Claret lean over Sage's and spit a glob of blood into her mouth. Their glowing eyes locked on each other. They grabbed each other by the backs of their heads and twisted their faces in to an impassioned, crimson-smeared kiss.

That's enough of this shit. Justin found himself sober instantly. He stopped the video and shoved the phone in his hoodie. The moment he let go it chimed with a new message. He slid it from his pocket just enough to see that Sage had sent another text. His guts coiled into nerve-wracked knots. The overwhelming urge to drop the phone and run like hell nearly overtook him before his vanity focused his thoughts. A viscous competition raged across the tech blogs. The first person to crush the rumor mill and break any genuine news on the Buzz 3K would be destined for instant tech celebrity.

All I need are a few clear photos in good light. He tucked his hands in his hoodie pockets and dashed for home to claim his fame.

The brilliant lamps safeguarding the front entrance of Triple Pines were just ahead. The phone chimed again. And then again. And then again. He stopped dead in his tracks, mere yards from the safety of the complex gate and pulled the phone out. A sudden knot gathered in his throat when he saw the oval stone clutched between his white knuckles. His sweaty thumb traced the intricate ancient symbols etched across its smooth surface. Blue light rippled through the patterns as the stone vibrated his finger bones.

Look behind you, her voice whispered within his skull.

Justin calmly spun on his heels to accept his fate. Shame hunched his shoulders. The story of the decade would have to wait for a more deserving soul to come along.

Green circles sparkled inside Claret's beautiful dark eyes. "I believe you have something that belongs to me," she growled.

The Misfits of Mayhem Meet Their Match

John Claude Smith

I had been following her for a few months, tracking her; not stalking. This had nothing to do with stalking. My agenda was of a completely different design.

Our orders had been placed. A single candle provided dim, fluttering light. The low murmur of disparate conversations surrounded us but never intruded.

I had officially met "Rachel" two weeks previous. That's what it said on her name tag—"Rachel"—though I know she goes by another name, something ancient that burns on one's tongue before it is spoken. A friendly smile and pat, insubstantial conversation sprinkled with the appropriate flattery during a handful of chance meetings at Lowell Art Galleries had led us to this dinner date.

I wondered how much she could actually gauge of my intentions.

I wondered if she could read that deep into my mind.

I wondered if she understood my fascination with her

freakish femininity: her impressive breasts, equally enthralling ass. Everything about her seemed channeled through the warped lens of an R. Crumb cartoon version of "woman" brought to life, exemplified by the show presently running at the gallery, a collection of underground art from the 1960s-70s. My initial impression was that she seemed like a more full-bodied Renaissance beauty, but seeing her amidst the artwork, it was apparent she had more in common with Crumb's bloated comic eroticism than any of my conquests from the past.

But she was more than this sophomoric perception. The general hugeness of her attributes was made wrong by the fact that this super sizing of her body was wide spread, as accentuated by her large head, in which each feature was made uncomfortably imposing. Satellite dish-like eyes to see right through you, or to hint at forgotten histories—in her eyes I saw my reflection, but it was a much younger me, before I'd been initiated into the Misfits of Mayhem. A prodigious nose, nostrils like caves, meant to sniff out your dirty intentions. A cavernous mouth, an oral abyss lined with too many large teeth, meant to devour your very soul—along with hands made for crushing, and prominent feet attached to tree trunk like legs, made to snap and break anything unworthy that groveled beneath them. She was in proportion, but her proportions were definitely, as noted, of a giantess' status.

I wondered if she knew I was here to help those she had taken, to rescue them.

I wondered if she knew that I knew what she was . . . and if she knew what *I* was as well.

I wondered if she knew there was a nine-inch blade pressed against my ankle, awaiting the pleasure of a to-the-hilt thrust, over and over again, like sex between pain and its mentor.

When she spoke her voice was a deep, resonant mutilation of the female voice. She tried to get it right, but I knew it was an act, artificial.

"I want you," she said, discarding with the small talk that

had dotted our conversations up to now. "I want you inside me."

I was not surprised by her candor. Rather, I thought it had taken her too long to get to the point. I mean, I *knew* of her purpose.

But I did have to wonder if she had infiltrated my mind, deciphered the heinous codes that scampered behind my eyes, and was aware of what we were engaging in.

War.

Her hand was as large as mine, maybe larger, as she held mine in her faux delicate fingers; the cool sweat of her palm made her seem desperate, greedy. She leaned forward, the low cut of her painted on black dress offering me quite a perverse indulgence as she almost spilled out across the table. Her attempts at being sexy were less sexy and more simply blunt, but I did not mind. I was aroused to the core, despite my knowledge of where this might lead if I did not keep control.

"Then why are we wasting our time here, when there is so much more to explore elsewhere?" I stared into those large eyes; they were devoid of true expression, blank as a computer monitor before the first word has been written, but not endowed with the endless possibilities the naked screen presented, revealing nothing of importance. Those dark blues shielded secrets.

And I really needed to know where she had hid my fellow Misfits of Mayhem: comrades in the pursuit of wanton lust and violence.

We had been here for centuries. I'd even gotten to play lead roles in this venture, once as Attila, once again as Vlad, and many times as minor purveyors of life's most insidious designs, meant to breathe deeply the stench of death and desire.

We left the restaurant, brushing past the waiter as he was bringing our salads, hastily waving down the valet.

She insisted we go to her place.

The game was officially on.

She lived on the top floor of Croscentor Towers, in the

penthouse suite. Gargoyles rimmed the edges, perched and ready to fly, to pounce, to swoop down and take whatever they wanted. I felt a kinship to those stone monstrosities.

I even thought I saw one smile, confirmation of our connection.

Had she flung each of my colleagues over the edge, sending them spiraling sixty-four floors to a most untimely, sidewalk staining death? It seemed not as my research had indicated that there had been no signs of any deaths of that nature in this city in the last eighteen months. So, what had she done with them?

The elevator ride up was drenched in misleadingly passionate kisses; kisses that revealed nothing of the beings we really were. They were a part of the expected. So when would things shift into that other realm, where expectations were rerouted in lieu of each of our objectives?

I suppose it had already started down that path.

I knew I had to be on my guard, no matter what. She had already taken four of my brothers; I could not let her take me. My purpose had nothing to do with the usual rape and murder— the expected. No, mine had to do with reconnaissance, with finding out what she had done with them.

After all, this was *war*.

Her bedroom was as large as her presence; the whole suite was sprawling. We continued to kiss, but my eyes flitted about, scanning everything, wondering what she had done with them.

Where were they hidden?

She knelt down and unleashed my erection. Its steely mass knighted her on the shoulder as it sprung loose from my leather pants. She actually looked as if she was impressed, but I knew at this point not to believe anything that she did.

She took my penis deep into that oral abyss. I tensed, uncertain if I had already erred. I sensed that she knew my intentions, knew what I was . . . and she was going in for the kill.

I wondered if I would have enough time to ascertain as to

the whereabouts of my brothers.

Her tongue wrapped around the whole circumference of my penis like a saliva slick fist, but just as abruptly she pulled away, releasing it, and stood up. She shrugged off her dress. It dripped like black ink, spilling about her huge feet. She wore nothing underneath.

She had already mapped out the evening's entertainment. (Of course she had, after all, *this is what she did.*)

I had to wonder how long she had known what I was.

I had to wonder if she really knew what I was or if I was paranoid because of what I knew, and what I needed to find out. At this point, most possessions lead to whatever I want, but I could not transfer my influence to her, just in case she did not know what I was. I could not just take her and torture the answers out of her. Otherwise this would already have been over.

Her reputation made me wary.

She spread herself on the bed like a flesh sheet, unfolding herself to me. My erection ached. I knew I wanted to take her, have her now, and kill her, choke her, break her windpipe, thrust the blade—whatever it took!

I was part of a different class of evil than she, yet we both existed amongst the humans, taking what we needed from them. My brothers and I reveled in the joy of mass slaughter, or the more stimulating breakdown of an individual's free will, bending it to need the primal cravings only we could fulfill, and filling it to the brink before disposing of the broken human with a slash of the blade. These were the singular manifestos that drove us, etched in blood and semen across the eons.

We'd heard—we, the Misfits of Mayhem—of the atrocities she was allegedly responsible for, sniffed them on the wind, sensed them in our bones, but had never seen the evidence— she was, apparently, good at concealing her misdeeds, masking them as something else: accident, murder between humans, mass suicide, mystery . . .

We'd thought she was rumor until eighteen months ago when the first of our legion went missing. The first ever.

We had stayed out of each other's way, until now.

What I wanted, what the nature of what I was wanted to do, had to be held in check until I knew what she had done to my brothers before I drew blood.

Her large hands plied her labia open; she was soaking wet. The bed already had a puddle beneath her ass.

"Kiss me here," she said, grinding emphasis toward her slick vagina.

I always had control once sex started. I always had my victims in a situation in which they had no say in what would transpire. This situation, because there was more at stake, put my internal instincts at odds. Still, I complied.

As I lowered my lips toward her vagina, she massaged and spread herself even more enthusiastically. I tasted her and was immediately aroused by the sensation that blood was so close to my tongue. There was sweetness as well, sweetness so sumptuous, so foreign to me, my enthusiasm grew frenzied as I suckled and swallowed the irresistible nectar.

That's when I heard them amidst her moans as my teeth gnawed her clitoris and my tongue darted about—*voices simmering from within her*. Like a radio station from afar, whispers filtered through her shimmering flesh, a bandwidth I couldn't quite tune into.

She moaned louder, pulling her labia more tautly. That's when I saw it, nudging through the nub of her clitoris—a nose! And furthermore, slits for eyes just above it; just below, the canyon echo of voices from within her vagina. The face moved up, as if swimming behind or beneath—*within*—her flesh, the indentation of mouth encompassing her clitoris. As the mouth swam up, a crater was momentarily scraped out, the clitoris puckering obscenely, the restricted lips a wide oval of distress.

It was not the only one. Another face pressed out just below her ribcage, moving across the swell of her belly. Pushing hard, its mouth also voiced something I could not make out.

My fellow Misfits of Mayhem seemed to swim within her monumental flesh, the disguise she utilized, her true self something much more horrendous!

She was a man-eater, soul devourer—succubus, lamia, Lilith: Eve's infernal doppelganger (temptation may have led Eve astray, but it had not instilled such vehement force in her as was present here)—one who roamed the blasted terrain of the earth after being spat from the depths of the ocean, the true essence of eternal feminine revenge—

—and my brothers were trapped within her flesh prison.

It was so simple: I knew what to do, how to get them out of her!

I reached back to my ankle and the nine-inch blade, my tongue gently teasing her vagina as I did. Once secured, I would raise it up, intent on bringing it down on her belly and releasing my brothers.

I would fuck her cooling carcass afterwards, in the light of their joyous smiles.

My fingers ached with the blade in their grasp, I held it so tight. I raised it, pulling my lips from her vagina . . . and she laughed. It was a throaty utterance full of confidence and spite.

The anger surged through me. I would derive more than pleasure from this, I would derive—

. . . *all thought melts, a riptide pulling me into its swirling gray matter maw. My essence turns liquid. My nerves are seared, lava kissed. She has done* . . . something. *The walls pulse, shadows move with intent, approaching me* . . .

"Do you have control?"

"Of course. With the first taste of the narcotic splendor that is my sex, he was a prisoner already . . . and one of the easiest."

. . . *tidal waves crumble like ash being shoveled into my throat—I cannot speak, my protest, impotent. My eyes take in her body—rubbery, elastic—her vagina stretching, tearing from clitoris*

to belly button, up through the torso, between those massive breasts,
a serrated path birthing something. I swim in confusion thick as
boiling mud in my mind, swirling still . . .

"Help me out of this abhorrent fleshy façade so we can let
me feed."

"Yes, my dear."

. . . gargoyles pace and prowl—everywhere—dripping into
the floor and hovering over me. She is one of them—blasted gray
sheen, oil stain luminescence. Another stands behind her as she
looks at me . . .

"You never had a chance, my dear. You and your kind are
all like mischievous boys, and boys are no match for a woman.
A woman always gets what she wants. And I want it all."

"Shall I bring over the vessel, my dear?"

"Yes, no time to waste. He is sustenance, nothing more. Let
me that hungers have it and let's move on to more stimulating
diversions."

. . . I flow as a river, rapids dying as water is slurped down a
starving drain, her hollow husk is draped over me, feeding, *sucking*
me in through hungry pores like miniscule rings of burning teeth
gnawing me, scraping me—a breakdown of self . . . disintegration.
The gargoyles, she and her companions, linger, watching me. I sense
their yearning . . .

. . . I am eroding into her, acidic corrosion, the flesh I wear
melting into her via absorption, the mere presence of that which
feeds. I see two gargoyles meld as one—a rhythm attained, arching
with insistence, a waterfall, turbulent, yet sinuous. Eyes crawl
across the ceiling. The night sky beyond the windows lets in many
voyeuristic stars as they peer into the room as well . . .

. . . I sense many here, my brothers, yes, and many more,
hundreds of thousands more, essence into flesh, her flesh, the one of
whom we do not speak . . .

. . . I hear the gargoyles meshing, tectonic plates grinding,
moans like waves crashing on a concrete shore, me a beach grown
dry, heat-blasted and dying inside, inside her *. . . but not death.*

Suffocation, desperation, but not death . . .
   My essence will swim inside her—forever!

Curfew

Eric Red

First time I saw her was the day she moved next door.

Her dad was all over her.

She wouldn't meet my gaze, but boy was she pretty under all those dumpy clothes. You could tell right away she had a body on her. They pulled up in their gray station wagon, she and her dad, but he hustled her inside before he even started unpacking. The dude shot me a mean stay the hell away from my daughter glance. He looked tired, and he looked like there was something wrong with him.

I didn't learn her name for two whole months.

Candy.

It was the house right next door to ours.

Saw my mom talking to Candy's dad in our driveway a few days after they moved in and welcoming him to the neighborhood. The guy looked uncomfortable speaking to her but when I asked my mother later she didn't get any weird vibe from him. Candy had been coming out of the house with her book bag for school. When she saw me, she gave me this sudden beautiful sexy beaming smile, and I smiled back, but her dad shot her that look, she dropped her eyes and mumbled a quick hello to us before getting in the car with her father and driving off. I felt the spark between that girl and me like somebody stuck my toe in an electric socket.

Guess I kind of followed her after the last bell rang at school.

Candy walked through the other kids in the hall with her head down, her shoulders hunched. I grabbed my book bag from the locker and tailed her into the parking lot, figuring maybe I could walk her home.

Her dad was waiting for her in his car.

She headed straight for it. He didn't see me, but I hid by the entrance and watched as Candy made a beeline for the station wagon. Her father was watching her like Daddy Dearest. I didn't like the look in his eyes. It wasn't the usual beaming or patient expression the other parents had around the parking lot as they swept up in their cars and loaded their kids in. His eyes were like red pebbles. There was no fatherly love in Candy's dad's face, but something else, not right. The blank middle aged face in that bland shirt and square tie had both hands gripped tight on the wheel until he leaned over and pulled up the lock plunger to let her get in, locked the door when she was inside, then drove off fast.

Like she was his prisoner.

That evening I was doing my homework and surfing the web. I heard the car engine, looked out my window and saw Candy's dad drive out of the garage off up the street. His daughter wasn't with him.

She sat at her open window, right across from mine, just resting her face on those freckled pale arms against the ledge. A summer breeze blew her blonde hair like wheat in a field. Candy was staring into space, daydreaming, wearing a distant expression but small happy smile as she sniffed the smell of leaves in the air. Glowing fireflies were starting to blink in the yard. I was hypnotized gazing at her. The way her long, lovely hair toppled out the window reminded me of that fairy tale, Rapunzel. I love medieval stories and fables. Probably comes from all those Brothers Grimm tales mom read me as a kid. I used to daydream about being a knight on a steed rescuing a beautiful princess from a fiery dragon. If Candy was my princess and I was her prince, I knew who the evil dragon was. Her dad must have left her to go get groceries. She was alone. Her eyes met mine in a flash of green. I didn't know what to do except not blink. Then she smiled at me, the most beautiful smile ever, white perfect teeth and shy warmth that filled me up like hot honey inside. If I was going to talk to her, now was my shot.

I opened my window and stuck my head out. We were across the driveway from each other. Maybe fifteen feet. I said hi, I was Ben. She told me her name was Candy and that's the first time I had a name to the face. The rest came easy. I don't know how long we talked, or remember all we talked about, just how comfortable it felt. I know we talked about the fireflies. They were everywhere, little yellow floating lights blinking on and off like fairies, which we both thought made the evening seem magical. I said a few friends and me were going to the movies at Citywalk on Saturday and asked if she wanted to go, but her face got sad and something strange passed across it, and she said she couldn't. I said some other time and right then we heard the noisy muffler of her dad's car coming up the street and she quickly said she had to go and ducked back inside the window. The garage door in Candy's house opened and that was the last I saw her that day.

Going back to my homework, I was happy I had such a pretty new neighbor and doubly glad her house was next to mine and her window right across from me, which meant there would be lots of time to talk to Candy and hang out with her and become friends and who knows what.

That's when I heard the hammering.

Looking out my window, I saw Candy's dad outside her closed window with a box of nails, hammering the window shut so she couldn't open it. As he turned to go, taking the box and tool with him, he shot me a glance. A bad look. His footsteps retreated around the driveway and into the house and I heard the front door slam.

Then lock.

At 3:30 every afternoon Candy's dad went for a run.

It took him twenty-five to twenty-seven minutes. He did it the same time every day, weekday or weekend. Monday through Friday he ran before he drove to pick his daughter up from school. But Saturday and Sunday he ran and left her home alone.

Where she was that Saturday.

Our houses shared a driveway and each of our backyards were separated by an eight-foot tall wooden fence. After her dad went out, I saw Candy in her room and gestured through the window for her to go out into the backyard. She made a mischievous face, nodded a lot, and disappeared. I went outside and got up against the fence. I heard her come out the back door and her soft footfalls on the grass in the yard.

"Hi Candy."

"Hi Ben."

We both stood with our faces pressed against the fence, peering through the slats. I saw just one big green eye. She said she was sorry she had to take off yesterday but her dad didn't like her being alone with other people. I asked why. Candy said it was he didn't want anybody to hurt her. I told her I wouldn't hurt her and she said she knew that. She said she wished the fence wasn't there.

"Can I come over?" I asked.

"Dad locked the door," she replied.

"You mean locked you in?"

"Sorta. Yeah."

"That's nuts."

"I know."

The big oak tree in back of our house was a huge fight with my folks and our last neighbors because my old man went to court to stop them from cutting the big branch that crossed over our property line into Candy's yard. Go Pop. It took me less than a minute to scale the tree, crawl across the big thick branch over the fence and drop down into the damp mowed grass of Candy's backyard. Standing in her yard felt dangerous and kind of cool, like I was a burglar breaking and entering. She stood there with a big wide grin in cut off shorts showing a lot of her long, pale legs. She wore an undershirt that was getting wet in the whizzing spray of whirling sprinklers. I noticed the pink of her breasts under her damp T-shirt. Candy put her hands on her mouth and laughed that her dad would call the cops and I laughed too. We both got a case of the giggles. Her father would be back in ten and I'd better be gone, so we made the most of our time. We listened to my iPod and shared the earbuds. She plucked a dandelion and danced around with it, and I watched her smooth, sexy body twirling in the fog mist of the sprayers. Her white shorts were getting soaked and the wet fabric clung to her soft skin. She was in a state of pure joy and with the golden light in her hair she looked like my very own princess. She even put a flower in my hair. Then, too soon, it was time to go. I pulled myself up on the branch. After I climbed down the tree and was back on my property, I spent the rest of the day thinking of my last moments with her in her backyard. She had stood there, smiling up at me.

And when I leaned down to kiss her, she kissed me right back.

Sunday I was raking leaves in the backyard with my iPod on listening to tunes so I didn't hear him come up and jumped when I turned and there he was. He had that uncomfortable expression on his face, with that tired way he had of standing and was wearing a shirt and tie even though the weather was hot. I saw the sweat stains in his armpits. Mom and dad weren't home and it was just him and me in the backyard. Candy's dad spoke to me for the first time.

I took off my earbuds. "Hi," I said because I didn't know what else to say.

"I need to talk to you," he said.

"Okay."

"Can we sit down?"

I nodded and we sat on the edge of our sundeck. His glasses were filmed with perspiration and he wiped them, looking out into the next yard, like he was trying to find the words. He found them. "You've been talking to Candy?"

"You guys live next door," I pointed out. "Hard not to."

He nodded. I smelled the bulk of him, the nervous sweat, under his neat clothes. "You seem like a nice young man. Your parents are very nice." I didn't say anything, just looked at him. Something was wrong with this guy. "But you shouldn't talk to Candy."

"Why not?"

"She's very shy." Okay, where was this going? "She doesn't have friends."

"When does she get a chance to make friends when she only goes to school and comes home. You're always with her."

"Excuse me?"

"Everybody notices."

"Who's everybody?"

I shrugged.

He went on. "She's not good with people." I felt a violent agitation building inside his bulk and his hands were trembling.

"How do you know?"

"I'm her father. I know her better than anybody."

"It sounds to me like you're being overprotective." I don't know where I got the nerve to say that to an adult but there it was out of my mouth.

He looked straight at me without blinking and I saw

emotions I couldn't understand in his moistening eyes. "You don't know anything about Candy or about me and my family."

"I know what I see."

Then he smiled and shook his head. "You think you know what you're talking about, but you don't."

"I know Candy is lonely. Everybody needs friends. If she wants me to be her friend I will."

"I was your age once, son. I know all you think about is sex. But not with my daughter. You'd say the same thing if you were in my position."

"I'd let her be herself."

He looked at me, furious. "You're not listening."

"You can't tell me what to do. Or her."

"You'd be surprised." He put his big hand on my arm and squeezed and was strong and it hurt. I got scared. "If you know what's good for you, you'll stay away from her." Then Candy's dad got up and went back into her house, slamming the door.

Boy, I wanted to tell him off.

I grabbed the rake, shoved the piles of leaves, put on my iPod and turned the music up so loud it hurt my ears. In my head, I was telling Candy's dad everything I wanted to say to him.

No way he was going to keep me away from her.

That night was the first time I saw Candy naked.

I don't know if she just forgot her curtain was open, or if she knew I was watching, but I had left the dinner table to go into my room and my lights had been off. I looked out the window and she couldn't see me because my room was dark but she was in her room taking her shirt off. Her window was just a few feet away from mine, her table lamp was on and her skin was soft and creamy in the light. Candy had on a lacey white bra and her bosoms spilled over the cups. Boy, she had good breasts. Reaching behind her, she unhooked her bra. She pulled her skirt over her hips and shimmied it down her knees and

ankles and stepped out of it, bare except for her white panties.
I was going crazy. I wanted so bad to put my hands all over her
when suddenly she took off her panties and was totally naked
just like that. Below her flat tummy and navel was a puff of gold
cotton candy. Nude as they day she was born but with a much
better body, Candy entered the bathroom and closed the door.

I was so horny I had get out to the track and go for a good
hard run to work it off. Jumping in my sweats and sneakers, I
told my folks I'd see them in an hour and was out the door.

That night, the whole time I was circling the Birmingham
High track I felt somebody watching me. I did my usual three
miles, breathing hard, sneakers pounding the dirt, under the
big klieg lights with nobody else on the school track but me.
Around and around I went, looking up into the looming rows
of gloomy bleachers in the giant shadows of the empty school
behind the link fences and felt somebody was there. Usually
I love coming here to run at night when the track is deserted
and it's just me and muscle and sweat and my head gets clear.
Sometimes there are one or two other people out there, but
tonight there were no other runners and I felt a tightening in
my stomach.

There was somebody.

I finished my run. Toweling off, I walked off the track
back to the parking lot and my car. Heading back through the
empty school grounds under the yellow mercury vapor lights,
walking through the rows of dark buildings, my shadow was
big on the gravel. I would get back to my house for a shower,
homework, some Internet surfing and bed.

Footsteps.

I stopped. Listened. Looked around. The footsteps had
stopped.

Figuring it was just me hearing the sound of my own feet,
I passed through the quiet dark between the school buildings
when the shape of the man in the dark clothes and ski mask
jumped out of the shadows so quick I couldn't react. The

baseball bat swung in a blur. Hit me below the knee. Never felt that kind of pain. Dropping to the ground, I lay on my side groaning, gripping my leg, and watching the figure flee behind the gymnasium and then he was gone.

I knew from the look he gave me the next day that Candy's dad had attacked me.

That little smile he had getting in the car with her that was just a warning. I couldn't prove it and he knew that. They kept me home from school all day. Nothing was broken. Just a bad bruise. My parents reported it to the school authorities. I got the day off. So Candy's dad had thrown down. I had been warned, but now it was war. I wanted Candy more than ever. And more than ever, I was determined to have her.

I waited in my room, biding my time. A few hours later, her old man had returned from dropping her off at school. Just after lunch, he went for his daily run and I made my move. Standing by my window, I watched the heavy figure in the black Adidas tracksuit and white sweatband shrink up the sidewalk and round the corner. I had timed him three times and he always ran for twenty-five to twenty-seven minutes. Grabbing the gas can and rubber tube, I limped across the divider between our two properties, lifted the garage door of Candy's house and went to their station wagon. I knew how to siphon gas from a prank two friends and I pulled in tenth grade. I opened the gas cap of the Ford and stuck one end of the tube in the tank, got the other end below the center of gravity, sucked the air out so the fuel started to go through the tube and drained the whole tank in five minutes. Huddling in the garage shadows in the cool smell of cement, painted metal and oil, I listened to the metallic plunk of the gasoline from the car run into the big gas can. Checking my watch, I saw I had about fifteen minutes. This was going to work.

As I stood there, I saw the door from the garage to the inside of the house was ajar. I couldn't resist. As the gas siphoned,

I crept through the door into the house to look around. The garage opened into the dining room. The air conditioner rattled. The house looked pretty normal. I passed the refrigerator and noticed it didn't have any magnets or photos or personal stuff families usually put on the icebox. Breakfast dishes were in the sink. An empty coffee cup sat on the kitchen table. I went to the mantle and looked at the photos there. They were all of Candy and her dad. She was smiling, but I couldn't tell if she was happy or not. I noticed that the city backgrounds of the photos were all different. Like she said, they had lived a lot of places.

A door was open and I stepped inside.

I was in Candy's room.

The bed was made. The duvet had pink elephants and looked like something she had from when she was a little girl. There were posters of rock stars on the wall. I saw that the door to her room had a custom built lock on the outside with a dangling padlock. To lock her in. That son of a bitch.

The front door slammed.

Someone was in the living room.

I crawled under Candy's bed.

My head reeled. Had I thought to shut the garage door? I didn't remember. The gas can and siphon were still there. Why had I broken into the house? Was I crazy? Her dad would find me for sure, and when he did he would kill me. Not just kick my ass but murder me and he could probably get away with it because I was breaking and entering and he could tell the cops I was an intruder. I was fucked, man, fucked!

The shower started.

I heard the stall door in the bathroom slide open and her dad step inside, grunting under the hot water. I made my move. Bolting out of Candy's room, I raced through the living room almost tripping on the sweat shoes and pile of sweat clothes her father had left on the floor as I blew through the garage door, and there was the car and the siphon into the gas can right where I left it so I gathered them up, shut the gas cap on the car, slid under the garage door, and ran next door not breathing until I was back safe and sound in my own room.

I listened to the sound of my ticking clock. There wasn't much time. School was getting out in twenty-five minutes. I grabbed my car keys. The drive to Birmingham High took me ten minutes. I pulled up in my convertible outside school and sure enough there was Candy waiting for her dad on the curb. I rolled my window down. Waved. She saw me. Her smile was like the sun, her hair wafting in the breeze. She came over, tits bouncing, and leaned on the passenger door.

"Hi."

"Hi."

"I thought you hurt your leg."

"It's better. I was just stopping off at school to drop off my homework to Ms. Jackson."

"I'm glad your leg is better."

"Can I give you a lift home?"

"My dad was going to pick me up but he just called and said he was having trouble with the car." Candy's beautiful eyes suddenly brightened and she swung into the passenger seat. "Sure. Thanks!" It worked. I took that drive slow. Man, I just wanted to spend time with her. I had the top down and the wind was blowing her hair and I snuck peeks to see it waft over her swelling breasts in her blouse as she undid her shirt. She snuck a look over at me. We stopped at a light. I kissed her. With tongue this time. Her lips were like honey and she didn't pull away, and my senses swam with her sweet musky scent as her hand reached up and her fingers touched the side of my face and then the honking horns broke us up because the light had changed. We drove on, big smiles on our faces, me still tasting her lips on mine. I reached over and held her hand. She put it on her thigh, stroking my fingers. Candy wanted me as much as I wanted her.

Then, too soon, we were home. I swung the car into my

driveway, looking straight at Candy's dad standing in front of the open garage by the AAA tow truck. He had his hands on his hips glaring at me, knowing I had taken his gas and gotten him back and boy was he mad. He'd be even madder if he knew I kissed Candy. I had my arm around her just to rub it in. "Ben picked me up from school, wasn't that nice, Daddy?" she said, oblivious to the war between her father and I.

He was looking at me like nobody had ever looked at me. "Go inside, Candy," was all he said as he followed her in, looking at me the whole time, and closed the door behind them.

I saw his bent, defeated expression.

I beat him.

Candy watched me pry the nails from her window with the toe of the hammer.

She was giggling the whole time. Her dad had just gone for his run. I'd have her and the nails back in so he wouldn't know in twenty-two minutes. It was Sunday. My parents had gone to my Aunt's. Candy and I needed some alone time.

The nails were out.

The window was up.

Candy slipped out onto the driveway.

We stole a quick kiss.

I helped her through my open window, and when my hand met the soft ass cheek of her jeans pushing her up, she didn't mind. I climbed in after her.

Candy and I both landed on the floor, intertwined.

I put my hand on her breast and felt the softness beneath the firmness of her bra. We stared into one another's eyes and her face got all vulnerable and serious as she stared into my eyes with those green and gold pools of hers. We kissed long, deep and hard. Her tongue probed its way into my mouth, exploring, and I stuck my tongue in her mouth, tasting her right back and was kissing her face and her cheeks and her neck, as her hands ran through my hair. Her sweet, musky scent filled my senses.

She took my hand squeezing her tit and pressed it down harder, pushing it under her bra and onto the soft boob so big and pliable in my fingers. I was so hard in my pants I couldn't stand it and she didn't need much help reaching in to start feeling and stroking me when I unzipped and guided her hand there. Her thin, rounded hips ground urgently under mine, as her breath accelerating as she sucked my face and pushed my hand under her skirt and her cotton panties as I slid my fingers up her.

She gurgled. I looked in her face to see if she was enjoying it and saw the awful death's head rictus grin. Her features, gone suddenly pale, were like a human skull, twisted in psychosis. Her eyes were rolled up in their sockets, showing marble whites.

With incredible maniac strength, Candy tossed me off her on the floor and rolled on top.

She grabbed the Bowie Knife on my desk and buried the blade to the hilt in the muscle of my leg. Screaming like a bitch from the unspeakable pain, I grabbed at her hands that were already slippery with my blood as she stabbed the knife again and again into my legs and hips, trying to hack off my junk. Candy wanted my balls literally, her lust turned into bloodthirsty bipolar psychosis like some evil switch had been thrown in her brain and I was wrestling with her fighting for my life. Blood spurted up, down and everywhere, like I was a zombie porn star ejaculating red semen. She tried to stab me in the groin but I rolled to the side and the blade hacked through the muscle and bone above my knee. I lay on the floor, retching, with my legs and thighs on fire. I was going to die. There it was. Sucked to be me.

Just then, Candy's father smashed through the door to my room in his running suit.

Grabbing his daughter off me, he wrestled her away in an arm lock. She was covered head to foot with my blood and stabbing insanely at me with the knife. The man threw the girl to the ground and pinned her in a practiced restraint with his knee in her back and elbow around her throat. In his hand, he produced a long and sharp hypodermic needle and jammed it in his Candy's flailing arm and injected her with some medication and then she wasn't flailing quite so much. Her eyes were rolled up in the sockets, revealing the whites. White foam poured out of her mouth, like a rabid animal. Sick gurgling noises escaped her throat.

Candy's dad looked grief-stricken and sorrowful at the sight of me lying there mangled on my own floor. "Oh no, no, not again," he groaned. "Oh God, not again. I warned you to stay away from her!" he blurted in remorse. Her father held his daughter down as the sedative kicked in and Candy became submissive and began to breathe regularly again.

Me, I just bled.

He looked at me with lots of sympathy, trying to explain. "I've called 911. The ambulance is coming for you. She's done this before, don't you see? I try to keep her away from boys. No matter where we move, the boys come and then there's all this blood, always all the blood. Her mother was the same way." I lay on my back and stared at them, the world tilted sideways. Candy's dad hugged his daughter's limp body is his arms, like she was the most precious thing in the world to him, and stroked her head and hair tenderly. "But she's mine and I have to protect her because she *is* mine, you understand, don't you? She's all I have. I know that in a few years she'll get better if I just love her and protect her. I couldn't save her mother but I will save her. Too bad about you, kid. I'm sorry. We're going away, son. Don't try to find us."

"Daddy . . ." Candy moaned, coming to her senses.

He picked her up and got her out of there before she saw what she had done.

Meaning me.

Candy's dad walked her out of my room like she was a zombie, eyes rolled up. I heard them close our front door behind them, then car doors slammed and their station wagon roared off up the street, gone for good. I was losing a lot of blood, aware I lay in a lake of it. Couldn't move below my waist. Going into shock, just before passing out I heard the distant sirens coming to take me to the hospital.

I sit at my window a lot these days.

I'm in a wheelchair.

The doctors say I may walk again after a few years.

So I sit here, all day sometimes, and look out the window at the house next door that used to be Candy's house. Nobody lives there now. But somebody will again someday. It doesn't matter. It won't be Candy. She lives someplace else. And her dad is there. I try not to think about it, but I do. Things aren't what they seem. You got to mind your own business, like my folks always said, it's safer that way.

Tell that to the next kid.

Blood, Sex and Eternity

Florence Ann Marlowe

Auggie watched a skinny yellow cat wander over to George's house and plop down on the porch to lick its anus. Auggie rested his cheek against the bark of the tree he hid behind and clutched the trunk, sinking his nails into the flesh. Auggie shut his eyes. At least he thought they were shut; he could never tell. With his eyes shut he could still see the front porch of George Rhednick's house and the scrawny cat licking at its balls. It was a dusky image, but it was there all the same. A lot of things had changed for Auggie.

He crouched down in the sticker bush and hugged the tree. Thorns caught on the flabby flesh of his ankles and arms, leaving jagged little tears that glistened red in the glow of the dim porch light. Another man would have fallen to his knees, his legs stiff and frozen from crouching for so long in one spot, especially a man of Auggie's great size with all the frailties that accompany living flesh. August Maxwell was no longer living flesh.

Rooting his toes in the damp soil, Auggie let out a wet laugh. The cat stopped mid-lick and stared up, its yellow eyes wide. In a fuzzy, amber blur the animal leaped from the porch and tore down the dark street. Auggie watched the cat retreat, heard it charge through the bushes a block and a half away and patter on the wooden steps of someone else's porch. He grinned, his long upper teeth hanging low over his lower lip. He could wait. He had time. Time was so unimportant to him now.

The most important relationship Auggie had ever had was with his Cherry Apple Red Camaro convertible. He had bussed his way to the Port Authority and then trained into Manhattan for four years before he could afford to buy that car. He changed the oil and oil filters himself every three months. Every Sunday he treated her to a warm sudsy bath and polished her glistening red coat with Turtle Wax Pro. He had even named her. Her name was Bianca. When Bianca came down with a case of engine hiccups Auggie panicked. Her yearly tune up and winterization was still several months away and Auggie felt real anguish when he found out his regular mechanic's shop had closed down. Apparently Carlos, his mechanic, sold a little something-something on the side that got him in trouble with the law.

Auggie searched the Net for a mechanic who specialized in sports cars. The name Superior Motor Works drew his attention. The shop was only a quarter of a mile from his house in Twin Pines and he liked the idea of giving Bianca "superior" treatment. Auggie drove his ailing convertible to the mechanic's shop which turned out to be part of an old Sunoco gas station. A bald headed man who grunted in reply to all Auggie's questions took the car in and wrote him up an order, promising the car would be fixed by Wednesday. It actually hurt Auggie's heart to leave the convertible for three whole days. He felt like he was leaving his wife at the hospital.

Those three days had been the longest and loneliest days of Auggie's short life. Later that week he got a message on his iPhone an hour before quitting time, that Bianca was ready to be picked up. Auggie felt a flutter of excitement in his breast as he left the building and headed for the train station. The shop closed at seven and he wanted to get there with plenty of time to spare, just in case they closed up early. He couldn't wait another day to see his beautiful Bianca.

The cab left him off in front of the pumps at Superior Motor Works. It was just starting to get dark and the shop lights were on. He walked into the crowded, dirty little office only to see no one behind the cluttered desk. The strong smell of motor oil and gas fumes wafted from the open door leading into the garage. Auggie dropped his considerable bulk into a small wooden chair. The arms gripped his oversized hips like an overzealous lover. He waited with growing impatience. He tapped his foot sharply on the tile floor, hoping someone would hear him. He listened for the sounds of engine work, dropped tools, anything that would indicate there was someone else in the building.

There was a soft, lilting moan from the garage area.

Auggie started to stand; the armrests clung to his girth, the chair rising with him. He fell back and waited. Clasping his hands across his belly, he sat feeling increasingly anxious. There were other people in the garage. He heard their hushed voices, the treble of a female voice and the coarse bass of man's. The nearly inaudible words they exchanged grew more and more urgent.

Carefully, Auggie lifted his body from the seat, fighting back the hugging armrests. He stood for a moment listening. There was just a muted creaking sound coming from the garage. He wondered where his Bianca was while this was going on. Was Bianca still in the odorous garage, waiting for him to take her home? With some trepidation, Auggie crept into the dimly lit garage. There was a caged work light hanging in the back of the garage, behind a pickup truck, its engine hood yawning like a gaping maw. Beyond the silhouette of the truck Auggie saw movement. He heard another breathy moan. He cleared his throat.

The muffled voices continued. Auggie heard the sound of scraping metal. He wanted to back out, hide in the parking lot and call the shop on his cell phone. He told himself that was the prudent thing to do. In the dimly lit garage he could make out two other cars, one on a lift high above his head. Could one of them be Bianca? His mind went white with panic. He stepped closer to the circle of light.

The two figures were entwined, their arms wrapped around each other, a female leg curling around the denim clad leg of the male figure. His head was pressed between her marble pink breasts hanging like plump fruit from her open red blouse. Above the man's sparse head of graying hair was the pristine face of a goddess. Auggie was shocked by the perfect oval of pale complexion. Her lips were the same shade of crimson as Bianca's shiny metallic coat. She clutched at the man's head with a handful of perfectly manicured nails.

The man was short and knobby. His wiry little body was riddled with lumpy muscles that were exposed by a torn sleeveless shirt. The squarish bulk of his upper body parodied the pointed insignificance of his lower torso tucked painfully into a pair of tight jeans that gyrated against the woman's slender thighs. Her skirt was drawn up. One of his gnarled hands slid up beneath her skirt, ferreting at her privates.

Auggie was dumbfounded. He couldn't find his voice. He tried to speak, but a choked squawk escaped and the woman's heavily lashed eyes flew open.

"Excuse me," Auggie squeaked.

At the sound of Auggie's strangled voice, the man's head whipped in his direction, his face a twisted visage of fury. A pair of tiny, ice blue eyes flared with cold heat and his mouth, a sloppy maw, jammed full of odd shaped teeth, worked spastically as he strode towards Auggie, his lumpy arms pumping at his sides.

The ugly mouth opened and sprayed a harsh voice, slurred

and scented with beer, across Auggie's face. "You fat tub o' shit, what the hell do you think you're doing?"

Auggie raised his hands up and back pedaled away from the angry man.

"I'm so sorry; I just came to pick up my car. I didn't know anyone was doing anything in here."

"You some kind of fuckin' perv? You think this is some kind of peep show?" The man grabbed Auggie's face, pinching his flabby cheeks hard between his fingers. His free hand was curled into a fist.

Auggie grabbed at his shirt and tried to pull himself free. He grappled with the knotty fist until the man threw him against the hood of the car behind him.

He barked into his face, "Who the fuck do you think you are, walking in on me and my girl?"

The girl behind him laid a hand on his shoulder. "George, he wasn't doing nothing! Stop it!"

George reached back and grabbed her by the wrist. With a shove he tossed her back into a metal table that was covered with tools. Auggie winced as he heard the girl's fragile body hit metal. She cried out as she slammed into the concrete floor.

George then jutted his finger under Auggie's nose, the long fingernail curled slightly at the end, cut into the fleshy tip making Auggie's face twitch.

He growled: "I oughta beat your fuckin' head into the ground!"

Auggie surprised himself when he gasped, "Get your fucking finger out of my face!" His chin quivered with amazement.

George's lip curled back and he poked at Auggie's nose again.

"I'll put my finger where ever the fuck I want, lardass." The gassy taint of beer rode on his breath, assaulting Auggie's face.

Auggie slapped the knotted hand away.

"I said, get your finger out of my face." His voice trembled and his prick withered between his legs.

George's jaw went slack and Auggie could clearly see into his rugged mouth, many rough-hewn teeth climbing piggy back one on top of the other before George's lips slid back in an angry slit. George's lumpy arm went back and swung out. His palm hit Auggie on the ear, knocking him to the ground.

"You fucking fat tub of shit," Auggie heard George whisper above him. His wounded ear rang brightly. George's heavy work boot caught him beneath the ribs and he puffed out an audible cough of air. His face hit the ground again.

Behind them the girl had gotten to her feet and threw herself at George's back. He shouted like a startled animal. Her slender arms were hooked around his neck. George swatted at her as she clung to him, screaming.

"Don't you ever fuckin' hit me again, you sonuvabitch! You treat me with respect!"

Auggie struggled to his feet. He swept his arm across his mouth which was full of blood. He sputtered, raising one arm over his head for protection.

"Look! I just want my car back. It's the red Camaro convertible. Please, I just want to go home."

George had managed to untangle himself from his angry girlfriend. Her face was still inflamed as she backed away from him. George motioned to smack her and then turned back to Auggie.

"The Camaro belongs to you? What would a fat fuck like you do with a car like that?" He laughed a hoarse wheezy bark that Auggie felt burning acid in his gut.

George turned to his girlfriend who glared back at him through strands of blonde hair that hung in her face as she buttoned her shirt.

"You stay here and be quiet, Tanya—don't give me that look, you little bitch! Lemme get this tub o' shit his car and I'll deal with you later."

His upper lip curled in a sneer, George pushed past Auggie and disappeared into the office.

Tanya pushed her hair back over her ears and wiped at the undersides of her eyes. She was staring at Auggie with curiosity.

"That red convertible is yours?" she asked.

Auggie was busy spitting blood onto the floor. He glanced up at her and nodded.

She smiled. "Fuckin' hot car."

He nodded again.

Her eyes were enormous. They were the moist, blue eyes that peered back at him from the pages of a magazine. Auggie had never seen such beautiful eyes in person. Her lips were slick and raw looking, as they sculpted every word.

"What's your name?"

She sauntered towards him, her hips rocking from side to side as she approached. The short black skirt that sheathed her legs was still rumpled, drawn up showing more thigh than necessary. Auggie watched the perfect figure eight that was her body as she drew closer. She had missed the upper two buttons of her blouse and her cleavage bobbed in front of him.

Tanya was standing in front of him, inches taller. Auggie forced himself to look up at her face. She was smiling, her lips a crescent bow.

"I asked your name," she giggled. The word came out as "axed."

"Auggie." His voice was a timid croak. Women didn't speak to Auggie never mind ask for his name.

Tanya ran a delicate fingernail down the front of his shirt.

"I never rode in a convertible. I wanted a VW Rabbit when I was a kid, but my folks didn't have the money." She caught the hem of his jacket in her hand, fingering the fabric. "Nice suit. You must make bucks, huh?"

Auggie could feel his shoulders trembling. Like an animal, he could sense danger as she drew even closer, so close he could smell her cologne, feel the warmth of her body.

She slid her hand across his chest. Auggie flinched as he felt her pass over his nipple. Her fingers landed on his lips. The caress was delicate. Auggie felt his mouth tingle.

"You don't talk much, do you?" She moved in, brushing the tips of her breasts against him. He could smell her skin.

"Please—don't," Auggie whispered.

"You scared?" she breathed on his face. "You're not gay are you?"

Auggie shook his head. He raised one hand to gently push her away and grazed her tit. She giggled and tangled her fingers in his.

"You'd be fun to tease." She ran her free hand down his thigh and burrowed beneath his belly at his crotch. "How big a dick have you got there?" Her lips shaped her mouth in a perfect "O" of mock surprise. "You're all swollen up and hard down there! You wanna show me what you got? You show me yours and I'll show you mine."

Tanya bent close and caught Auggie's lower lip with her mouth. Auggie groaned and opened his quivering mouth, accepting the taunting kiss.

"You fucking tub o' shit!"

Auggie's entire body flinched beneath the assault. Tanya broke off the kiss and turned away from him, making Auggie an open target for George's wrath.

"I'll fuckin' break your skull open!" George's face was an ugly contortion of furious hate. He flung Auggie's car keys at him, hitting him full force in the stomach. Auggie gasped and fumbled to catch his keys.

"I'm gonna rip your head right off your bloated, fat body and shove it up your ass!" George was moving towards him with rapid speed, turning over a metal cart loaded with tools. He dragged himself forward between the cars lying in his path, hauling his drunken body past obstacles using his hands like an ape to support himself. His mouth was working, but no clear words came out, only animal like snarls.

Auggie clutched his keys so tight in his hand he could feel the metal biting his palm. He raised a hand to protect his face.

"Hey, wait! I didn't do anything!" He pointed at Tanya. "She—she was the one!"

Tanya stood, both hands clasped beneath her chin. She was staring wide eyed at George who was snorting like a mad bull.

"George! He made me touch his thing! He forced me to put my hand there!"

Auggie gagged. He watched as tears forced themselves from Tanya's blue eyes.

"That's a lie!" He backed up into a wall hung heavy with power tools. There was no escape. "She's lying! I swear!"

George was only inches from his face.

The smell of beer and sweat and axle grease made Auggie ill. He turned his head away, his open palm the only thing between his face and the enraged mechanic, Auggie was sure George would rip out his throat with his jagged teeth.

The tension from George's body seemed to fade and he eased back. His eyes were still fixed on Auggie's face, his breath still ragged, he moved a few feet to the side.

His voice was low and very calm when he spoke.

"Get your fucking Camaro and get the hell out of here."

Auggie's neck felt wobbly as he inched his way around the perimeter of George's position. He turned so he could face the man as he exited. The overturned cart nearly tripped him and he stopped, swallowed hard and managed to ask, "I don't know—uh. Where's my car?"

George's eyes never left Auggie's gaze. In the same low, calm voice he answered.

"Outside beneath the Sunoco sign."

Auggie nodded and carefully found his way out to the parking lot, positive George would follow him with a shotgun aimed for his ass.

Auggie had gone home and found his little address book.

He dialed a number and made a decision he would soon regret many times over.

He pressed charges against George Rhednick, the owner of Superior Motor Works.

A few weeks later Auggie had pulled into his driveway after a busy Friday at work. Auggie parked the convertible in front of his garage door and left the car running. He hauled his bulk out of the car and pulled up the top of the convertible. The driveway was dimly lit and he squinted in the dusky light to find the catches. With the top secured he waddled to the garage and lifted up the door. George's ugly face beamed at him just before he saw the baseball bat swing down on him.

The bat struck Auggie between his shoulder blades and he flopped to the ground like a dead fish. He barely had time to say "oof" before the toe of George's Wolverines stabbed him in the kidney. The force of the blow turned Auggie onto his back, his huge stomach rising like a mountain peak.

Unclenching his eyes Auggie stared up at George and two other men. The taller of the two was completely bald, the dome of his skull forming a nearly pointed cap of shiny skin. The other wore a reddish beard that crawled down his neck and disappeared into his shirt. The two of them were grinning.

George's face was wrinkled with a cheerful smile that worried Auggie. He grunted and tried to pull himself up. The bearded thug placed a boot on Auggie's neck. Auggie gagged and lay still.

George turned his back to Auggie and pulled the garage door shut, for a moment the garage was in complete darkness. Auggie felt his face grow hot and his eyes fill with terrified tears. A second later the garage filled with light.

"What's the matter, Auggie Dawgie? Hah? You scared or somethin'?" George smirked. His lower tooth caught on his upper lip, folding his face into the grimace of a bulldog. George bellowed and sliced the air above Auggie's crotch with the heavy bat.

"Wh-wh-wh-wha . . ." Auggie's mouth vibrated uncontrollably as he tried to clear his head of the panic that rushed through his brain.

George's eyes widened and he bent over Auggie's body. His voiced dripped with rancid honey. "Wh-wh-wh-what's a matter, Auggie? Yu-yu-yu-you gonna pee your pants?"

The other two men brayed with laughter. He poked Auggie's big belly with the bat. The mound of flesh rippled beneath the neatly pressed shirt.

"So you suing me, Auggie? Hah? Is that what you're doing? You're suing me?" He stood tall; gazing at Auggie's steadily reddening face. "You put your limp, little dick in my girlfriend's hand and you're suing me 'cause I harassed you? Is that what you told your lawyer? I 'violated your rights'?" George leaned against the bat with one hand. "Is that what he told you? He told you, you had rights? What rights does a fat pile of shit like you got?"

A jolt of terror ripped through Auggie's bowels as George shifted the bat to his shoulder in a business like way.

He stabbed Auggie's side with the toe of his boot. "I bet you got ribs under all that lard, maybe even a backbone and couple of shinbones that need breakin'." He took the bat in both hands and regarded it respectfully. "Yeah, we can put things in order right now if we have to."

"I didn't touch her!" Auggie struggled beneath the heavy shoe at his throat. "She was just making fun of me and you know it!"

George smirked. "So? Can't take a joke, hah? I don't give a fuck what she was doing, you should've been grateful I didn't break your neck right there and then. Like I'm gonna do now!"

Auggie gobbled, his face twitching madly, "You'll go to jail!"

The bald headed thug whooped and turned to look at George. George raised his furry eyebrows and shook his head with sudden sobriety.

George pushed the bearded man back and dropped to his knees onto Auggie's chest, resting all his weight on the fat man's lungs. He grabbed Auggie by the hair and pushed his face close to Auggie's.

"I don't think so, Auggie. There ain't gonna be much left of you to testify in court." His lips came together in a thick, homely smile. "You sure as hell ain't gonna be able to talk!"

George dropped Auggie's head to the cement floor and moved away from him. He motioned to the two men.

"Go ahead. Start him for me."

The one with the beard kicked Auggie in the face. Auggie rolled to one side with a girlish scream. The other one landed on his stomach with both knees and brought a fist down on Auggie's left cheek. George leaned against the garage door, the bat swinging lazily between his legs. He peered out the small window into the dusky evening.

The Beard kicked Auggie in the side over and over. Each time his foot met flesh a series of bright flashes exploded in Auggie's brain. He grunted, his jaws snapping together. The tip of his tongue was snipped by his incisors and a tiny plume of blood spurted out.

In a few agonizingly long minutes the beating was over. Auggie lay still as the men backed away. George bent over and jabbed Auggie with the end of the bat. Auggie moaned and twisted away from its metallic touch.

"Auggie! Hey! Auggie!" George roared and pounded the bat against the floor. Auggie twitched. "Listen to me, you fat faggot! I'm gonna let Kelly and Nichols here carve you up like a turkey if you don't listen to me."

George motioned to the bald man standing behind him.

"Kelly here collects tongues."

The bald man pulled a huge black folding knife from his pocket and flicked the blade open. A gurgling laugh exploded in his throat and his own tongue popped out of his mouth and danced wildly on his lower lip.

Auggie sobbed. Tears leaked past his clenched eyelids and streamed down his puffy cheeks. His entire body rose and fell with each gasping breath.

"You listening to me or do I have to bring this bat down on your fat face?"

Auggie shook his head. "Listening," he croaked.

"You're gonna call off your fuckin' lawyer, understand? You keep the fuck away from my bitch, you understand?"

When Auggie failed to answer, George rapped him sharply on the knees with his bat. The pain scooted up his leg and into his spine like an electric eel.

"I said, do you understand, you fat tub o' shit?"

Auggie grated his teeth and nodded.

George knelt down by Auggie and grabbed his chin in his hand, squeezing his face like a plump tomato.

"Get the fuck off me!" Auggie hissed, worming out of George's grip. Surprise and shock darted past his heart. Why, in moments like this, did he suddenly have brief rushes of idiot courage?

Quietly George got to his feet. He hitched his pants up around his hips. His tiny gray eyes never left Auggie's as he motioned to his companions.

"Grab him," he said simply.

The two men each latched onto one of Auggie's arms and propped him up. George lifted the bat over his head and brought it down on Auggie's stomach. The bat bounced off his belly with a resounding boom. George brought it down again. Auggie heaved and gurgled. He began to pant. He could smell the two men by his sides. A waxy smell of unclean skin and whiskey mingling with the usually comforting smells of car polish and engine oil, aroused a powerful wave of nausea deep in Auggie's bowels. He dry heaved, doubling his body in half and dragging the two men forward. He then slumped back between them, his teeth chattering.

He heard George rumble, "Hold his mouth open."

His eyes darting about in panic, Auggie finally focused on George who was standing over him, pulling at the belt strapped around his waist.

He struggled to stand. Auggie's feet slipped on the floor of the garage, his knees too weak to lift him off the ground. Sputtering and flailing his arms about uselessly, he flopped back between his two captors.

Nichols was behind him now. He grabbed Auggie's plump cheeks and pried his mouth open. Auggie wailed and bucked. Kelly bent a pudgy arm back and pinned Auggie between his knees and the floor.

George ripped his fly open. The buzz of the zipper shocked Auggie into another spasm of useless bucking and pitching. Nichols pulled at his cheeks as if he would tear Auggie's face apart.

Then George's hand disappeared into his jeans and pulled out his member. His penis was stout and stubby and struggling for an erection. He pointed it at Auggie's face, a malicious grin sliding over his lopsided mouth.

"Drink up, Auggie."

A yellow arc of urine traveled over Auggie's chest and landed directly on his lower lip. He gurgled and whined, his legs kicking as George relieved himself into Auggie's mouth.

"See what happens when you piss me off?" George cackled.

The pee splashed off Auggie's chin and ran down his chest. George adjusted his aim and made contact with the roof of Auggie's mouth. The taste was foul and bitter and the smell was caustic. Auggie's stomach bubbled and forced up its contents. He lurched forward and a flood of vomit filled his throat and mouth. He gagged and swallowed and lurched again. Nichols let him go, exclaiming in disgust. Auggie doubled over, the last of George's urine spilling onto his head. It felt nauseatingly warm as it ran down his ears and dribbled into his collar.

Auggie vomited between his legs, puke splattering over his shirt and pants. The smell made him sick again and he dry heaved. He heard George's zipper buzz into place again. He shuddered, his head bent over his knees. One of the men called out: "Shit! What a fuckin' mess!" The other laughed shrilly.

George picked up his bat and sneered at Auggie. "You fat slob! You make me sick!"

Auggie continued to stare at his knees. He heard the garage door slide up. George stopped half way out the door and called back at him.

"Call your lawyer, Auggie. Call him or you'll be drinkin' your own piss next time."

The garage door rattled shut and a spasm ran across his shoulders shaking his gelatinous body. The sour taste of vomit sat in his throat and he felt another dry heave threatening his diaphragm. Auggie crawled away from the puddle of vomit, spitting strings of puke from his lips. His body hiccupped as he fought off the urge to wretch. He peeled off his piss soaked jacket and began to unbutton his shirt. On the third button, the glittering sound of glass breaking outside made him pause. Auggie listened as the windshield of his convertible collapsed under the assault of George's aluminum bat.

Auggie sat on the floor of his garage and continued to undress. His pudgy face crumpled as he began to cry.

A pair of headlights sped down the dark street and turned into George's driveway. Auggie's eyes glowed ember-like and he hunkered down into the bushes. The black pickup bounced to a stop. The driver's side door opened and George stepped out. Auggie smiled a long, reptilian smile. A deep rumbling began in his chest, a guttural purr of anticipation.

George pulled a paper bag out of the cab of the truck and tucked it under his arm. He adjusted the peaked cap that sat on his head and removed an expensive pair of sunglasses that were perched on the brim, folding them into his shirt pocket. He swung the cab door shut and strolled up the driveway to the front porch, blowing a tuneless whistle.

Auggie crouched and watched as George disappeared into the house. The porch door banged and bounced against the door jamb before closing behind him. Inside a light flickered on and a TV set noisily came to life. Auggie had pictured this moment a thousand times in the past week. He had pictured various, brutal, creative ways George would die.

After cleaning himself off, Auggie had sat in his kitchen and withdrew to a part of himself he hardly knew existed. His mind and his heart withdrew into the deepest part of his soul, the primitive part of the spirit where all the foulest emotions are harbored and festered. Here, where hurt hides, not to lick its wounds, but to nurture them in the darkest dungeon of the human psyche, August Maxwell sat and welcomed each painful memory, each humiliation and indignity he had ever suffered.

Hours past and dawn shed its palest light on the little valley. Auggie stepped outside in his bare feet to pay his last respects to his Camaro. The convertible sat, bent and twisted like the remains of some fossilized animal caught in the agonized throes of death. Her windows were empty of glass. Her soft rooftop had been shredded. She had been disemboweled, raped. Auggie's only lady friend was dead.

In less than a month Auggie's bank accounts were all empty and he'd sold the condo. His family was paralyzed with shock at his behavior. They were all convinced he was on drugs. Only his oldest brother had come close to guessing what was on Auggie's mind. He had called Auggie and hesitantly asked him if he was planning suicide. Auggie had laughed dryly and answered, "Probably" and then hung up.

He had gotten the idea from a magazine he had picked up in the Chicago airport a few years back. The magazine was a colorful publication, a chronicle of the supernatural and occult. The article that had drawn his attention was about modern day vampires. The article intrigued him. But this article was not about your typical "Bela Lugosi-in-a-Tux-and-coffin" vampire. It was titled, "*They're Selling Immortality In Mexico.*"

He loved it. For the price of a few hundred grand he saw himself as a new age Dracula (considerably less portly in Auggie's mind's eye) surrounded by beautiful vampire women who often enough resembled Cameron Diaz, Megan Fox and on one rare occasion after finishing half a bottle of Tequila, a befanged Ann Coulter entertained him for many lonely nights that winter.

After a while the novelty of the fantasy wore off, but on certain occasions when he was bored or down, he would happily summon up the vision of Scarlett Johansson in a skimpy tank top and a pair of delicately honed fangs.

Through a complicated series of phone calls and carefully worded letters, Auggie traced the author of the article to a local paper in Milo, Florida. Angus Dougherty was decidedly loathe to discuss his conversation with the woman he had interviewed in Los Gallos, Mexico.

"I don't know why I make such a big fuss," Angus Dougherty sniffed. "Most of them don't go through with it any way."

Auggie thanked the writer after getting the contact information and then quickly asked him, "Mr. Dougherty? When you wrote the article—when you interviewed this," his eyes darted to the name on the legal pad he had been scribbling on. "Llorna Jueana. Did you believe what she told you? Did you think she was telling the truth?"

The other line was silent. Auggie thought for a moment that the man might have hung up on him. As he was about to whisper a tentative "Hello?" into the phone the writer spoke.

"Well, let me tell you this much, my friend." There was a long pause as the man on the other end coughed loudly. "If you do happen to find this woman and you do make this transaction, keep in mind, that there's no turning back. There are stiff penalties to be paid for breach of contract in this business."

Auggie became distinctly aware of an icy pain in the soles

of his feet.

"And of course there are no refunds." Once again he hacked and the receiver clicked leaving Auggie holding the phone on his knee until his buttocks fell asleep.

In a steamy Georgia home office, Llorna Jueana sat behind a large cherry wood desk, her childlike hands folded in front of her. Her shiny, black hair was wound around her head tightly, creating a smooth, gleaming helmet. She gazed at Auggie with deep onyx eyes as he answered all her questions.

"Now, Mr. Maxwell, you have taken time to prepare all your affairs with your family and your finances, yes?" Her accent was delightful. She ended each statement with a pleasant "J-yes?"

Auggie nodded and handed her his paperwork. She took the papers, glanced at them and set them aside.

"Very good." She smiled and turned to her computer. Her bright red nails clicked on the keyboard. Above her head was a tiled plaque bearing the image of a curvaceous woman with colorful butterfly wings. Auggie noted a pair of elongated fangs protruding over the figure's full lips.

"Mr. Maxwell, I must tell you now, before we go any further, that once you have paid your money, and I have left you in the presence of the vampire you no longer have the option of changing your mind. Do you understand what I am telling you?"

Auggie nodded. He felt the chill of invisible fingers tickling his spine.

"Very good. Then we can continue." She smiled, pertly, her dark lips bending into a benign 'V'. "Barbara told you to bring cash only, yes?"

Auggie reached into his briefcase and extracted a manila envelope that bulged at the center. He passed it across the desk. She glanced inside and ruffled through the bills.

Closing the envelope she laid it on top of his paperwork.

"I cannot give you a receipt, you understand, yes?"

"Yes," he quoted.

"Then I will see you this evening at fifteen minutes past eight o'clock. I believe it was eight fifteen, please, check with Barbara before you leave." She stood up and took his hand in hers. "Also, please, Mr. Maxwell, do not be late. That is important. It will be much easier for you if you do not keep my employer waiting."

He stared at her for a moment and then nodded. Auggie started for the door.

"And Mr. Maxwell, I always recommend to my clients before they leave, to be sure they enjoy the rest of the day," she purred as he closed the door behind him.

At ten minutes to eight he found himself on a very secluded street. The house he had been told to meet Llorna Jueana at sat on the end of a cul-de-sac where new houses were being built. The circular driveway that curved in front of the house was covered with white gravel. The grounds themselves were empty of foliage save for a tremendous weeping willow tree whose branches swept the dusty ground.

Auggie strolled around the side of the house. The windows on the lower floor were covered with ornate metal grills, painted white. A heavy link chain was threaded through the handles of the cellar doors and held together by a huge padlock. He took it in his hand and felt the weight of it. Was this to keep people out or to keep something in? He dropped the padlock with a disturbing clunk.

Auggie looked at his watch. He still had time. He glanced back at the cellar doors. Everything will be fine, he thought, staring at the chains and the hefty padlock. The chains seemed to jingle and the cellar doors seemed to part and buckle where the chain and padlock met. Everything will be fine, he thought again, as long as I don't have to go through those doors. His eyes remained fixed on the cellar doors until Llorna pulled up in a white Prius at eight o'clock sharp.

"Good evening, Mr. Maxwell. You have had a pleasant day, I hope, yes?"

Auggie quickly padded to her side, glancing back at the cellar doors. "Yes, ma'am."

"I am glad to hear that. Are you ready?"

Auggie nodded.

"Very good. Are you wearing any silver jewelry, a silver watch?"

Auggie shrugged. "No, ma'am."

"Very good. Then come with me." She started up the path to the house, made a swift turn to the left and headed for the cellar, fiddling with a monstrous collection of keys.

Auggie stood at the curb and stared up at the house. Auggie realized his neck had suddenly gone rubbery and his head was quivering.

The heavy chains fell to the ground and Llorna pulled the doors open, a huge black mouth opened at the side of the house. Llorna daintily stepped down into the dark chasm. Auggie followed.

Llorna removed a brand new candle from her purse and began to strip the plastic off. She turned to Auggie and smiled. "How are you doing?"

Auggie shrugged. "Me? Fine. Just fine."

Llorna flicked a lighter in the darkness with a click that made Auggie's heart jump. She lit the candle and warm, yellow light illuminated the cellar. The walls had been lined with ash gray panels that gave the cellar a cool, cave like atmosphere. The room was bare save for a few ladder-back chairs, sorely in need of paint.

Auggie chuckled to himself. What had he expected? Moldering bodies and caskets full of dirt? He turned to Llorna to share his thoughts when an amorphous shadow near the back wall caught his eye. He zoomed in on the figure. A naked mattress lay on the floor and a woman was stretched across it, obscured by the shadows.

Auggie drew in a sharp breath of air. A hand fell on his shoulder. He jumped, letting a little squeak escape his lips. Llorna smiled and patted his shoulder.

"I must leave now, Mr. Maxwell," she murmured.

Auggie nodded and glanced back at the mattress, just in time to see the woman sit up in one liquid motion.

Llorna set the candle down on to a stool he had failed to see when they first came down the steps. There was a small mountain of wax on it, evidence of other candles gone in its wake. Auggie silently thanked God. He thought for sure he would have dropped to the floor, cold dead, if she had walked out with the candle and left him and the figure on the mattress in the dark.

"I will see you in three days, Mr. Maxwell," Llorna told him as she collected her purse and her keys. "It is best to be cooperative."

Auggie heard Llorna go up the stairs and then the doors falling closed behind him. The chain rattled and he could hear Llorna snapping the lock shut. He wanted to call to her, to stop her, but all he could manage to utter was a soft spoken, "*oh, boy.*"

He glanced over at the mattress and his heart fluttered like a pigeon against his rib cage. The mattress was empty. The woman was gone.

Where was she in the darkness?

A shadow fluttered close to his face and Auggie gasped. The air was suddenly cool and wet. It slid across his cheek leaving a damp path. He had a sensation of being sampled, tasted. His mouth went cottony.

And then she was standing in front of him, a vague figure in the candle light. She stepped forward and let the light fall on her face. Something heavy dropped into Auggie's groin. She was shockingly beautiful. Her skin was stone white porcelain. The flame of the candle glittered in her eyes, golden amber orbs filled with fire. She moved smoothly, gliding towards him. A cascade of red hair slid over one side of her face as she studied him.

A silky, thin slip of clothing clung to her pale body. Auggie could clearly see her nipples straining against the filmy material. His eyes moved over her breasts down to her legs and then traveled back up her body to meet her glowing eyes and her tightly curved lips.

Auggie finally allowed himself to breathe, forced a chuckle.

"I sure hope I didn't spend all that money on a very expensive hooker or something." The woman's smile widened and Auggie's voice died in his throat. He could see her red lips surrounding what looked like way too many teeth. The smile itself was nothing, but her mouth moving flesh. It was like looking at a face hidden beneath one of those transparent, plastic masks.

She said, *"I was a prostitute once."* And Auggie nearly wet himself. It was a voice so dark and moist, a voice so very feminine and yet so rich with age and life and death. It thrilled along his spine, teasing his nerves.

"I was," she assured him. *"Over a hundred years ago. In Ireland. A village called Doire."* A bit of Irish brogue worked its way into the dark voice. *"I was given the Gift when I was only sixteen."*

"The Gift?" Auggie whispered as she lifted a snowy hand and grabbed the tip of his tie.

She laughed, dragging Auggie closer to her. Auggie reminded himself to be cooperative.

"The Gift I am about to give to you."

Auggie cried out and placed a hand in front of her face. A frosty breath chilled his palm. It reminded him of ice cream bars hidden in the back of the freezer.

"Wait! Just wait a minute," he pleaded. The smile faded from her lips. "No, no! I haven't changed my mind. I just want to know. I always need to know—like when I go to the dentist,

I have to know—if it's going to hurt. See what I mean?" She brushed his cheek with a tender finger. The smile returned. "See, I can't take pain," he said honestly.

She laughed, a deep warble. He started to say something else and her lips gently fell on his and she kissed him long and sweet, his chin cupped in her hand.

"*I will never cause you pain,*" she soothed, her mouth leaving his and then returning, taking his lips inside her own. "*I want to love the part of you that hurts the most in this world. It's this world that causes pain. There is no pain in my world. I will give you the Gift and all the pain will end. You will become one with me and my world. We will be one.*"

Her voice was like a wave of chocolate, dark and thick, surrounding him. It caressed him and filled him. His mind left him as he returned the kiss eagerly. Her hands fell down his rounded hips and found his ample rump. She gathered his flesh in each hand and kneaded gently.

He found himself on the mattress. He thought she may have carried him there, but couldn't remember. He may have floated there. Her white hands slid inside his jacket and she massaged his chest and stomach. Slowly, she stripped him, allowing her fingers to wander over his nipples and disappear into his navel. For the first time in his life, August Maxwell lay naked before a woman. His crotch was liquid fire, his penis felt like a living thing. In his mind's eye he could see it writhing and searching the air for a partner.

The woman stood up and removed her clothing. She pulled it over her head, her hair emerging in a red explosion.

He exclaimed over her breasts, pink veined marble peaked by two pink pebbles. She ran her hands over them and then brought her body down on Auggie's, her breasts resting on his face. His hands moved sluggishly, in wonder, gathering them up to his mouth. She gazed down on him, blissfully content, her lips curved in a generous smile.

Auggie laughed as she continuously pressed her lips to his

face, trapping his tongue in her mouth.

He giggled. "It's really sad, you know?"

She purred in his ear and caught his fat cheek in her mouth, gently nibbling. "I mean, you're dead, right? It's just really sad."

His laugh ended in a sob.

She licked his lips and then ran her tongue over his cheek, pausing to kiss his eyelid. Somehow her snatch had caught his penis and she pressed her pelvis into his.

"*I am not dead, Auggie.*"

He was shocked to hear the dark, velvety voice speak his name.

"*We are those who exist between the living and the dead. You will be one of us as well.*"

She snapped his chin between her jaws. The needle-like teeth reminded him of puppy teeth. "You're going to kill me now?" he asked her.

"*No,*" she crooned. "*You will first become one with me. Then you will be a part of me. You will be mine and you will return to me when I call to you and again we will become one. You will always belong to me. We will be together forever.*"

Tears swelled in Auggie's eyes without warning and he sighed.

"Do you love me?"

"*For all eternity.*" She licked the tears from his face and wrapped her hands around his head. Auggie felt his penis being sucked inside of her.

For more than an hour she loved him and then she bit his neck.

He had woken naked on the mattress in the cellar. His eyes may have been open. He was not sure. The cellar was deeply black and yet his vision was perfect. He could not only see the painted grain in the ash gray paneling, but he could see the lathing behind it and the tiny winged ants that crept between the plasterboard and the wood. His eyes traced the bareness of the cellar. He knew he was alone; the red headed vampire he had given his life to was gone. He could still feel her lips on his neck and the soft pressure of her tongue on the wounds she produced as she drew his blood into her mouth. His hand crept to the side of his neck and felt for the marks. There were none; not even a swelling where she had pushed her teeth beneath his skin. Auggie was disappointed.

He craned his neck suddenly and snuffled the air. The gentle odor of—what could it be—something warm, flesh. He sat forward with more ease then he had ever experienced in his obese life and his eyes fell on the cellar doors. They parted and the sweet scent of the outdoors wafted in along with the smell of skin, oils, blood. From the dark opening he saw a face peer in and Llorna Jueana entered the cellar. He slowly turned his head to greet her.

"Good evening, Mr. Maxwell. It is eight fifteen and it is Thursday. Three days since I last saw you. I trust you are feeling well, yes?"

She stood in the doorway of the cellar stairs, a dainty silhouette against the twilight sky. Draped over one arm were his pants and jacket and in the other she held a lit candle. He smiled at her benevolently.

"*Hello, Mrs. Jueana.*" His voice was softly thunderous. It surprised and pleased him. She stepped into the basement and placed the candle on top of the stool, adding to the pile of molten wax.

"I have brought your clothing back from the cleaners. They were slightly soiled." She laid them on the back of one of the chairs and then stood in front of him, folding her hands at her waist.

"It is time for you to leave, Mr. Maxwell."

Auggie nodded and stood up. There was a delightful lack of effort involved in the motion. He reached for his pants and began to dress. He was dimly aware of the fact that he stood in front of this very professional woman with no embarrassment over his nakedness, his pendulous belly hanging over his penis and his nipples resting on almost womanly breasts that jiggled as he dressed. He had thought he would have to ask for instructions or a list of rules and regulations, like stay out of the sun or avoid eating garlic, but somehow all he needed to know was already knowledge to him. He knew everything.

Except how to knot a tie.

He swung it around his neck and stood stupidly clinging to both ends of his tie. He searched his mind for the memory and then quickly abandoned the search tossing the tie back on the chair. He slipped his arms into his jacket.

He turned to Llorna and studied her a moment before speaking. He could actually see the outline of cells in her skin and the minute lines in her face hidden from the human eye. It made her even more beautiful. The smell of her was intoxicating.

"Is it possible for you to arrange for me to be sent back to New Jersey? I've got something to do back there."

"Of course," she demurred. "It is one of the many services we supply for our customers."

A wave of nausea rippled through Auggie's great girth and he threw his head back, snarling. His entire body jolted as a fierce pain ripped through him. Anxious, he turned to Llorna, who stood patiently watching him.

"It is just the hunger," she reassured him. "You know it is necessary to feed each night, yes? If you will follow my directions, you will see I have already made arrangements for your first meal."

And it had been a beautiful meal, Auggie thought as he climbed the steps to George's porch, the wood complaining beneath his heavy body. She had been young and black and smelled tantalizingly of cocoa butter.

By Sunday Auggie was back in New Jersey. He searched Pinetree for Mark Kelly, the bald headed tongue collector. He found Kelly in his own garage, peering under the hood of his Maverick. In the morning the paper boy found Mark Kelly's body, his spine severed by the weight of the Maverick's engine, still resting on his back. Clutched in his hand was his own tongue, the bloody root dripping on the floor.

Nichols was cornered on his bowling night in front of the Shannon, his favorite bar. Through the dirty block glass windows, bartender Jimmy Wilkes could barely see the huge man approach Nichols. He craned his neck and squinted.

Jimmy motioned to a tall man who had just dropped a jigger of bourbon into his beer. "Hey, Ron? You wanna peek outside and tell me what the hell is goin' on out there?"

Ron nodded and pushed the heavy wooden door open and out into the street. Lying on his side in front of the bar was Cliff Nichols. Ron poked at him with the toe of his shoe.

Ron bent over Nichols and then noticed the odd angle the man's face met the sidewalk. He grabbed the man's shoulder and turned him onto his back. Nichols' jaws had been pulled wide, his mouth stretched into a taut "O". Along the side of his face, his skin had been torn into long, bloody strips, the white of bone peering through in spots. Something black, shiny-dull, bulged from Nichols' mouth. Helpless to do anything else, Ron promptly vomited on Nichols' body. The man was undeniably dead. No one eats a bowling ball and survives.

He stood at George's front door and watched his stony finger stab at the doorbell. He heard George's feet scrape the floor as he pushed himself away from the TV. Auggie could smell the poignant odor of George drift through the door jamb. He heard the door knob turn before seeing it actually move and then George stood there.

George's face filled with stupid surprise at first and then his lips curled back from his gums. He rested his forearms against the door frame and stared down at Auggie with undisguised contempt.

"Auggie-doggie. What the fuck are you doing on my front

steps?" He shook his head, in mock amazement.

Auggie grinned, exposing his long, white teeth. He watched with growing satisfaction as George's face drooped a little.

"What the hell are you doing here, Auggie?" George growled.

"*Oh, George!*" Auggie gushed. "*I missed ya, buddy!*"

Auggie watched George quiver at the sound of his impossibly deep, bass voice. The knobby, little man straightened his back to have a good look at Auggie.

"What the fuck is wrong with you?" He glanced down at Auggie's pudgy bare feet and took a step back. "Are you drunk or something?"

"Something, George," Auggie agreed and took a step towards George. "Something."

George back pedaled into his living room and Auggie was two steps behind him. In the room sat a huge color TV on top of a pair of milk crates. An ugly, putty colored recliner and a sagging sofa were the only other pieces of furniture in the room. On the floor was an eight pack of nips, two already emptied.

In the bright electric lights of the living room George got a good look at Auggie. His eyes were jelly red, sinking into the squishy, pale pudge of his face. His lips were stretched in a mad grin, baring his newly acquired canines that gleamed in the flicker of the television screen.

"George. Oh, George!" Auggie chortled darkly. "When's the last time you and me got together, eh, buddy?"

George simply shook his head, fear spreading across his homely face.

Auggie beamed at him, his eyes two bloody slices in his fleshy cheeks. "How's Tanya, George? You still seeing that lovely girl? No? Well, if you don't mind, George, I'd like a crack at her. Is that okay with you?"

George's voice trembled. "Get outta my house—before I kick your fat ass!"

Auggie leaned forward and thundered at him. "*Answer me!*"

Auggie's bellow threw George back against the recliner. He slid down the slick vinyl side and landed on his rump. Auggie hunched over and balanced his hands on his knees.

"Let's try this again, George."

George pulled himself up and darted away, heading for the kitchen door. He slammed it shut behind him and leaned against it, panting. Auggie was suddenly by his side.

"You're not paying attention, George, ole pal. I'm talking to you."

George bleated in terror and threw the kitchen door open. He bolted through and slammed into Auggie's meaty chest. Auggie's white hand clamped onto George's T-shirt and hoisted him to his feet.

Auggie leaned into George's face and pressed his nose against George's nose. "*Don't ignore me, you sonuvabitch!*"

The blast from Auggie's voice assaulted George and he flew back into the kitchen, knocking over a bag of trash. The door swung shut and he found himself sitting in a pile of garbage, staring at the closed door. Auggie walked through the door as if he were walking through a waterfall.

George screamed, his trembling finger extended in Auggie's direction.

"Jesus fucking Christ! Get outta here, or I'll shoot your fat ass!"

Auggie's pasty face brightened. "Have you got a gun, George? Have you? Oh, go get it, George. Please?"

George struggled to stand, his feet slipping on coffee grinds and mashed potatoes. He gripped the side of the kitchen counter and reached over his head. A cabinet door flung open and he drove his hand inside. Coffee cups clattered and fell out, crashing to the floor. He withdrew his hand and a .44 pistol.

"Oh, George! You do have a gun!" Auggie squealed, clasping his hands in front of his chin.

George's frame shook as he held the gun in front of him, the barrel pointed at Auggie's chest. Sweat plastered his hair to his scalp and ran down into his eyes.

"I'm warning you, you crazy fucker! This thing is loaded!"

Auggie raised an eyebrow in comic curiosity. "You wanna shoot me now George, or wait 'til we get home?"

George squeezed the trigger twice. Auggie's abdomen jumped twice and he looked down at the gaping holes that appeared in his chest. George dropped the pistol and leaned back against the counter. His eyes were glued to Auggie's wounds. Tiny ribbons of blood began to leak out.

Auggie looked up and smiled winningly at George.

"Shit. And I swore I wasn't gonna get any blood on this shirt!"

"What the fuck—what the fuck?" George puffed as he stared at the torn shirt and the dead white flesh of Auggie's round stomach. Auggie stood with his arms open wide like a statue of Jesus. His mouth curved into a benevolent grin that made George's teeth chatter.

"You're quicker than you look, George!" Auggie laughed. "It took you all of fifteen minutes to realize I ain't the old Auggie-doggie you know and love." He grinned, exposing his needle like fangs, his mouth widening. "How do ya like the dental work? I'm new and improved—and I'm really pissed off!"

George's weight shifted to his rear end. His knees finally called it quits and he dropped to the floor.

His mouth flapped open and he whispered, "What the fuck."

Auggie smiled. "Very good, George. You got that line down good! Now let's try something really hard." He strode up to the frightened man and leaned against the wall with one arm, his puffy face close to George's. Every limb of George's body quaked. His lips quivered and his eyes rolled back into his skull showing only his bloodshot whites.

Auggie took George by the arm with his free hand and

lifted him off the floor.

"No, no, no. Don't leave yet, George. We've got things to talk about, you and I. George? Are you in there, George?"

George's head lazily flopped to one side. A puddle of drool was forming on Auggie's hand.

Auggie pressed his mouth close to George's ear and roared, "HEY, GEORGE! WAKE THE FUCK UP!"

His body shuddered and George's eyes swam into focus. He stared at Auggie's grinning moon face and gobbled weakly.

"Oh, fuck me."

Auggie clucked sympathetically, "George, George old man! You and me, we're both men of the world, right? You were doing what you had to do. Nothing personal, right, George?"

George shook his head and then thought better of it, nodding vigorously.

Auggie's maroon eyes narrowed to slits. "*You had two of your fuck monkeys hold me down while you pissed on me!*" he roared, lifting George over his head and shaking him like a bag of marbles.

George wailed, his eyes popping alarmingly. His knees hitched and a dark, wet patch spread across the crotch of his pants.

Auggie stopped shaking George and then drew him close to his face, staring into his eyes.

"You peed on me again, George," he whispered and then threw his head back and bellowed with laughter, the glasses and dishes in the kitchen cabinets rattling.

Auggie hauled George through the rooms, his toes dragging along the floor. He threw the terrified man onto the sofa and then bent over, his face close to George's sweat soaked cheeks.

"It's ten P.M., George," Auggie said. "Do you know where your girlfriend is?"

George's rheumy eyes rolled in Auggie's direction. "Jesus Christ, Auggie!" His voice was weak and breathy. He sobbed, his arms wound tight around his chest.

"That's all right, Georgie," Auggie replied around a toothsome smile. "I do."

Auggie stood up and his massive shadow blanketed George. One large waxy hand reached out for George. He had little time to do much more than draw a noisy breath before Auggie gripped his head between his cold, rock-like fingers.

With George securely grasped in his hand he flung the little man's body against the wall, cracking his torso like a whip. George made no sound as his back snapped. Auggie dropped him to the ground, peering into the watery gray-blue of George's eyes. He bent over and with both hands grasped George's wrists and bent his arms at the elbow—in the wrong direction. The joints audibly crackled and popped. A thick gurgling sound escaped George's lips. His face was stretched in a rectus of agony.

Auggie let go of the now useless arms and gripped one of George's legs. He held it up and studied it. He then placed his other hand on top of the sole of George's foot, eagle claw style and began to grind the leg into George's hip. George's mouth opened wide and he hissed as the bones of his legs crunched and shattered. Auggie released his foot and George's eyes glazed over.

Auggie sat down on his haunches in front of George's ruined body and studied him. One of George's eyes slid in Auggie's direction. Spit glittered on his lips.

"That's okay, George, old buddy," Auggie said, patting George's crushed shoulder. "You can leave now; just make sure you stay alive, I want you to live a long time."

As good as his word, Auggie sought out Tanya. He followed her scent, a combination of acrid perfume and her own unique odor, and wound up on the tiny balcony of her apartment down town. She was sitting at her dining room table nursing a cup of coffee. He gently tapped at the glass sliding door. She glanced around the room and froze as her gaze fell on Auggie's pale face.

Auggie smiled. He instinctively knew to hide his true appearance with a glamor. He could see Tanya's face already softening, accepting. She rose from the table and opened the sliding doors.

"Auggie?"

"Hello, Tanya." He forced his voice to be gentle, comforting. "My God, you're beautiful."

A smile played on her lips. Confused, she shook her head. "How did you—what are you doing here?"

"Aren't you glad I'm here?" Auggie moved closer, his arms extended. Tanya lifted her own slender arms to him.

"Yeah," she said. Her eyes were large and moist as she reached for him. Auggie could feel the greed emanating from her.

He ran his hand along her chin and stroked her blonde hair. She sighed and slid into his arms.

"George is going to kill you," she said, her voice barely a whisper.

"Nah," Auggie chuckled. He ran his hands down her smooth body. She was quivering. "George and I have an understanding. He admitted that he could never give you what I could give you."

There was still a trace of resistance in her, struggling to surface.

"Why? 'cause you got money? George has money."

She was in his arms, leaning on him for support. Auggie slid a hand beneath her breast and cupped it. "I don't have money. I have power."

She laughed, lifting her chin so that Auggie could massage her neck with kisses. "Yeah, well George thinks he's powerful," she sighed. "He's just an animal. He doesn't really give a shit about me."

Auggie's fingers disappeared beneath the shoulder of her nightgown. He teased the sleeve off, allowing it to drop, revealing her pink nipple. He caught it in his mouth, rubbing it between his lips.

Tanya's body shuddered with pleasure.

"Oh, wow. You really know what you're doing! See, George never did stuff like that. He was such a—selfish lover, you know what I mean?"

She gasped as Auggie nipped the tender flesh of her nipple. He lapped at the tiny tears of blood that leaked out.

Auggie slipped one hand between her legs and cradled her shoulders in the other. With no effort he lifted her in his arms and carried her to the bed. Tanya's golden tresses flowed onto the pillow, spreading like the petals of a flower. With both hands Auggie slid her nightgown down to her waist and pulled it free. He ran his fingers over her naked body, a slow smile spreading across his face.

She was so beautiful, he thought as he pressed his mouth to her silken belly, sucking gently on her skin. Her pubes were covered with flaxen down. He marveled that she was a natural blonde after all. How could such a beautiful shell contain such an ugly soul? He grazed her thighs with his cheek and heard her sigh again. He cupped her buttocks in both hands and drew her groin to his face like a piece of fruit. His lips caressed her vulva and she gasped. He spread her mound with his tongue and tickled the tiny button of sensitive flesh beneath.

Tanya's hips bucked and she made a breathy sound. He teased her clit again and she hitched her body in response.

"Oh, my God! Oh, please, yes! George never does that for me!"

Auggie sucked one lip of her vulva into his mouth and then the other. He reveled in every audible squeal of exaltation Tanya made. For a moment, he thought, he could keep her for his own—but she was not worthy.

Auggie lifted her hips higher, forcing her legs to open wide. He kissed her twat, just brushing his lips against her clit. Tanya moaned with appreciation. Auggie unhinged his jaw and drew the entire mound of her pubic area into his mouth, running his tongue along the pink tenders before clamping his jaws shut, his razor sharp teeth piercing the fleshy mound.

Tanya's entire body jack knifed and she emitted a shrill bird-like sound. Auggie clenched his jaws and pulled back, the skin tearing, blood spurting. He amputated the entire mons pubis and sucked the blood into his mouth as if draining half a lemon. Tanya's limbs began to spasm and Auggie sat up on the edge of the bed. He spat the bloodless flesh onto the floor. Between Tanya's legs was a raw, ragged wound. Blood spewed in a stream from the hole, soaking the mattress.

Auggie allowed the blood to dribble onto his open hand.

"What a waste," he thought.

He turned his attention to Tanya's face. Her eyes were open and her lips parted. Jagged breaths escaped her as her chest hitched and her arms jerked spasmodically.

"Are you in shock, sweetie?" Auggie reached over and grabbed one of her tits. He squeezed it and then twisted it until the skin rung tight in ropey circles.

"Oh, yeah," he said. "You're in shock."

Auggie stood up and licked the blood from his fingers. He stepped out on the balcony where he could see the silhouette of the New York skyline far in the distance.

Such a beautiful woman, he thought. But there were many beautiful women out there. He could share the Gift with some of them, but most he thought he would enslave and reward them with pleasures beyond their own fantasies—if he deemed them worthy. He had all of eternity to find them.

Little Miss Sanguine

Terry "Horns" Erwin

She loved lots of things.

The gentle touch of a warm summertime breeze flowing across the curves of her naked body. She loved that. So she spun around in a giddy manner, the way she often did, inside the waving curtains, right in front of her open bedroom window.

She also loved—probably more than anything else—to write.

Life had just inspired her.

With one last spirited twirl, she laughed and then tumbled into the nightstand. The book was lying on top of it. The best book ever. It was a gift to her from the man. Inside its leather covers were pages she had read time and time again. It was the only book she'd ever need. The only one she wanted. A famous dead writer's autobiography.

She said the words aloud, "We write what we live."

She adored those words.

Hugging herself now, she grinned and glanced at the mirror

on the wall, noticing most of its surface had been blocked out by the red. The sight of it was an awakening.

Reaching out with one hand, she slowly slid her fingertips over the book until they reached an edge where she stopped suddenly.

We write what we live.

She would write.

Then letting her hand fall flat beside the book, into a red pool that was there, she hesitated. A stickiness swallowed her palm, squishing between her fingers as she pressed down.

She lifted up her hand and turned it over to see all the beautiful red covering it now. Then with it, she grabbed one of her breasts. Slippery, it plopped out of her clutch when she squeezed and pulled.

She curiously looked down at herself. Amazed at the glossy coating, particularly where the red had collected thicker on the nipple.

Knowing she must write before she would forget, she bent down and scooped up more red. She walked over to the other side of the room and began to write. Her fingers were perfect. It was about her, and she would touch the words, form the story with her fingers.

But first she had to remember where the beginning began.

The two boys walking across the lawn.

Yes.

That's how it had started.

With an excited motion, she began to scribble.

She didn't know the boys. And it was strange how they had managed to come inside the property without being stopped. Of course the man wasn't home. But the ones who worked for him should've kept them out.

She stopped writing in need of more red. She got some quickly and rushed back to go on.

Why were they there? What did they want?

Pulling back her hand, she paused. Blurred images played

in her head for a while. But once the pictures became clear again, she continued.

She'd watched them walk below her window. Saw the one with a beard look up at her and smile as they'd moved out of sight together.

She needed more red.

She got some and went on.

The jingling of keys had caused her to jump and spring out of bed. Then the door opened and they'd walked in.

"Hi," the unshaven one had said to her.

The other one didn't speak. His shirt was black and had a big faded skull on its front.

Details were important. Someday those who read her story would want to know and appreciate her even more for it.

At first she'd thought they were there to force her to take the pills. She hated the pills. Had the man found out she hadn't been taking them? Were they there to find where she'd hidden them?

But it only took a minute or so before she caught on that they were not welcome. Two intruders. Trespassers.

What had she told them?

She stopped writing and smacked her forehead over and over to jog her memory, cursing her forgetfulness, unintentionally painting her face in red. She turned and threw an angry stare at the door. Then she remembered. Too quickly she went to write it down, and found her fingers dry.

More red.

She dipped them and returned.

"Private!" she had warned them.

Her eyes had concentrated on the unshaven one's dark hands as they'd unclasped and slipped the belt out from around his pants. And because of this, his companion had been able to surprise her and take hold of her arms, wrestling her backward and down on top of the bed with his strength.

Stretching the belt with both hands, he'd stood over her

and said, "You've gotta be a nympho. We watch you, you know. We see you flashing what you've got under that robe you're wearing now. Dancing butt-ass naked in your window. Teasing us." He'd leaned down close to her. "You're not just a tease. Uh-uh, I can tell you're not."

As she wrote out his words, she could hear his deep voice inside her head and almost smell his sour breath. She stopped and saw the last word was hard to make out, coming off her fingertips too light. Fast, she needed more red. And as she scrambled to get more red, the next words screamed at her.

"Hold her down!"

The boy on top of her had let go of one of her arms to take something out of his hip pocket, and while doing so she'd reached up and scratched his face.

He'd cried out.

The bed had jerked up and down when the unshaven one got on it, crawling over on his knees. Then the belt had been strapped forcefully around her throat.

A click had gotten her attention. And she'd seen the knife in the hand of the boy on top of her.

She quit writing.

Things inside her head went dark again.

She stuck two fingers in her mouth and sucked them, gradually harder, tasting the unique sourness of the red, until her teeth were tempted to bite.

Then the story came back to her.

She took them out of her mouth. Saw the stain of red that she knew would not create words, so she got some more red and kept at it. Fearing she'd forgotten a detail, her hand shook now as she wrote.

The knife had been pressed against one of her wrists, and his hand over it. He'd suddenly let go of her other arm, but only after the one holding the belt had trapped it beneath the force of his knee.

Her heels had beaten the side rail as she kicked and fought.

She'd stared at the skull design on his shirt as he opened her robe.

"Nice," the unshaven one had said.

Then the skull had started to move up and down. He'd put himself inside her.

"Yeah, you like this, huh?" the unshaven one had said, taking the belt away and positioning himself right next to her head.

The sensations of his hand playing with her breasts had caused her to become still. She'd watched his dark fingers find a nipple and stroke it until it grew big. Then next he'd. . . .

The red had stopped again. She needed more of it and now also realized she was running out of space.

He'd laid his boy thing across her lips.

"C'mon, it's what you want," he'd told her.

The boy rocking on top of her had begun to cry out. At that moment, something inside of her where he was joined changed. And he'd fallen on her, his chest heaving against her.

She'd felt the knife loosen too, and with furious speed, she'd grabbed it and jabbed the blade into the side of his neck.

"Why?" the unshaven one had shouted. Then he had jumped off the end of the bed, and without delay, he'd ran to the door, thrown it open and vanished.

Clutching his neck, she'd watched the boy's head strike the nightstand. And she'd seen the way the skull on his shirt had laughed after he'd stood up with the knife still there and stumbled across the room, where he sat down hard on the floor with his back up against the wall.

She stopped writing. And with a frown, she looked at the limited space around her.

Would she have the room to tell it all?

She walked over to the body and yanked the knife free.

It made his limp head shake.

Using her fingers, she wiped the red off the blade.

She tossed the knife down and walked over to the bed.

Her eyes were trained on the space on the wall above it where a picture was hanging.

With her feet, she moved aside the robe lying on the floor, noticing the red spattered on it she couldn't use. Then she climbed on the bed and balanced herself as she walked across the mattress. The belt the unshaven one had left behind made her angry when she stepped on it, so she kicked it off the edge. She took down the picture frame and set it on the bed.

Not much space, she thought. But she put her fingers on the wall anyway and began to write.

Just as she was losing the red again, she heard a sound outside.

She quickly got down off the bed and hurried over to the window.

Holding onto the metal bars, she pressed her face between them. The sunlight tingled her skin.

She saw the man.

Yes! He's home! she thought with joy.

He would see the work she'd done. Treasure her inspiration. *We write what we live.*

He understood. He'd given her the book. Now maybe he would see there was no need for the pills. No more need at all.

She loved lots of things.

And *he* was one of them.

She sat down on the edge of the bed and waited. And she imagined him coming inside her room and saying, "Little Miss, I am so happy!" A smile swollen with pride and cheerfulness trembled on her face. And it stayed there even when the shadow began to dim her mind once more. She wasn't sure how long it would affect her. She never was.

She looked up and saw the man standing inside the doorway.

"What have you done?" he asked.

She watched him as he stepped slowly and carefully into the room. And she noticed the muscles in his face shifting and forming different expressions as he took it all in. The magnitude and brilliance of the red everywhere, telling him her story.

She expected him to cry tears overflowing with delight once he realized the significance of what she'd done and read the words until there was nothing left to possess.

She blinked when she saw a small badge on his jacket.

"Come here," he persuaded her, holding out his arms.

Dr. Christopher Thanner.

Why was he wearing those words?

She glanced at the body of the boy.

Her smiled faded.

Was that the reason something was wrong? she asked herself. The boy? The intruder?

The man grabbed her and, all at once, the cloud in her head went away.

She hugged him tight. Thrilled because he was so happy with her like she'd believed he'd be. Then she tugged on him so he would give her his full attention.

With tears in her eyes and a breathtaking sense of belonging, she whispered the words to him, "We write what we live."

She peered into his wide eyes and yearned to never look away again from the love and happiness she found swirling within their blue depth.

After he had talked on his phone, the others came.

She couldn't help but laugh from all the excitement bursting out of her as he carried her with him through the hall and down the stairs.

The others would erase her story, she had no delusions about that, but it didn't matter now because he knew it. The man she loved would always know it, and someday share it with the world.

The Line-Up at Buddy Milam's Trailer

Walter Jarvis

Sometimes when I lie in bed at night, unable to sleep, the sheets soaked with sweat, I go over in my mind how different things would have been if I had taken Joe Mayes' advice and gone home to take a cold shower. Oh, he hadn't been serious when he suggested it, and I can't blame Joe for talking me into going to Buddy Milam's trailer either. Poor old Joe. I hear he underwent shock therapy again last week. It got to all of us, no matter how tough and macho we thought we were at the time.

It seems like part of me is still stuck in that trailer, trapped like a fly in a spider's web. And the more I struggle to break free, the more entangled I get. It's my soul that's caught, maybe, or whatever it is that separates man from the beasts, and I can hear Buddy laughing from the grave about my plight.

Don't get me wrong. I appreciate you trying to help me, Doc, I really do. Only don't lose too much sleep over the end results. I guess you know you're not the first, and you probably won't be the last. Sometimes it almost seems that therapy will make a difference, then my thoughts start beating against that web again, and I'm back where I started.

Logically everything you're going to tell me makes sense— that it's guilt that I feel over what we did at the trailer that's messed up my life, not anything supernatural—but then you didn't know Buddy Milam. You didn't know the power he had over Cissie. And you didn't see that figure crouched on its knees in the back of the trailer, waiting in the dark. I see it every time I shut my eyes, and probably will until the day I die.

I don't sleep very well anymore, and hardly eat a thing. Sex is the last thing on my mind. Maybe that's all I deserve. Maybe all any of us deserve. I'm sure that's what Mary Alice would say, if you asked her . . .

I had heard the rumors that Cissie Maxwell was going to take on the whole football team on Thursday night, but I was more concerned about how far I was going to get with my own girlfriend that evening to pay much attention to the logistics.

My buddies called Mary Alice a prick teaser. You know, somebody who acts like she wants it, but who really uses sex for the power it gives her over a guy. They did it because they knew it would piss me off. Half the reason it did get under my skin was because I suspected they were right.

I used to talk a good line in the locker room about how Mary Alice and I were doing it every chance we got, but I think most of the guys saw through me. I was desperately afraid that one of them would say something to Mary Alice, calling my bluff, but nobody ever did.

The thing was, I was willing to let her boss me around because I really did love her. Part of it was the way she looked: I was captivated by her firm little breasts always shown off to their best advantage under tight cashmere sweaters, or by the curve of her hips which seemed to be poured into the gray wool skirts she wore to school. Her ash-blonde hair always smelled good.

Her smile was beautiful, too, even though there was something a little flinty behind the dimples and perfect white teeth.

Her kisses were deep and passionate, and her murmurs of "I love you" when we went parking bordered on moans of ecstasy. But one thing I have to say about Mary Alice: She always knew how to put on the brakes before things got out of control.

"Nice girls don't do those things," she told me once, after a long bout of French kissing during which I had tried clumsily to move to the next plateau, "and nice boys don't ask them to."

"Well, maybe I'm not a nice boy," I had answered, wiping her spittle off the side of my cheek with the back of my hand.

"You're a very nice boy," she had said, patting me with almost motherly fashion on the knee. "We go to church together every Thursday, remember? If you weren't nice, you wouldn't do that. Anyway, you don't want me to be like that awful Cissie Maxwell, do you?"

Actually, I did. Lord, how I wished she were more like Cissie.

We had stopped for a light on Main Street on our way to park at Grover's Point. Mary Alice, who had been chattering away about a dress that one of our classmates had worn to church ("Have you ever seen such a god-awful color, Bobby? Even our maid Mattie wouldn't be caught dead in it!") suddenly sucked in her breath. "Look over there!" she whispered dramatically. "You see that person standing in front of Norma's Dress Shop? You know who that is, don't you?"

I turned my head and saw a rather nondescript girl in a light green carhop's uniform. She was a little on the heavy side and had her hair cut in a careless pageboy. She was staring at a sharp-looking dress in the store window as if there were nothing else in the world that mattered.

"That's Cissie Maxwell!" Mary Alice hissed. "No need to ask what she's doing out on the street!"

"Aw, she's just got off work and is waiting for her ride," I said.

"If you want to know what kind of work she really does, just ask Buddy Milam," Mary Alice said with a knowing little smile.

I had heard all the rumors, too. How Cissie had taken on two boys at the same time in the back of Elmo's Pool Hall after hours under Buddy's none-too-gentle encouragement. How, if you were real nice to Buddy, and lent him twenty bucks which you would never expect to see again, he would arrange a very special date with Cissie. Lately I had heard that Buddy had matched her up with complete strangers, traveling salesmen who stayed at the aging Hughes Hotel in downtown Boulton, or even GIs stationed at nearby Ft. Hood.

Let me tell you a little about Buddy. He was the kind of kid you learned early on to stay as far away from as possible. He wore his hair in a long, greasy ducktail and always had an unfiltered Camel dangling from the corner of his mouth, drawn from a cigarette pack conveniently folded away in the upturned sleeve of his T-shirt.

The rumor was he was into all sorts of vices: booze, tobacco, even a little dope. Some people said he even played around with black magic, which would have been a first for Boulton's ne'er-do-wells.

"She's looking in our direction!" Mary Alice said. "Pretend you don't see her."

Impossible under the circumstances. Our eyes met for a moment and then she gave me a sad little smile like she knew what I was thinking, and that she wished that somebody else besides Buddy was going to pick her up. The light changed, I looked hurriedly away without smiling back and drove off.

A harvest moon was just breaking over the horizon when we pulled into the point. There were four cars that had arrived ahead of us, parked far enough apart so that each couple could maintain a minimum of privacy. Before my hands had left the steering wheel, Mary Alice was all over me, kissing me, nibbling at my ear, her arms clamping leech-like around my shoulders.

I hadn't expected this. Mary Alice had never come on to me so strongly before. Maybe she finally felt guilty about stringing me on for so long.

I responded by kissing her deeply and passionately. With matching moans of pleasure, we twisted against each other in the front seat of my Fairlane while the windows steamed over, turning the drops of moisture pumpkin-yellow as the harvest moon grew brighter and brighter in the autumn sky.

My fingers wriggled under the edge of her blouse and brushed up against the soft, warm skin of her belly. Emboldened, they crept upwards until they came to rest on the curve of her breasts. I could feel her heart thumping beneath the sheer material of her bra.

"No, don't," Mary Alice groaned, pushing my hand away. It wasn't a very heartfelt push, though, and it only spurred me on. This was the furthest I had ever gotten with her, and I wasn't about to let the opportunity slip away.

Pressing my other hand between her legs and exerting pressure, I began to force my way up her thigh. She tried to wiggle away from me but I had left her no room to maneuver.

Mary Alice grabbed my wrist and tried to pull my hand away; but that only made me redouble my efforts. It suddenly struck me through a pounding red fog of passion that tonight might be the night I had waited for so long.

My fingertips found the elastic band of her panties and slithered inside, plunging triumphantly in the mass of her pubic hair. A few seconds later my index finger entered that mysterious place that I had dreamed about so longingly but which had been uncharted territory until now. She moaned with what I took to be encouragement and my free hand began wrestling with my zipper. I was almost beside myself with the realization that the moment had arrived.

Suddenly she jerked her head away. "Oh, Bobby," she sobbed, "that's not nice. That's not nice at all." I tried to kiss away her reservations and felt something wet and salty on my lips. She was crying now with great gulping sobs. My passion wilted immediately and I shifted away from her with a sigh of remorse.

"I'm sorry, Mary Alice," I said in a voice of utter dejection. "I didn't mean to make you cry."

"You must think I'm terrible," she said in a choking voice, covering her face with her hands. "A real little tramp."

"No, no," I protested. "It wasn't you, it was me."

"I just couldn't face myself if I went all the way," she went on. "You wouldn't respect a girl who did that, I know. That's true, isn't it?"

I said it was, and sounded convincing when I said it, but respect for Mary Alice or any other girl was the last thing on my mind.

After I took her home (we barely said two words the whole way back), I cruised over to the All Star Drive-In and went up to the window to drown my sorrows in an ice cream float. A car honked repeatedly and I looked around to find Joe Mayes grinning at me from the driver's side of his black '48 Ford coupe. Some other guys from the team were piled in the back.

"Well, did you get any tonight?" Joe asked. His question was greeted with guffaws of laughter from the back seat.

"Oh, screw you," I said, which only elicited more hoarse merriment.

Joe hopped out of the car, ran up to me and pounded me on the back. "Hey, don't take it so hard, son," he grinned. "Everybody knows ol' Mary Alice is the queen of prick teasers. And speaking of pussy, we're on our way over to Buddy Milam's. Wanna go?"

"Gee, I don't know," I said doubtfully. I remembered then that tonight was the night that Cissie was supposed to service the football team. "I'm afraid I'll get the clap or something."

"She's just goin' to give us blow jobs," Joe said. "All you got to do is give Buddy Milam a ten-spot going in, and everything's cool."

Buddy Milam. Just the thought of having to look him in the eye while handing over a $10 bill so I could be blown by his girlfriend sent an apprehensive chill down my spine.

I was about to say no when Joe added, "Hey, look at it as a way of getting back at Mary Alice. You'll have the last laugh. Otherwise, be pussy-whipped and go home and take a cold shower."

"I'm in," I said, my jaw tightening.

When we arrived at the trailer where Buddy lived with his alcoholic father, there were already half a dozen cars parked in a semi-circle around the run-down double-wide. Even with its worst excesses masked by the moonlight, the Milam residence was still a pretty sad sight. The body of a rusting Desoto sat on cinder blocks in the front yard, and a television antenna tilted dangerously from the sagging roof. I noticed right away that no lights were on inside, and that the front door gaped open. I could barely make out a ghostly figure slouched against the door frame. It was Buddy Milam himself.

The other football players waiting their turns were sitting on their car hoods, drinking beer and talking in low, excited voices.

I got out and looked around for Joe. "Hey, look who's here," someone called out in the darkness. "Mr. Straight Arrow."

"If Bobby's here, I know my mom would approve," another player chuckled.

"Go fuck yourself," I said, but without much conviction. I walked over to Joe's old Ford that had pulled in just ahead of me.

"This is the way it works," Joe said, nervously lighting a

cigarette. "We go in one at a time. Buddy, he takes your money
at the door. You don't need to say nothing, just fork over ten
bucks. He's real late gettin' started, so it's gonna be down and
dirty."

Buddy suddenly stepped out on the trailer's little porch.
He was sporting a T-shirt that gleamed with a bleached bone
whiteness in the moonlight and a pair of Levi's that seemed
glued on to his bony hips. I didn't know if it was a trick of the
moonlight, or just my own anxiety, but Buddy looked worse
than usual. His hair, normally fashioned so lovingly into a
complex ducktail, stood out in spikes, and his pale skin was
covered with a sheen of sweat. I clearly could see the whites of
his eyes, like a horse that has been spooked.

"You," he said, pointing to the next in line, which
happened to be Joe.

"Well, here goes nothing," he said with a sigh, pushing
himself away from the hood of his car.

As I watched him pause at the entrance to pay Buddy and
then disappear into the blackness of the trailer, I was tempted
to get back in my car and drive off. I knew I'd get a lot of crap
from the other guys, but they'd forget about it soon enough. In
the long run, who would really care?

Then Buddy was pointing at me, and I knew that the eyes
of the other players were on me as well. It was too late to back
out. Reluctantly I trudged toward the trailer.

"So you're here, too," Buddy said when I stepped up to the
door. "Cissie said she saw you in the car with your girlfriend,
and y'all pretended she didn't even exist." His voice sounded
really weird, as if each word was being torn out with forceps
from his vocal cords. "Now that she's got a little pussy to sell,
you can't get here fast enough, can you? You know what, Jock?
It don't matter. Your money's as good as anybody else's."

I was careful not to look at him as I handed over a ten-spot,
but we were close enough so that I could feel a kind of heat
radiating off his scrawny body, as if Buddy was burning with

a fever. Easing sideways, glad to get away from him, I stepped into the darkness of the trailer.

It smelled of too many unwashed bodies and moldy carpets, and my nose wrinkle in disgust. There was also another, underlying smell, coppery and faintly acrid, which I could not identify but which was disagreeable enough to make me want to turn around.

The almost total darkness was disorienting. I thought about waiting there a few minutes, and then letting myself out as if I had done the deed. Who was going to know the difference? Buddy had his money, and Cissie would probably look at it as a favor: one less guy to service.

Then I heard the floor creak. Peering into the darkness, I could barely make out an indistinct shape at the end of the hall. At first I thought it must be a child, and then realized it was someone foreshortened for a purpose. Cissie Maxwell. On her knees and ready for business. Well, you've paid your money, I thought glumly. You might as well get your reward.

"Cissie?" I called out softly. I was answered by something that sounded more like a gurgle than words. Taking that as an acknowledgment of my presence, I took a tentative step down the hall. I knew I was getting close to her because I could more clearly make out her outline in the faint light seeping in through the curtained window. For a second, I felt bad for her. I remembered the girl staring dreamily at the new dress in the store window, and was sure that Buddy never rewarded her with anything nice like that. What kind of existence was it when you were reduced to giving blow jobs to the football team to satisfy your boyfriend? Then to have to face those same boys at school, knowing that they were whispering about you behind your back, laughing at you?

I stopped in front of the crouched, motionless shape. What was I supposed to do next? Say something to get her started? Acknowledge her presence in some way?

While I was debating my next move, I felt fingers, light as

crawling spiders, touch my thigh and begin to work their way up my jeans. The unexpected shock made me gasp a little, and then I gave a nervous, uncontrollable giggle. "Sorry, Cissie," I said in a choked voice, "you surprised me."

No reply. Instead she began working at my zipper. I distinctly heard a cold metallic hiss as the braids separated. Then fingers inside the opening, probing.

Instead of becoming aroused, I grew more and more uncomfortable. At that moment I felt anything but horny. If there had been any way I could have gotten out of there without hurting her feelings, I would have, loss of face or no.

But then she began to massage my cock in a mechanical, almost indifferent fashion. Surprisingly enough, I felt it go erect. I forced myself to look down at the same moment she took it into her mouth. She took it in so far that I thought surely she was going to choke on it, but she didn't. With a feeling of disgust I looked away, even though I could barely see her in the darkness.

The piston-like suction of her enveloping lips made me shudder, and not with pleasure, either. I would never have imagined that a mouth could feel so cold and dry.

Feebly I tried to withdraw, but one of her hands clamped firmly around the base of my cock and held it in place. Her head began to bob faster and faster to a rhythm of its own.

"You know you really don't have to do this if you don't want to, Cissie," I choked. She made an unintelligible noise in reply—a kind of gurgle (but then, her mouth was full, wasn't it?)—and I knew that she was going to bring me to a climax no matter what.

I felt myself approaching orgasm and, not wanting to come in her mouth, tried desperately to pull away. Her jaw tightened almost imperceptibly and I froze, afraid for a horrifying moment that she was going to bite down on me.

Then it happened. I ejaculated before I had a chance to pull out. Not worried anymore if I were going to hurt her feelings, I reached down and pushed her face away. I was disgusted to feel my hands all wet from touching her. Hurriedly zipping up my pants, I fled the trailer, pushing my way past Buddy, not caring whether it angered him or not, and rushed to my car. "Well, you feel like a new man?" Joe called out to me as I stumbled past the old Ford. There was an odd, forced note in my friend's voice that I had never heard before.

"It was good," I answered in a strangled voice.

"They don't call ol' Cissie Hoover Mouth for nothing, do they?" Joe said with a curious high-pitched laugh. "Hey, what's that on your hands? They look all wet."

I looked down. In the moonlight, the spots on my hands were almost black. Quickly I wiped them off on my jeans, but a kind of sticky, salty smell stayed with me. It wasn't until two days later, when my mom complained about being unable to wash out the stains, that I made the connection. I've wished ever since I hadn't.

It took another twenty-four hours before the town learned how busy Buddy Milam had been that night.

First he had killed his old man. The sheriff's department found Gilbert's body in the woods behind the trailer. His head had been bashed in almost beyond recognition. No one ever found out what prompted the killing, but most of us believed that Gilbert must have aroused himself from his semi-comatose alcoholic state long enough to balk at using the double-wide as a portable whorehouse, and the ensuing argument drove Buddy over the edge.

Cissie was found slumped over at the end of trailer's hallway with her throat cut. She was still wearing her carhop's uniform, although it was more red now than green. Maybe she had tried to stop Buddy from killing Gilbert, only to suffer the same fate at his hands. Just before dawn, and long after we had left, Buddy had hanged himself from the oak tree in front of the house. The rope was too long, allowing his toes to touch the ground after he jumped, so he must have endured a long, painful death that night. That would have been poetic justice in someone else's case, but was simply one final screw-up by a classic loser in Buddy's.

Of course, our visit to the trailer could not be kept secret, and in due time all of us were interviewed by the Boulton police. Surprisingly enough, although word of the scandal flew through the school like wildfire, it was never discussed publicly. None of the players were ever censured. Nobody wanted to do anything that would decimate the team and ruin our chances of winning the district championship.

"It gives me the shakes every time I think about it," Joe said to me long afterwards. "I mean, one minute she was giving us all blow jobs, the next minute she was dead. Jesus Christ."

Joe was never very good at math, or maybe he just didn't want to do the numbers, but I figured it out. Years later, I got a hold of the coroner's report. Cissie had her throat cut about 10 P.M. Church let out about eight. It took about half an hour to drive out to the Point. Mary Alice and I probably used up a good hour once we were there. We'd be pushing ten by the time I took her home. Then I went to the drive-in, and from there, to Buddy's. Given driving time and waiting in line, that would have put me in the double-wide's hallway well past eleven. Buddy would have had just enough time to do his mischief from the time he picked Cissie up downtown until the first of the team arrived. Unless the coroner was wrong, Cissie had been dead at least half an hour before my arrival.

My nightmares began about six months later, long after Buddy and Cissie Maxwell were laid to rest. In the dream, which was repeated over and over again, Cissie would look up from the floor and give me a slow, satiated smile. At least one of her mouths did. The other one, the one that ran from one side of her throat to the other, would pucker up a little before bubbling out more blood.

Mary Alice and I broke up for good as soon as she discovered I had been at the trailer. "It was a disgusting thing to do, and I don't ever want to see you again," she said, throwing my senior ring at my feet. "You're not a nice boy after all."

You know, I was almost relieved by her decision. Somehow it seemed to be what I deserved. As the years went by, and I found myself unable to have a long-term relationship with any woman, it was easy to convince myself that Mary Alice had been right. It was disgusting, it was wrong, and it was only fair that I pay the price for it.

All of you experts say that Cissie was alive when she performed fellatio on me. You ignore the time line from the autopsy report because it doesn't fit "reality"; you say I must be mistaken as to what time I left the Point. Still, none of your arguments, none of these therapy sessions, has convinced me that she wasn't already a murder victim when we met in the hallway of the trailer. If it had been anybody else but Buddy and Cissie, you might have changed my mind. But the more I found out about Buddy, the surer I became that if anybody could make her perform tricks after her throat had been cut, it was he. Buddy was a low-life Svengali, and Cissie his willing slave. Dead or alive.

Maybe he did it for the money—after all, the event had been planned long in advance, and Buddy was never one to turn down a greenback, no matter how ill-gained—although the wad of ten dollar bills must have been far from his mind when he wrapped the noose around his neck. Or maybe he did it as one final poke in the eye at the football team, guessing what our reaction would be once we learned of Cissie's fate. Buddy always hated jocks.

The reasons don't matter now, I guess. Buddy and Cissie are both gone. Joe Mayes mumbles a lot when you try to have a conversation with him. And I'm left with the memory of the stains. When I hold my hands out in front of me, I can still see them, as if they were tattooed indelibly on my skin.

My fingers were wet all right, but not with sweat or spittle or semen or anything else that I could live with now. It was blood that spotted my skin, the same blood whose coppery scent I had smelled when I first entered the trailer. Cissie's blood, which has left a permanent, cancerous mark on my life forever.

Legacy of the Bokor

Walt Hicks

Silver Chalice Peyroux—for nearly eight decades known as Miss Silvie—was born outside New Orleans in Plaquemines Parish circa 1897 to a *gens de couleur libres* housemaid and her wealthy white employer. The event had been shrouded with some secrecy in those days, but her great-great grandfather Cage Peyroux nodded with satisfaction upon hearing the news. "Dis gone make her one pow'ful woman chile."

Now Silvie Peyroux sat, withered as old leather and wheelchair-bound, not so far away from her birthplace, in the Sunset Acres Assisted Living Facility, shrouded by the suffocating Gulf humidity and ancient oaks drooling gray Spanish moss.

Miss Silvie's head was bowed, her old neck too tired to hold position long, her clear, pale gray eyes intently studying her knitting needles. The colorful yarn slowly but surely weaved together as her skeletal hands patiently worked the needles.

The night attendant, Obie, already annoyed at having to cover the dayshift, shook her chair harshly.

Hands still working, Miss Silvie's eyes glanced up from beneath arched eyebrows and glared at Obie with undisguised hatred. A slow smile spread her wrinkled face. The last thing Obie saw was a metallic flash as the knitting needles pierced his eyes, impaling the pupils, the needles traveling effortlessly into his brain. Vitreous fluid spattered Miss Silvie's face and she lapped at it greedily. With a deft economy of movement, Miss Silvie's wrists twisted and Obie's eyeballs popped out of their sockets onto the needles like meat on a pair of shish kabob skewers. She had both oozing orbs in her mouth before Obie's corpse hit the hardwood floor. She chomped down on them and they burst in her mouth like large overripe grapes, the delightfully thick viscous fluid filling her mouth like some perverse nectar. Miss Silvie savored the taste for a moment, chewed the rubbery eyeballs, and then swallowed after first peeling the stubbornly tough optic nerves from each.

What a lovely appetizer, she thought.

Miss Silvie's warm and dark reverie burst suddenly, like capillaries in a strangled corpse's eyes. Obie was standing next to her chair, his heavy-lidded eyes intact.

"You deef ol' bitch. I said, 'do y'all want the rest of yo' Jell-O'?"

She smiled up at him, her leathery visage warm, pale eyes sharp and dangerous.

"No, dearie. You go riiiiiight ahead."

Before she had even finished her reply, Obie had slurped down the cubed gelatin from the plastic cup.

In spite of his obvious flaws, the boy got decent technique, she thought, as Obie wheeled her into the day room.

The day room was not unlike the rest of the facility: a hastily applied cheap façade over ancient underpinnings. The sprawling facility had once been a massive antebellum Victorian manse on a ten-acre plantation at the edge of a bayou swamp, but had been converted in the 30's first into an insane asylum, much later to an old folks' home. It reminded Miss Silvie of a whitewashed crypt, nice and shiny on the outside, but if you squinted just a little, you could still see the squirming rot within. The day room did have the advantage of a haphazardly installed bay window, allowing in some sunlight filtered by the lazy oaks. At a table in the corner nearest the bay window, Miss Silvie's new friends sat awaiting her entrance. The six of them had arrived (committed or imprisoned, as each would have it) at nearly the same time and despite their disparity, had become friendly, taking meals and playing cards together. All of them found themselves sitting in Death's Waiting Room, patiently awaiting their respective appointments with some primordial hooded bugler.

"Ah, Miss Silvie arrives," Colonel Edgar Carver, U.S. Air Force, retired, boomed happily. "Welcome, dear."

Colonel Carver was a still handsome man of African descent, tall and lanky with sharply defined features, whose principal vice and downfall had been a surfeit of women over the years. Six times married and divorced, his sizable savings mostly wiped out by alimony, child support and later a severe gambling habit, Colonel Carver unexpectedly found himself a ward of the parish and had been committed to Sunset after being diagnosed with mid-stage Alzheimer's disease. The assisted living facility claimed the majority of his military retirement and all of his remaining savings. Most days, he was incredibly lucid, but sometimes, his face abruptly became a mask of abject terror, as if he were unsure of where he was—or *who* he was.

Beatrice Rae McSimmons—Miz McSimmons to most, particularly to those of *color*—sat at a respectable distance next to the Colonel, smiling tolerantly through her carefully applied scarlet lipstick. Once a striking Southern beauty, her face had been lifted so many times, she nearly appeared Asian in ethnicity. Beatrice Rae, hailing from Biloxi, Mississippi, was a lifelong racist, although she would categorically deny that. She was positively certain that the Good Lord had intended the *white* man to have dominion over the earth and all the beasts of the field, and that included people of color. Of course, being a genteel lady of the South, one never spoke of such things, and one conducted oneself at all times as a lady in such vulgar matters. After the death of her beloved husband J. Harold and her subsequent and inevitably melodramatic meltdown, the McSimmons children had placed Beatrice Rae at Sunset, assuring her that it was the absolute best place for her, as they viciously fought each other in court over the family fortune. Upon arriving at Sunset, she thought to herself that the place was rather rundown, likely rodent and insect infested, plus there were far too many people of color to suit her. However, if her little darlings said that it was the best place for her, that was well and enough for her; she would keep those reservations to herself.

Recently freed Hosea Rothstein came to Sunset almost directly from Louisiana State Prison after doing a double dime for insider trading, investment fraud and DUI manslaughter— convicted long before such things became fashionable, he would allow almost proudly. His family had long ago disowned the wraith-thin old man and moved on, and his crippling arthritis mandated special care, so he was shuttled from one form of prison to another. At least this one had decent television, you didn't have to work the farm like at Angola, plus trips to the shower weren't nearly as dreadful.

Nancy Hwang had been a highly sought after escort in 1950's New Orleans. The petite, porcelain-featured North Korean expatriate had worked as a high-priced call girl amazingly until the early seventies, when she transferred her considerable talents to the station of *la mère des prostituées*, running a stable of nearly one hundred girls. She had made millions over the years in her underground trade, most of it cash finally seized by various government agencies after she was ultimately turned in by one of her girls, a crackhead nicknamed Jezebel. Mentally damaged by syphilis and deemed unable to care for herself any longer, she was unceremoniously deposited at Sunset by the

Department of Social Services in conjunction with the parish.

Portuguese immigrant Gusmao Guzman came to the U.S. in his youth as a promising lightweight prizefighter. He neared a world championship title as a young man, only to suffer a number of concussions, leaving him confused and punch-drunk. After a long career of lawn maintenance work, Gusmao's addled mental state deteriorated into mild dementia and he was placed into Sunset's care and custody. Somehow, Sunset made him happy and he often softly sang beautiful Portuguese lullabies at night.

De One Momma, Buluku, sure picked 'em right for moi, Miss Silvie thought, and she uttered a quick prayer of thanks for the incredibly fortuitous confluence of events, people and nature's own divine elements.

When she was settled in and Obie trudged away sullenly, Miss Silvie addressed her friends. "Folks, I got a biiig surprise for us all this evenin'. Y'all know Friday's dey let us stay up extre hours, and tonight, I got us a special treat in mind. It gone be a biiig surprise, but tonight we gone merry make like we's all young folk ag'in!"

The group became visibly excited; any break from the droning monotony was enthusiastically welcomed. Particularly if there was the possibility that food other than the bland Sunset menu might be served. And Miss Silvie had been a notoriously superb Creole chef.

She glanced slyly around and lowered her voice conspiratorially. "Can't tell y'all what all I got in mind, don't wanna spoil no surprises . . . but I managed to sneak in de white rum!" Beatrice Rae tittered excitedly, demurely covering her lipstick-caked mouth, Colonel Carver smiled broadly and Hosea's eyes filled with tears of sheer joy. "Now y'all get in an extre few winks dis afternoon. Be good and ready for tonight!"

Conversation during the otherwise uninspired lunch was light and chatty, anticipating the night's exciting new events. They all agreed to break early for a long nap, so they would be fresh for the evening. Miss Silvie knew she would be too excited to sleep. She did doze off for a bit, dreaming of a young girl with dark cinnamon skin, long dark wavy hair and bewitching pallid eyes dancing the night away in old New Orleans, seducing every hapless man who came under her preternatural spell. And with the Holy Grace of the One Mother, that girl would dance again.

"*Buluku* and me, we gone bake us up somethin' *right* tonight!"

The gang of six reassembled again at 5:30 sharp, anxiously awaiting Miss Silvie's promised surprise. They were slightly disappointed that she hadn't prepared a full course meal, but Colonel Carver noticed a covered serving cart off to one side, and he rubbed his hands together in anticipation. After supper was finished and the dishes cleared away, Miss Silvie motioned to Obie, who rolled his eyes and shuffled to the serving cart.

"Bad 'nough, I gotta work a flippin' double . . . now gotta be a damn manslave to that crazy ol' bitch," he murmured as he wheeled the cart to the table.

"Thank you, Obie," she said as he uncovered the cart and wandered away, grumbling to himself. Other than Obie, the night crew consisted of an additional two beefy orderlies, a grumpy overweight night nurse, and a mousey young administrative assistant named Abigail, who surreptitiously watched the group from her desk a few yards away. The group stared in awe at the serving tray.

"*Uau!*" Gusmao said softly.

"Oh my," Beatrice Rae whispered, with a hand to her sagging throat.

The Colonel smiled broadly and placed the large carafe in the center of the table as Nancy carefully situated the silver platter next to it. Hosea grabbed a stack of old chipped china plates and set the table, with Gusmao on silverware.

The clear carafe was filled with a strange light green liquid that seemed to shift, shades sinuating slightly in the light. It appeared to have a darker green skim at the top, resembling a murky algae bloom. The aroma, however, was astonishing: a weird combination of freshly mown grass and pulped citrus, along with a faint but powerful undercurrent of alcohol— white coconut rum. Neatly stacked on the silver platter were dark squares of spongy material that at first glance appeared to be brownies, or slices of a dark fruitcake. The scent from the triangular stack was of freshly baked bread with a slight meaty base. Everyone was salivating like crazy.

Colonel set the teacups and poured the elixir. "Miss Silvie, I don't know what this is, but it smells wonderful!"

"Well, a couple ol' family recipes from my ol' great-great granddaddy. De nightshade tea and black bread. Ever'thin's nat'ral, so no worries dere." She smiled at each one of them in turn. "For y'all take a sup, I got to tell y'all that the ol' stories said dat dis here tea could make you young again and live *forever*. Now, I ain't sayin' it will . . ." Miss Silvie paused for dramatic effect. "But I ain't sayin' it *won't* neither. The drinkin's gone be up to each of y'all."

The Colonel grinned innocently. "Well, in that case, Miss Silvie, I say, 'I hope I live forever and you never die!'" He downed the contents of the cup like a quick shot of whiskey. He smacked his lips together and grimaced exaggeratedly. "Damn and begone was that smoooooooth!"

The rest chuckled gamely and followed suit, the Colonel quickly refilling empty teacups on demand. Miss Silvie declined the drink and snack, but encouraged the others. "Don't forget the black bread; it go down real good wid de tea."

The group enthusiastically followed her apothegm and under her watchful pale gaze, devoured the snacks and drained the tea amid a few hours of joyful conversation. A number of the other residents eyed them curiously, but kept their distance; the night crew stayed away as long as they didn't get too loud. Abigail actually smiled sheepishly because they all seemed so uncharacteristically happy.

The conversation began to wane after a few hours, as did

the blood red moon peering into the bay window through the gauze of Spanish moss. Obie came around to half-heartedly enforce lights out. Abigail offered to clean up what little remained of Miss Silvie's savories.

"Thank you for a lovely evening," Beatrice Rae said to Miss Silvie and actually meant it. It didn't hurt that she was more than slightly tipsy. "I am absolutely stuffed!"

"You more than welcome, Miz McSimmons. Jus' remember, we all bleed red . . . ever' last one of us."

Beatrice Rae smiled stupidly and nodded. "Oh please, Miss Silvie, please call me Beatrice Rae." After all, Miss Silvie seemed to be of *mixed* heritage. What was that called? Mutilato? Mulatto? Matata? She chuckled to herself.

Miss Silvie's eyes narrowed dangerously above her warm smile. "Miz McSimmons will do just fine, *cher*."

Beatrice Rae was well beyond being offended. "Well, okay. Night, dear." She staggered off toward her room.

They each thanked her in turn, all of them slightly drunk and their bellies full. The Colonel waved Obie away and wheeled Miss Silvie back to her room.

"Miss Silvie, that was wonderful. How on earth were you able to procure the ingredients to make those delicacies?"

"Oh, it was lots easier than you'd think . . ." she replied coyly. It had indeed been child's play to bribe the simple-minded Obie and trick eager-to-please Abigail into obtaining the various items she required. Some of them readily available in voodoo shops in New Orleans, some from just a few yards away in the swamp, some had to be recovered from the remains of her old home in the Lower Ninth Ward. Obie was happy to do that, along with a little impromptu burglary on the side. He was completely unaware of the treasures secreted in the hidden compartment of the seemingly empty jewelry box he'd retrieved, including dried and powdered swamp grass, mangrove roots, amphibian and reptile innards, tetrodotoxin, datura and other wondrous substances collected by Miss Silvie over the decades, following the teachings of her great-great-grandfather, the mighty *bokor*. Cage Peyroux was thought to be over two hundred years old when he abruptly disappeared. There were even whispers that it was his powerful magick that had actually *started* the Civil War.

"I ain't sayin' it did . . . I ain't sayin' it didn't," he rumbled, drinking frothy fresh blood from a sterling silver plated human skull. That homemade mug had been the inspiration for Miss Silvie's given name.

Seeing the pleased smile and her closed eyes, Colonel Carver gently kissed Miss Silvie's leathery forehead. Abruptly, his head began to spin and he felt his balance start to give way. His stomach tightened and his knees nearly buckled. Carver closed his eyes against the surge of dizziness and nausea; Miss Silvie's coarse flesh beneath his lips seemed to go silky smooth, and fever hot. His various aches and pains melted away like bayou fog in the spring. His muscles felt strong, his head clear, hot blood pumped urgently through his veins, particularly to his groin.

The face that looked up at Carver was familiar, but impossibly young and beautiful. Her cinnamon skin was smooth and lustrous, with a hint of slick perspiration. Passion and fire burned in clear gray eyes and her wet tongue slid suggestively over full lips. Carver's groin ached.

Miss Silvie's porcelain hands glided quickly over Carver's fly and extracted his engorged member from his boxers. Carver's eyes widened.

"Damn. Looks like an eight-year-old makin' a fist," he murmured.

Miss Silvie locked Carver's gaze with her bewitching pale eyes as she took him into her moist, fervid mouth. Carver's eyes unexpectedly filled with tears; he was experiencing a level of mind-bending pleasure he hadn't known since he was a young man, if then. Miss Silvie expertly worked him with tongue, lips and mouth until he could no longer hold back. She fiercely grasped the thick base of his cock with both hands, squeezing hard to stem his explosive climax. She lithely arose from the wheelchair, her old robe falling away from a perfect body. Carver's mouth watered as his eyes swept her. Small globes of pert tight breasts, topped by erect, quarter-sized brown nipples; supple, taut belly flesh leading to a wispy thatch of pubic hair covering moist, perfect folds of pink flesh.

Miss Silvie kissed him almost savagely, her tongue exploring his mouth greedily. She abruptly mounted him, wrapping her shapely legs around his waist, impaling her soft folds on his turgid erection. She buried her face in his chest and neck, licking and biting him as she rode him furiously. Her silken folds were tight and almost unbearably hot and she clenched him fervently, bucking uncontrollably against his once again muscular body. She grasped his face in her hands as he tautened to climax.

"Look at me when you cum," she demanded, her breath sultry against his neck. The voice seemed familiar, but . . .

As Miss Silvie slowed her rhythmic pace agonizingly, she pulled her face away from his chest, pausing mere inches from his face. "Cum for me," she whispered, her breath sweetly scented with rum. "Cum *in* me."

Carver felt the lightning bolt ebullition building, surging through his core and he opened his eyes as a flooding ejaculation poured from him like a torrent. The face, inches from his own, was no longer that of a lusty and vital Miss Silvie, but the dazed, passion-addled visage of young Abigail.

Carver gasped and stumbled backward. Once his swimming vision cleared, he could see old Miss Silvie dozing peacefully in her wheelchair. His abrupt vigor was gone, his arthritis was back with a vengeance and his genitals once more felt like shriveled fruit. His breathing was labored and harsh. His eyes were wet with tears.

"Damn, that was some wicked fuckin' hooch . . ." He staggered then shakily returned to his room, his heart crushed beneath the weight of an agonizing nostalgia.

Meanwhile, Miss Silvie waited impatiently like a kid for Christmas. The hours oozed by slowly, like molasses during a cold snap, but near midnight, she heard the first effects of her carefully conjured treats. Hosea, she thought, uttered a long, chattering death rattle. Nancy, perhaps, a weak sigh. Someone farted explosively. The staff would ignore these sounds, she knew, since most of the residents were heavily medicated and often made strange noises at night.

Within a few dragging ticks of the clock, other noises: harsh grinding of teeth (Gusmao, the only one of the group with his *original* teeth), pained groaning from bones reforming hard as stone and some fitful shifting in beds as the result of muscles and tendons tightening like steel cable. The transformations, Miss Silvie knew, were nearly complete.

One by one, they slowly entered her room. Each scarcely recognizable as themselves; each changed profoundly in a similarly ghastly way. Withered flesh pulled back and drawn, various shades of frost gray, as pale and pock-marked as a forgotten crypt. Lips split and flaking, gums black and receding, jagged shards of bone erupting from the gum line for those without teeth, Gusmao's natural teeth ground into uneven spiked points. Their eyes were sunken and hollow, but blazing with an unnatural fire behind them. The irises had vanished, replaced by a milky off-white, a nervous pin-point pupil in the center, surrounded by a thin black spider webbing of dead capillaries. Shambling as they walked, they were straight away clumsy because of the relentless tightening and contraction of steely sinew and compacted tendons. Movement was hellishly painful.

Worse, their minds were completely clear and lucid, yet filled with unspeakable longing and hunger.

"I don't know what you gave us, Miss Silvie," Colonel Carver said pensively, "but, by God, I think you found a cure for Alzheimer's."

Beatrice Rae was unimpressed. "Well, it hurts and I'm

absolutely famished." If she could've seen her own face, she would've fainted dead away, Miss Silvie thought happily. Beatrice Rae's askew scarlet lipstick made her look like she'd just consumed a small animal.

"The soreness'll go way once y'all limber up some. As for food, well, I'm fixin' to make y'all de happiest gourmets in de whole of Lou'siana."

Miss Silvie nonchalantly explained to them the most efficient method of draining a human body of blood, then delicately opening the skull just prior to death to extract the 'sweet meat' since the taste is *sooooo* much better when the brain is teetering on the dark precipice of death. They all nodded sagely, as if Miss Silvie were giving them a new recipe for crawfish stew. Her hideous instructions made perfect sense to them.

"Miss Silvie," Abigail said, surprised. "It's after midnight, you should be in your—" The five no longer living denizens of Sunset Acres shuffled into the dim pool of her desk lamp. Abigail opened her mouth to scream but nothing came out; she stumbled over her desk chair, pissing herself as she fell into a dead faint.

"Leave her be for now," Miss Silvie whispered. "Dem big fellas be here shortly . . . talk about a *meal*!"

Obie shuffled into the day room about that time. "Goddammit, y'all need to be in your . . . what in the flyin' fuck?"

Gusmao descended on Obie from behind, pinning his arms and slamming him repeatedly against the wall violently, then forcing him to his knees. Nancy slid a large kitchen pan beneath him then nicked his carotid artery with a kitchen knife. Hosea helped hold Obie as he struggled, blood spurting into the pan with the harsh rhythm of his heartbeat. Obie's eyes began to flutter and roll back into their sockets.

"Now, chil'lin," she said.

Colonel Carver retrieved an electric carving knife and

deftly engraved a circle around the top of Obie's head. Beatrice Rae inserted a butter knife into the ragged cut and popped the top of Obie's skull off with a wet slurping sound.

The five of them tore greedily into Obie's exposed brain, ripping it to shreds with sharp jagged teeth, swallowing chunks while scarcely chewing. Within moments, the interior of Obie's skull had been licked clean. Nearly as an afterthought, Gusmao popped Obie's dull eyes out and tossed them to Miss Silvie.

"Thank you, Gusmao—you know dey my fav'rites."

Within a few hours, the two other orderlies, the night duty nurse and twenty-five other residents met gruesome fates similar to that of Obie. Tubs of frothy blood were everywhere; bodies with hollowed-out skulls littered the day room, the hallways and most of the individual rooms.

Miss Silvie was dreaming about soaking in all that fresh blood, lounging in an old claw foot bathtub, sprinkling in additional herbs, roots and spices. Once the lifeblood had healed her tired old body, she would drink down the entire glut of blood and she would be young, forever young again.

Her small army of zombies would, in the meantime, skeletonize the remainder of the bodies; from the voraciousness she had witnessed, she imagined that they might even consume the *bones* of the corpses as well.

There was one final and important matter to consider: Abigail.

The frail girl lay shivering in the corner behind her desk, her jeans dark with urine, her teeth chattering together so hard Miss Silvie thought they might shatter. She was such a pretty young girl, Miss Silvie thought . . . if she'd only take proper care of herself.

"*Mes bon hommes*," she called to the men. "I need y'all."

The Colonel, Gusmao and Hosea formed behind her.

"Her brain?" Hosea inquired hopefully.

"*Mais non, cher*! No, not hers, not *yet*. De numbers of de ol' rituals say dat six ain't hardly done yet. Seven is de number makin' us perfect. She will make us seven. And seven be de one must bear fruit. I need y'all to do something' *else* to her," she said, smiling malevolently.

Colonel Carver immediately caught her suggestive intent and said, "*That?* We can?" Carver stole a covert glance at his own crotch. "I mean, does it *still* work?"

"Oh yeah," Miss Silvie enthused, "y'all been blessed wid de angel lust, each of you. Dey works reeeal fine!"

In all the excitement before consuming multiple brains, Carver had failed to notice the tent pole in his pajama bottoms. Blue steel. Just like when he was a young stud. Just like in his *dreams* . . .

"Go have you some fun, boys," Miss Silvie said. She had declined to inform them that they would ejaculate something that looked like spent motor oil—just like she hadn't told the ladies that Beatrice Rae's precious 'li'l kitty kat' and Nancy's legendary 'snapper' had both grown voracious, razor-sharp teeth. Too much knowledge was indeed a dangerous thing.

In a deep, ancient voice, the old *Momma Lois* murmured, "Partake of *my* blood, partake of *my* flesh, that *I* might receive life everlasting."

The women wolfing down gobs of ragged flesh behind them, the men slowly advanced on a cowering Abigail. She whimpered, a keening sound like a small animal, and tried clawing through the wall. Her mind was mostly gone.

Gusmao shambled to a pained stop, his face suddenly illuminated with a devastating awareness. His misshapen face twitched and tremored and he held up his hand. "*Meus amigos*, wait." Miss Silvie flinched in her chair. "We can't do this. None of this. None of this is right. Poor Miss Abigail was nice to all of us. She's the only one here who treated us with respect. *Tal como os seres humanos.* Like humans."

Hosea's curdled-milk eyes glistened with tears of blue-black blood. He nodded solemnly.

"You're right, Gusmao. Right." Colonel Carver's jaw

tightened—a sound like grating stone on metal. "We can't. We *won't . . .*"

They all gathered in their usual places at their familiar table. Beatrice Rae and Nancy had set the table with a fancy linen tablecloth they recovered from the supply room along with some decent china and silverware. Hosea filled the wine glasses with thick, frothy blood. Colonel Carver, appropriately enough, stood at the head of the table with the electric knife in hand.

"Friends," he said, balefully regarding the carnage surrounding him: skeletons stripped of nearly every last shred of flesh, muscle and organs, entrails dangling from the overhead lights, blood spattered everywhere and brain matter caked around each of their mouths. "I think we have come to understand that this must be our last meal together. Our last meal, *period.* We all agree in substance that it's better to die human than it is to live as monsters. For this noble group decision, I salute you all."

"*L' Chaim*," Hosea said and drained the glass of blood. The rest followed suit.

"At the very end, we can all at least be somewhat civilized," Beatrice Rae said softly.

"Somewhat," Nancy echoed with an ironic grin.

The electric knife whirred to life and Carver dissected the brain on the platter into four equal pieces. After generously salting the portions, he carefully placed them on the china plates in front of his friends. The unnatural urge was to tear into the tasty morsels, but they all neatly folded linen napkins on their laps, cautiously sliced small portions of the spongy meat and slowly chewed, savoring the delicacy.

From her wheelchair, Miss Silvie watched them with pale glassy eyes, her slack jaw agape, the top of her skull—and her brain—removed.

Colonel Carver watched his friends dine, absently sipping at a wineglass of blood and nibbling at a sizeable chunk of flesh from the fat night nurse's thigh. He had avoided eating any of Miss Silvie Peyroux's diseased brain, for he had theorized—correctly—the dangerous finality of that. Besides, there was one last mission he had to accomplish.

Beatrice Rae finished first. "My heavens," she said, "am I ever stuffed!" With that, she abruptly farted—loudly—and her friends all laughed heartily in the still carnage. What might've been a blush appeared blue-black on her sunken cheeks. "In some cultures," she said primly, but not without humor, "that's considered a compliment after a meal."

"I think that's a belch," Hosea shrugged, "but in the same general neighborhood."

Nancy chuckled softly; without warning, she doubled over in a violent seizure, and convulsively vomiting a gray-scarlet soupy mess onto the floor at her feet.

"Miss Nancy?" Gusmao said, concerned then tossed his own Technicolor cookies as well. The four of them began writhing on the floor in horrific pain, vomiting and shitting the vile meals they had consumed. Ultimately, they all died. Again, and for one final, agonizing time.

Carver's hollow eyes misted, black sludge trailing down his face. He would go to the caretaker's shack out back, retrieve all the gasoline he could find then burn this unholy place to the ground. Along with his friends, the devil known as Miss Silvie—and himself. As he walked away, he stole a backwards glance at the table.

Miss Silvie's corpse was now smiling.

As Colonel Carver left the room, Abigail unsteadily made her way toward the exit, pausing only for a moment at the table of horrors. Without realizing it, she plucked a pulpy pink-gray piece of matter from a plate and popped it into her mouth. Munching absently, she vanished into the gathering dawn.

The Sunset Acres Assisted Living Facility burned with an ungodly ferocity. Firefighters from several nearby communities and parishes were called in for assistance, to no avail. The old building burned to the foundation, which cracked irreparably from the inferno. Sifting through the ashes, a number of skeletons were found, most with the tops of their skulls missing. The old coroner theorized that the incredible heat had boiled their brains, causing enough pressure to explode their skulls from the inside out. A most unfortunate accident all round.

All of the deceased were accounted for and the only survivor was the young night assistant, Abigail. Regrettably, the poor thing was initially catatonic, became a ward of the parish, and had to be institutionalized.

Remarkably though, Abigail seemed to affect a slow recovery over the passing months. Her appetite improved, she appeared to respond to external stimuli, particularly off-color jokes told by some of the night staff. She would often absently stroke her stomach, muttering *"puissant femme enfant,"* whatever that meant. Curiously, veins of silver began to streak her mousey brown hair and after a just few days outside, her skin tanned a lustrous dark cinnamon.

Inexplicably, her brown eyes had abruptly changed color to a startling pale gray.

The Eye of the Devil is Brown

Owen Z. Burnett

"**What** do you mean?"

"I mean just kiss my butthole, silly," she snorted. Alan looked at the small brown spider that sat below her vagina, and for a second, just a second, he swore it winked at him. "You don't get *any* access until your lips touch my asshole."

He shrank back in horror. This wasn't the kind of thing he was used to. He'd ignored the existence of the female butthole ever since he walked in on his sister letting loose a big, wet turd on the mailman's forehead.

"Oh come on! I hardly thought this would be a big deal for you. When I first saw you I thought you were the kind of guy who used to jack off in front of a mirror wearing Mommy's dress," Tina said.

Alan had a flashback. He was wearing his Grandma's dress and jacking off in front of a mirror. "Hey! Are you going to do it or not?" Tina asked, her voice squeaking. Alan watched his reflection disappear. In place of his young face was a glistening butthole. He swore it blew a kiss.

"Okay . . ." he said, his mouth *already* tasting of shit. He leaned forward, eyes closed, to kiss Tina's once harmless, now malicious butthole, and then stopped short. "Did you hear that?"

"Hear what?"

"I thought somebody whispered my name . . ."

"No. No, I don't think so. Now kiss my ass or these legs close up shop."

Alan peered at the butthole. He'd certainly seen more disgusting ass openings in pornography. He'd seen withered, drooping masses of bleached flesh with strings of semen hanging from them, and black, yawning craters that looked like they'd been pounded with a concrete slab and then filled with steroids.

This anus, however, was a moderate one. It wasn't immaculate looking, nor was it a poop coven. It had that familiar brown of a place that had known the passage of turds. Alan closed his eyes tight. Even a moderate poop disposer was still, in essence, a dirty butthole. But it would have to be done, or he'd never get his penis, maybe not even his fingers, into that beautiful pocket of flesh—Tina's puss. With a quick peck it was all over. His lips lightly pressed into Tina's rear and then he drew himself back, wiping his mouth cautiously.

"That wasn't so bad now, was it?" she asked him.

"No, no I guess not," Alan said, his member growing stiffer as he realized snatch was on the menu. This was more attuned to his tastes. He parted her labia and began to work his tongue inward. Tina let out a small moan, her hands reaching down and pressing his head into her vagina. For a moment he felt he was tainting his favorite part of Tina with his least favorite part, but the thought was nothing but harmful so he expelled it from his mind.

Tonight was the first time he'd seen Tina naked, though he'd known the day would come as well as he knew he wouldn't pass math class. He'd known her for a few semesters, seen her around and talked—small talk, really. She'd flirted with him here and there, and he'd flirted back. But tonight had been different. Tonight she had that tigress look in her eye, the one reserved for the sighting of prey—a snake, in this case. Alan wasn't sure what had taken so long and when they finally got to her dorm, if he hadn't known better, he'd almost guess there was some hesitation before she decided to take her clothes off. Maybe it was just nerves. He'd only been with a handful of girls. It seemed possible that most of them would be shy.

After some very hurried foreplay, Alan gained entrance. He thrust with quick, deliberate attacks, his member gaining speed, taking over his body. Tina lay beneath him, her head sinking into a large white pillow, her faced flushed and her mouth open, a series of small breaths assaulting Alan.

Tina screamed, her face a portrait of red. "I'm almost there," she said. *Almost there?* This was new to Alan. He pumped harder and hoped he didn't win the race.

"Would you please . . . put it in . . . my butt?"

"What?" Alan stopped. He looked at Tina, her eyes open now, staring back at him like a stray puppy-dog. He glanced away from her, instead focusing on a heap of dirty laundry that was scattered across the floor.

"Don't stop now!" So he started again, picking up momentum. He tried to get the speed and rhythm that he had achieved before. It seemed unlikely that he'd push Tina over the edge. Still, she was enjoying herself more than he had expected. He tried to ignore her request. "I'm still close," she told him. "Just. Stick. It. In. My. Butt. Hole."

It was all over. Alan pulled out and fell lifelessly beside Tina. His penis had wilted at the second mention of butthole. "I'm finished," he lied. "I'm sorry. I'm not used to . . ."

"Getting a girl so close?"

"Yeah. Sorry."

"It's okay. Maybe we'll try again later. But," she yawned,

"I'm tired." Alan watched her for a moment. She closed her eyes again and fell silent, her stomach rising and falling. Her brown hair spread across her pillow like a net, ensnaring the casing of down feathers and keeping it from going on a soft and pleasant rampage.

Alan leaned to the edge of the bed and grabbed his clothes, slipping them on. He liked to be dressed in case a fire alarm went off. He got up and hit the lights, then crawled back into bed with Tina and pulled the covers over the two of them.

A faint but unmistakable whispering woke Alan. He listened hard, straining his ears. At first the sound was muffled, distorted. He searched the room with his eyes, shivering a little. Who was that? The window shade was down and the whispering seemed to come from *inside* the room. He got up and went to the window anyway, hoping that he would see a friend on the other side, playing a prank on him. Did anybody know he was in Tina's dorm? He didn't think so.

He drew the shade up. Nothing. He turned and slipped back into bed. The whispering had stopped. He listened again, wondering if it would return. When it didn't, he began to dismiss the idea that he'd ever heard anything.

When Alan's lids were creeping down, his muscles relaxing and his heartbeat slowing, his brain fizzling out, the whispering began again.

It was coming from under the covers.

A soft burst of warm air hissed at his leg. Alan whipped the blanket away from himself and Tina. He turned his gaze on her rump. She lay with her butt slightly in the air, her face buried in her pillow and her stomach smashed against the bed. "Alan," the butthole whispered. "I want you."

"Jesus Christ!" He watched, frozen. The butthole pulsated, contracted, and convulsed, trying to operate as a tiny mouth.

"Alan. Come inside me," it said. He stared at the brown circle as it cooed at him, asked him to do dirty things. He couldn't stomach looking at the shit stain.

"Alan. Alan!"

"Shut up!" *Did I just tell an asshole to shut up?* He wiped a dense layer of sweat from his face and then slapped himself. Not a dream.

"Alan just . . . just put it in. Please. I'm so . . . I'm so lonely here. *She* gets all the attention. Everybody always wants that *cunt*, but never *me*," the butthole said, and then, to Alan's disgust, it began crying. Or was it drooling? It was hard to tell—it had no tear-ducts, and it certainly didn't have eyes.

"Please!" The voice of the thing was something like Tina's, if her throat had been filled with dirt and shards of glass. Alan stared, still frozen. Tina's anus began to swell outward and lurch forward, her rump and body gliding behind it like a cape of skin and bones. "Please fuck me," it begged. *Maybe if I fooled it,* he thought.

He spied a half-eaten carrot lying on Tina's headboard. He picked up the carrot, turned it over to the fat end, and stuck it in the butthole.

It began moaning. Alan momentarily imagined himself taking a knife to his penis, then his eyes, then his throat. The moans devolved into an agonizing *schlupping* sound. He flung himself from the bed, tripping over his mud-crusted boots. Without a second thought he clambered out into the hallway. He blazed out the entrance of the building.

He thought long and hard about his distaste for the female anus. The word was so ugly. *Anus.* He said it out loud four or five times, revolted at himself for allowing his tongue to be poisoned by such ugliness.

In his head he could still see his sister's turd sliding out of her ass and landing with a moist thud, right onto the mailman's forehead—that sick motherfucker. The turd left a print, a greasy, shining print. What had she been eating?

The mailman picked up the turd and—

Alan stopped. He shook his head, the memories tumbling

into each other until they were a mess of thoughts. His feet were freezing, grass and dew all over them. He didn't stop until he arrived at his apartment.

He trudged up the driveway, the rocks getting stuck in his feet. The front door hung halfway open, one of the hinges long ago broken. He pushed open the screen door, letting it slam behind him. A gust of wind started up and the front door banged into the doorframe a few times before lazily retreating. Alan spun around and looked through the screen. Both doors seemed pointless.

Alan retreated to his bedroom, walking up the stairs past posters of James Dean and Jack Nicholson, their eyes glaring at him, their smiles masking laughter for the man who'd kissed a butthole that wanted to kiss back. He nearly turned around to tell them to shut up, but then he realized they weren't *actually* laughing, that they never could.

He lay down on of his ALF comforter, which was ripped in the corner, but the best purchase eBay had to offer. His mind flickered, for a second, to the mailman taking the turd and—

"Fuck!" Alan opened his dresser, pulled out some sleeping pills, and took two. Tina had no idea where he lived. Maybe he was safe.

For now.

The sky was flesh toned, with clouds of brown skidding across the horizon. Alan found it tricky to keep his footing, the ground below him squishy, like walking on water balloons. He went forth into a haze of thick, vaporous mass.

Inside the mass he saw fleeting images, scampering, rousing images that darted in and out of his spectrum of sight. He got down on his knees, trying to keep from inhaling the mist, which was beginning to burn. He crawled forth, the darting images in full view now. They were hard-faced infants, covered in boils.

"The one who wore his grandmother's dress as a child! Quickly, show him his fate!" burped a surly infant, with red-opal eyes. Alan swatted at the thing as it charged for him. When his hand landed on the babe's head he screamed as his arm turned into an explosion of spiders. He watched as his forearm, now a pillar of spiders, fell to the ground and scuttled away in fifty different directions.

"Jesus," Alan cried. Then the ground beneath him began to give way and the infants began swooping upward, flying through the fog and disappearing somewhere among the clouds.

He was falling. Falling down some enormous chasm, his hair blowing right off his head. Alan looked down and saw beneath him a giant, looming butthole.

His screams were useless, his fate already determined. He tried to close his eyes but his lids came off his face, fluttering away like paper. Suddenly he was falling head first, the foreboding cavern welcoming him with a thunderous fart.

Alan woke up with his groin fully bathed in piss. He stood up, covered in sweat, and took off his pants and underwear. A steady vibration was coming from his pocket. He took his phone out and opened it, without bothering to see who was calling. "Huh-hello," he said, his voice wavering from the nightmare, the images still strong in his mind. Sleep had granted him the ability to question the events he thought had happened earlier in the night. Maybe he'd never had sex with Tina.

"Hello, lover boy."

"Who . . . who is this?" Alan pulled the phone away from his ear for a moment. He saw Tina's name on the little screen. "Tina?"

"No. My friends call me Buckeye."

"What?"

"You don't remember? That was a smooooth move with that carrot. You didn't think I wouldn't know it was a carrot?"

"Tina, is this a joke?"

"Honey, a carrot can feel good if you know how to use it. Don't think I don't know that. But why don't you come back and give me the real thing?"

"Stop it! It's not funny!"

"Please come back. I'm very lonely. And . . . well . . . I was lying. I don't have any friends, Alan. Just Tina. Just *you*." The voice was familiar. Dirt and shards of glass familiar.

"Leave me the fuck alone!" Alan slammed his phone shut and tossed it across the room. He fell on his bed and cried all over his ALF comforter. How could *it* have called him? He didn't understand. He wanted all of it to go away. He'd never been butt dialed quite like this.

Alan went downstairs, still naked from waist to feet. The front door had now somehow fallen part way off its hinges, hanging loosely. The screen door flapped. He went over and slammed it hard to make it stop. He started for the kitchen—food might quell his fear, though maybe he'd eat himself to death.

His big toe touched something soft. Looking down, Alan saw a trail of rose pedals. *Oh God. Motherfucker.* He looked up. On the kitchen table sat Tina, her eyes full of tears, her lip quivering. "I'm sorry. She made me do it."

"How did you get here?"

"She knows your scent now, she can sniff you out. Let's get this over with."

"Please just leave . . ." Alan said, his penis shrinking.

"Do you think I like being here? I'm lonely too, but *she* makes it difficult. I'm not normal. I know that. And I know she's lonely, but god damn it! I have a life!" Tina stopped, lowering her head. Her hands sat on her inner thighs and she couldn't keep her fingers from shaking.

She was wearing nothing but a yellow pair of panties. Alan backed away.

"All my life I've had to deal with this. Do you know how hard it is to get a date when you know you have a talking asshole? It's like trying to pull one hair with wet fingers."

"Tina . . . please . . . just . . ."

"Just what? I had to come here. She won't shut up. She never does. If I feed her then she stops for a while. She goes away. I don't know how, but . . ."

Alan was inching towards his living room; the coffee table close to his heels. Tina looked at him, her eyes narrowed. "Stop!"

He didn't listen. Tina reached into the back of her panties and pulled out a knife. "I'm sorry. It was worse this time. If you won't stay still long enough, well . . ."

Alan went for the coffee table. Tina dove at him with a surprising amount of force. He fell down on his knees and she began clawing at him with her free hand, trying to turn him over. He winced, reaching for the table.

His hand was pinned down. Tina held the knife to his throat. "Turn over," she said. Alan did as he was told, his penis limp. It would have been mush if it got any softer. Tina reached down and began touching him, and to his disapproval, despite his best efforts, he began to feel aroused.

Tina ripped her panties off, and the voice, the sound of the *devil*, called out to him. He could see the anus reaching down, squeezing itself from its hiding place. "Alan! I'm sorry, I just want you. I want you so bad!" He looked away as Buckeye was lowered down onto the head of his penis. He felt his member being eaten up by throbbing, pulsing tissue. Did the thing have teeth? Would it bite his pecker off?

He found himself traveling, again, to that moment where his fear had begun. He saw the mailman, his grin growing wider, as he held his sister's turd in his hand and tried to force it back into her asshole, his other hand grabbing at his crotch. And then he—

"No! No! I won't let you do this!" Alan threw a punch, hitting Tina square in the stomach. She dropped the knife and it landed with a dull thud. He swiveled over and his hand snatched the only weapon in sight: a pair of scissors on the coffee table. He lifted himself as best he could and threw Tina on the floor. Before she could stand up, he bent down and jammed the scissors deep into her ass, pushing until they stuck there, the blood coursing out around the blades. His hands were on the handles so tight that he could have broken them if he squeezed and pressed any harder.

He scrambled out of his apartment, laughing, and left Tina behind.

Alan ran down his driveway, into some nearby woods, crying and laughing. Twigs snapped beneath his bare feet and hanging branches clawed his head. The morning sky grew clouded. The sun disappeared.

The other side of the woods birthed him—a new portrait of terror for the 21st century. He fell onto the road, shivering and moaning. He picked himself up, rocks embedded in his back. Torrents of rain burst down from the sky, showering Alan as he zigzagged on the road. A UPS truck came rolling down a hill, the driver not yet (nor would he ever be) prepared to see a half-naked psychotic running around, his penis flapping, blood on one of his hands.

He swerved, trying not to hit Alan. He pulled over immediately and got out of the vehicle. Alan looked at him harshly. "Hey, watch where you're going!" he shouted. Then he looked at the UPS truck, the company slogan in bold letters across the side: WHAT CAN BROWN DO FOR YOU?

"No, you watch where *you're* going, Asshole! And put on some clothes."

Asshole? Ass? Hole? It was too much. Alan couldn't get the word out of his head. It just kept repeating itself, over and over. He forgot about the UPS truck, about its driver, about the road, about everything but *asshole*.

Asshole. Asshole. Asshole. Assholeassholeassholeasshole.

Alan made it all the way downtown. People stared at him, confused. One woman covered her son's eyes. Somebody else yelled something about a tiny dick. Their stares and insults meant nothing to him. For a brief moment he came back to reality. He saw the rush of cars coming down the street, water flinging up from deep puddles and splashing all over him. Then, from the ass-end of a Chevy, he caught a glimpse of a tail-pipe sputtering exhaust. Is this what life had come to?

He threw himself into the throng of vehicles. Horns blared and tires screeched. Bones were shattered and a streak of blood spread across the road. Alan lay howling, a mess of tendons and sinew, his fingers twitching.

When the ambulance arrived he felt his lids grow heavy. "Please let me die," he told them. "Please, whatever you do, don't save me." His words broke off into a child-like sobbing and he lowered his bloodied head.

They hauled him away on the stretcher, barely alive, but still alive enough to feel defeated. Still alive enough to be haunted by blubbering, lonely assholes.

The House of Pain

Wayne C. Rogers

Sergeant Frank Morrow of the Las Vegas Metropolitan Police Department was a little antsy as he headed out the entrance of the Blue Bayou Hotel & Casino and made his way through the large parking lot out front. This was the first time he'd ever spearheaded a raid without a handgun and badge, and it worried him like a toothache throbbing in the back of his mouth. The head of the vice squad, Lt. Jim Robinson, had told him not to sweat it. Few policemen, if any, ever got hurt in vice. The owners of the clubs expected the occasional raid and were used to seeing two-dozen cops filling the doorway of their establishments. It was simply a part of doing business. They took the fall, paid the fines, and were back in action within twenty-four hours. There was no profit in shooting a cop. Something like that brought too much heat down on everyone and disrupted their profit margins.

Morrow didn't believe it for a moment.

He'd wanted to carry his Glock 9mm semi-auto and gold

star, but the information vice had was that two big bouncers stood at the entrance to the elevator, delivering people down to the House of Pain. They swept every person who entered the elevator with an electronic wand to make sure no one was carrying. Any metal in the pockets set the wand off.

That meant no pistol or badge.

The lieutenant had also made it a point to tell him that if someone got in his face, for him to use his martial arts skills to kick some serious ass. Morrow remembered one of the other sergeants laughing and telling him to *Bruce Lee* anyone who got in his way. The team had been making fun of him, but he didn't care. Morrow had been studying the martial arts since he was fourteen and was damn good at it. He could kick anybody's ass in vice without breaking a sweat. Still, he knew as most good cops did that a 9mm pistol balanced out the unexpected and offered better protection than any fighting skills.

Fuck it, he thought.

It was after midnight and traffic was still heavy on West Tropicana as Morrow jaywalked across the wide thoroughfare, ignoring the honking horns and the middle fingers being flipped at him.

He wondered if people still slept in Las Vegas.

Well, at least the night was mild for February. There was only a slight chill in the air as he made his way down the sidewalk to the Arville intersection. He'd dressed lightly for the raid, wearing only a brown leather bomber jacket, a pull-over knit shirt with short sleeves, a pair of jeans, and some running shoes. He didn't care if he looked like an enlisted man from Nellis with his clothes and short haircut. The main thing was that he could move fast in what he had on, and he needed that edge.

Morrow made it across the intersection before the light changed and headed over to the Adult Entertainment complex on the southeast corner. It was a large center comprising of four businesses that catered to horny men and sometimes their wives or girlfriends. There was an adult bookstore in it that sold everything under the sun, a lounge with pole and lap dancing, a building consisting of nothing but peep shows with glass cubicles to separate the paying clients from the female performers, and a movie house where a man could watch a thirty-minute flick in the privacy of a booth for ten bucks. The center had been open for less than a year and was doing a booming business. The parking lot in front of it was jam-packed with cars. Walking over to the lounge, he thought no matter how bad the economy was, sex always sold.

To get into the House of Pain, one had to enter the lounge, walk to the far back area on the right, pay a hundred dollar cover charge, and then enter a long hallway through a black curtain. The elevator was at the end of the hallway. From what little intelligence they had on the place, the club was supposed to be below ground in a vast cavern of epic proportions. Everything involving pain and degradation went on down there. There had even been some rumors of single men disappearing, but no hard facts to back it up.

Morrow was supposed to check out the place before the cavalry arrived.

Stepping up on the sidewalk in front of the Jade Lounge, he pulled open the curtained door and entered the dark interior where loud music immediately blasted him over the speaker system.

"The cost is ten dollars, sir," a male voice said to his right.

Morrow turned to the voice and saw a maître d' dressed in a shiny tuxedo, standing behind a wooden podium.

"I'm looking for the House of Pain," Morrow said.

"There's still a cover charge for getting into the lounge."

Shaking his head, Morrow took out his billfold and gave the man a ten-dollar bill. The maître d' stuck the bill down an opening in the top of podium, grabbed Morrow's left hand and stamped *Jade* on the back of it. He then handed Morrow a packaged towelette.

"You can wipe the ink off when you're finished."

"Thanks."

"Follow the right side of the lounge down to the front," the Maître d' said. "There's another gentleman standing at the end behind a black curtain. It's a hundred dollars to enter the House of Pain."

"Yeah, I know."

Morrow moved past the maître d' and followed the rear wall over to the right side of the lounge. He forced himself not to look at the near-naked women doing lap dances for guys sitting in booths without tables. The ladies had on G-strings and high heels. There was little left to the imagination. Unfortunately, some of women in the club were rather nice looking.

Morrow saw three of them dancing up on the front stage to the left of the black curtain. They were moving around the metal poles like gymnasts. One woman had her black hair tied into little girl pigtails and was wearing a white cotton blouse with the sleeves rolled up, a short black-and-white checkered skirt, white thigh-top stockings, and black high heels. She caught Morrow looking at her and winked. He gave her his best cavalier smile.

Closer to the curtain was another booth on the right with a woman down on her knees in front of a male customer, performing oral sex on his exposed member. He must have slipped her a couple of hundred dollars because she was really working her lips around the hard piece of flesh as if there was no tomorrow.

Reaching the black curtain, he pulled it aside and stepped through. He saw another tuxedo-dressed man standing behind a different podium.

"Are you here to visit the House of Pain?" the man asked.

"Yes," Morrow said.

"It's a hundred-dollar cover charge."

Morrow gave the guy a hundred-dollar bill and watched while he made sure it wasn't counterfeit before slipping it down the rabbit hole in the podium.

"You understand that if you see something you're interested in," the Maître d' said, "there will be an additional charge that's negotiated between you and the other person. Don't be hesitant in asking, if you're curious."

"What if I just want to watch?"

"That's not a problem as long as you don't interfere with a session that's going on."

"Are there restrooms below?"

"Of course," the Maître d' said. "They're down a tunnel on the upper right-hand corner of the cavern."

"Thanks."

The maître d' nodded and pointed his finger in the direction of the hallway.

"Follow the corridor around to the elevator," he said. He then stamped Morrow's right hand with the words—House of Pain. The bold letters were in blood red. Removing the stamp, he gave Morrow another sealed towelette. "Enjoy yourself."

Nodding a *thank you* at the maître d', Morrow made his way down a long, winding corridor. Its walls were covered with black felt curtains and the floor had a thick blood-red colored carpet on it. He followed the corridor to the end and turned left. He saw an elevator door about twenty feet further down. The two bouncers he'd heard about were standing in front of it, guarding the entrance to the House of Pain as if it were the tomb of a pharaoh. They looked like twins. Both men were around six-and-a-half feet tall and in the two-hundred-and-fifty pound range. They had chiseled faces with hard jaws and long wavy hair that reached down to their broad shoulders.

There was a short table to the right of them, covered with more black felt. A round cocktail tray sat on top on it.

When Morrow reached the two men, the one closest to the table said, "Would you please take everything out of your pockets, sir, and place the items on the tray."

Taking out his wallet and car keys, Morrow laid the stuff

in the middle of the cocktail tray and then waited. The guy on the left swept a metal detector wand up and down his body. After a few seconds, he looked at his partner.

"He's clean," the man said.

"What were you looking for?" Morrow asked, grabbing his wallet and keys off the tray. He stuffed them back into his pockets. "I hope not weapons."

"Unfortunately, some customers try to get into the club with a handgun or knife hidden on their body," the other man said. He pushed a button on the wall and the door to the elevator slid open. "We have to also watch out for the police. The wand picks up their metal badges."

"It is *safe* in the club, isn't it?" Morrow asked.

The two men thought that question was hilarious and laughed out loud.

"What's so funny?"

"Nothing, sir," the one on the left said as he held his hand out to the opened elevator. "Have a good time."

Morrow looked at them for a moment, and then stepped into the elevator. He turned around and watched as the door closed in front of him. Pressing the bottom button on the inside panel, the elevator started descending.

Down and down it went.

When the elevator didn't stop after several seconds, Morrow began to wonder just how deep the cavern actually was. The cost of blasting through hard rock below the top soil in Las Vegas was astronomical. That's why so few homes had basements. The owner of the Adult Entertainment complex would've had to lay out millions to go this deep. That estimate, however, instantly quadrupled the moment the elevator stopped and its door opened. Morrow stepped out of the cubicle and stared in awe at the unbelievable space before him. The cavern was the size of football field with a forty-foot high ceiling. There were hundreds of red and black lit candles attached to the walls, or placed at the top of black metal stands located throughout the underground club. Shadows were cast over the nightmarish domain by the flickering lights. The whole scene gave Morrow a shiver of dismay as he realized the fifteen men in the vice squad wouldn't be enough to corral all the perverted people down here.

He had no way to warn his team, either.

Morrow stood there and allowed his eyes to adjust to the dim light inside the humongous place. He could feel the touch of fresh air hitting his face and knew there had to be a large air-conditioning unit somewhere. Taking another step forward, he glanced up at the painted murals on the ceiling. It reminded him of the cathedrals in Europe. The scenes, however, weren't angelic in nature. Rather, they were right out of the mind of someone like Hieronymus Bosch. They depicted man's cruelty in every imaginable way. The beautifully hand-painted murals set the tone for the House of Pain, letting each incoming patron know that he or she was in store for something that would stay with them for years to come.

Moving further away from the elevator and looking around with obvious curiosity, he took in the massive stone columns rising from the polished stone floor to the decorated ceiling. There seemed to be a column every twenty feet, and they were also painted with a vast array of murals that displayed men being flogged, burned at the stake, hung upside down over a roaring fire, and being tortured in all manner of gruesome and original ways. A few even showed groups of men kneeling before an evil-looking, but extremely beautiful Goddess with a rolled up whip in her hand. Between many of the columns were thick wooden beams that were put together in such a way that willing victims could easily be hung up by their wrists or ankles. Other spots along the central walkway had elegantly crafted whipping benches with black padded cushions on top, or old timey electric chairs made out of thick oak, where men could be tightly bound into them with electrical wiring attached to their genitals.

Ouch!

All the spaces between the countless columns appeared to be occupied by people doing their bizarre *thing* with eager relish. In other words, there were the *givers* and *takers* of pain. Both parties were in their own little world of pleasure with little thought as to what was going on around them.

Walking past one particular area, Morrow could see a naked man tied face down over a curved bench. He was being whipped repeatedly on the back and bottom by a stern-looking woman dressed in only black high heels. On the other side of the walkway was a naked man chained down across a heavy, varnished block of wood as a woman pressed a red-hot branding iron to his buttocks. He screamed loudly from the pain of the burning iron to his bare flesh.

"*Jesus!*" Morrow said.

He saw another male hanging by his ankles being whipped by two women wearing black leather fetish garb.

Further down, a nude woman was strung up and being erotically teased by a beautiful dominatrix. It seemed that one's sex didn't actually matter as long as you could pay the price and then take the pain. There seemed to be something different going on in each section between the columns and most of it appeared to be heavy S&M that was tailored toward masochistic men and women.

His eyes drifted over to another male victim who was strapped down over a padded whipping bench. While a stern Mistress wearing a black corset with black nylons and high heels watched, two muscled men sexually used the slave for their own pleasure. One of the men forced his impressive erection back and forth inside the slave's opened mouth, while the second man sodomized him with long, fast strokes. The woman's eyes were filled with excitement as she ordered the two men to fuck the slave even harder.

No one is tying me down, Morrow thought with conviction. *I'm not having some guy's dick shoved up my ass.*

He walked past another section and saw an upside-down hanging slave with his hands bound behind his back. A lovely blonde-haired Dominatrix was standing right up against him, sucking his hard-on. The woman was dressed in black thigh-top stockings, high heels, and nothing else. Morrow made himself do a double take because the woman wasn't actually a complete female, but rather a dominant pre-opt transsexual. She had her erection buried deep inside the slave's mouth. She held the back of his head with one hand while fucking his mouth with rapid thrusts of her heart-shaped bottom. His cock was held with the other hand as she sucked him off with loud slurping noises. She reached her orgasm first and forced the slave to swallow the heavy load she squirted into his mouth.

"This is a fucking den of perversity," Morrow said to himself, shaking his head.

Glancing at his watch, he saw there was still at least fifteen minutes left before the raid commenced. He'd have to find a way of killing time without participating in the sexual activities taking place. The thought then occurred to him that maybe he should stay close to the elevator door for when the cavalry arrived. That would be the smart move to make.

"Are you late for a meeting?" a heavy accented voice asked from behind.

Morrow turned around and saw a statuesque woman dressed in skin-tight black leather and knee-high boots with four-inch heels. She towered over him, causing him to take a step back.

"Who are you?" Morrow said.

"I am the Countess Antonova."

She had long black hair that flowed freely down to her shoulders. Her face was expertly made up with blood-red lipstick, black eye shadow, extended lashes, and a type of foundation that gave her a slightly pale complexion. It seemed to work because she was ravishing. Hell, she was probably the most beautiful woman Morrow had ever seen in his life. It also didn't hurt that her body was shaped like the classic hourglass figure. He could feel a slight stirring in his loins. The last thing he needed was an erection, but it was as if his body was no longer under his control. This woman gave off some type of hormonal scent that stimulated his senses. He had to fight himself to keep from getting a hard-on.

"Cat got your tongue?" she asked, smiling seductively. Her eyes dropped to the front of his jeans and noticed the growing budge. "I can see you like me."

"I think I'm in love," Morrow said.

"All men say that to me and my sister."

"You have a sister?"

"She lives in San Francisco," the Countess said.

"Is she as beautiful as you?"

"Yes."

"I bet thousands of men fall in love with both of you."

"I always demand proof of their so-called love," she said, smiling at the compliment. "Would you be willing to prove your love?"

"And how would I do that?"

"Didn't you come here to suffer?"

"Yes," Morrow lied.

If he wasn't careful, he'd find himself hung up like a slab of beef. Still, Countess Antonova was different. He'd never wanted a woman as much as he desired her . . . not even his ex-wife.

"What would you like to experience?" the Countess asked.

"Maybe I'll look around first," he said.

"Are you sure?"

"Yeah, that way I can see what you have to offer."

"You disappoint me," Countess Antonova said, shaking her head. "I thought you were serious about your love." She then gave him a laugh that was deep and throaty. "No, it would be better if you didn't walk around like a man out for an evening stroll. Men who do nothing but gawk make the other patrons nervous. We wouldn't want that, would we?"

Morrow didn't know how to answer that question.

"Perhaps you should kneel at my feet for a while and honor me as your Goddess?" the Countess continued.

"What would I have to do?"

"You could polish my boots with your tongue. Who knows? If you did an excellent job, I might accept you one of my personal slaves. Does that appeal to you? Are you good with your tongue?"

"I haven't had any complaints."

"I'm sure you haven't."

"What's your name?"

"Frank."

"Follow me, Frank."

Morrow wanted to check his watch again, but instead stared at her heart-shaped bottom as he followed her down the walkway to the rear of the cavern. It made him realize how much he needed to start dating again. Nine months was long enough to be celibate after an unusually cruel divorce.

"Who owns this place?" he asked.

The Countess glanced back over her shoulder and said, "The House of Pain belongs to me."

"It must have cost a fortune to build."

"Yes, it did."

"Are you from Eastern Europe?" Morrow asked. "I'm trying to pinpoint your accent."

"I come from Russia."

The Russian mob, he thought. *This could get bloody.*

The Countess led the way to a throne up against the far wall. It was resting on a raised platform. Though exquisitely designed in style, the large hand-crafted chair looked old . . . like a king had once sat comfortably within its armrests. What really caught Morrow's eye, however, were the two men standing at the top. They were over seven feet tall, built of solid muscle and had a hard, serious look in their dark eyes. They were also trying to fit in by wearing black leather pants and an opened leather vest, but it didn't work.

"The important thing," the Countess continued, "is that my club is out of sight so it draws less unwanted attention."

"How do customers find you?"

"Submissive people find me by word of mouth, talking to each other or writing to one another on the Internet. You'd be surprised to discover how difficult it is to find a sadistic woman to fulfill your desires. The men flock here by the thousands each year. Nothing is taboo and every fantasy is enacted. How did you locate the House of Pain?"

Morrow followed her to the dais and then stopped as she went up the wooden steps to her throne. He had his eyes on the two men above, hoping he wouldn't have to fight them when the time came. They'd probably beat him to a pulp.

"You didn't answer my question," Countess Antonova said as she sat down and crossed her long, slim legs. Her right foot was swinging back and forth as if she was anxious for something to happen. "Wouldn't you like to lick my boots clean?"

He glances at her boots and saw they were already polished to a high glossy shine. In fact, they looked brand new.

"Yes, I would, your worshipfulness," Morrow said.

"That's not how you address a Countess."

Morrow couldn't help but give her a silly-ass grin.

Turning to the man on her left, Countess Antonova said, "Would you please teach this new slave some manners, Alexei?"

"It would be my pleasure, Countess," Alexei said.

The grin Alexei gave Morrow was far from silly. There was a degree of cruelty and meanness in it. This man was looking forward to hurting the cop. As he started down the steps toward Morrow, a sudden alarm sounded over a hidden intercom system. It sounded like the type of emergency alarm you might hear on a sinking ship. The Countess and her two guards looked up at the ceiling for a moment, and then shifted their attention back to Morrow.

"All three of you are under arrest for soliciting in sexual

favors and prostitution," Morrow said, flashing them his brightest smile. "Just sit still, and it will all be over in a matter of minutes. You'll be out on bail before you know it."

"Kill him, Sergey," the Countess ordered the man on her right.

Sergey didn't hesitate for a second. He swiftly started down the steps with the intention of ringing Morrow's scrawny neck.

"Oh, shit," Morrow said, spinning around and running for his life.

Morrow didn't know where he was headed, but his primary thought was on getting away from King Kong. He wished he'd had his Glock. It would probably take all seventeen rounds to stop the fucker behind him. A crazy thought popped into his mind as he ran past a tall metal stand with a lit candle at the top. He screeched to a halt, grabbed the weighted stand, and turned around to face his adversary.

Sergey's smile grew bigger when he saw what Morrow was holding.

"That won't save you, police officer," he said with distain. "You may as well give up and let me rip your head from your shoulders. It will only hurt for a few seconds. I promise."

"Fuck you," Morrow said, jabbing the end of the stand at Sergey's face.

As Sergey dodged the jab, the flame went out and hot wax flew off of it and into the Russian's unprotected face. He threw his hands to his eyes and screamed out in blind pain as the candle came loose from the stand and fell to the floor.

"You sound like a little girl," Morrow said.

The cop then drove the end of the stand hard into the man's groin. He must've hit pay dirt because Sergey bent over in agony, one hand leaving his grimacing face and moving down to grab hold of his crotch. Not wasting any time, Morrow whipped the metal stand around and whacked the Russian in the side of the head. The blow, however, barely fazed him. Morrow aimed lower and hit him squarely in the kneecap with everything he had, bending the stand from the sheer force of the contact. The bodyguard grunted loudly and then collapsed to the floor in a fuddled heap.

Dropping the stand, Morrow looked around for anything else that could be used as a weapon, but was hopefully smaller than a candle stand. He saw what he wanted across the walkway. Running over to one of the sections between the stone columns, he got a branding iron out of a bucket and held it in his hand, liking the weight of it. He swung the iron around a couple of times, and then nodded his head. The iron was only two feet long, but it felt great for knocking the shit out of someone.

While everyone else seemed to be headed to a tunnel in the upper right-hand corner of the cavern, Morrow started moving to the left. That was the direction Countess Antonova and Alexei had rushed off in. He hadn't gotten five feet when he suddenly heard a gunshot behind him. Turning around in a crouch, he saw his lieutenant and some other cops standing in front of the elevator door at the opposite end of the cellar. His boss was holding up his Glock 9mm in the air and waving it at him.

"*Everybody's headed to the right!*" Morrow yelled.

"*I see them,*" the lieutenant hollered back. "*Wait for us.*"

"*No time. I'm going after the owner.*"

The lieutenant motioned him to go ahead as more police officers emerged from the small elevator.

If the Countess hadn't sicked both Alexei and Sergey on him, Morrow might have allowed her to escape. Cops sometimes did things like that if it was personal. As it was, he intended to catch her one way or another, no matter what it took. No one walks away after ordering the death of a cop.

Now, *it* was personal in a big way.

Morrow found a tunnel in the upper left-hand corner of the cavern. He figured that was the way to safety if you happened to be Countess Antonova. He didn't know what was down the long corridor, but he ran as fast as he could, hoping to catch up with the two people before they vanished. After zigzagging through two hundred yards of candle-lit, rock tunnel, Morrow rounded a curve and saw them fifty feet ahead. He was just about out of breath and had to lean over to keep from passing out. When he looked up, he realized they were headed to a set of stone steps, leading upward to ground level.

"Hey, guys, you're leaving without me," Morrow shouted, keeping the branding iron down behind his right leg. "That's not nice. I thought we had something special going."

Countess Antonova and Alexei stopped in their tracks at the sound of his voice.

"I'm still in love with you, Countess," Morrow said.

They looked at him. The expression of their faces wasn't a happy one.

"You don't look glad to see me," Morrow said as he walked closer to them. He kept the branding iron hidden. "I hate to pass on bad news but I had to bash Sergey's head in with a candle stand. I think he's still alive. His body was twitching when I left him. Ah, hell, he's probably dead."

The Countess whispered something to Alexei.

"What was that?" Morrow asked. "I couldn't hear you."

Alexei starred hard at Morrow and started approaching him with purpose. The look on his face reminded Morrow of Sergey.

"Were you and Sergey brothers?"

"I *bash* your head in now," the huge Russian said.

"That doesn't sound too friendly," Morrow said. He stopped, took a deep breath to calm himself, and waited for Alexei to get within striking range. "It's only a raid, guys. You go downtown, pay the fine, and you're back on the street in a couple of hours. Killing a cop is the worst thing you can do in Vegas. Of course, if you're doing something worse than selling sex, then you're in trouble."

They weren't listening, or else they didn't care.

Morrow thought about fighting the Russian, but this

wasn't a movie and he didn't want to end up in the hospital. Instead, he waited until the giant was within twenty feet and then started running toward him at full speed. He figured Alexei would be expecting a tackle of some kind, but Morrow had something else in mind . . . something he'd seen in a movie. When he was only four feet away and the big guy was reaching out to grab him, Morrow dodged Alexei's hands and jumped in the air to the left side of him. He hit the Russian with a hard swing on the side of the neck with the branding iron.

Alexei stumbled and then went down on one knee. He knelt there, rubbing his sore neck, and shaking his head in confusion while Morrow stepped up behind him. This time Morrow slugged the giant in the back of the head and watched him go face down on the floor.

"Fucking stay down, asshole," Morrow said.

He turned to look at the Countess and saw her darting up the stone staircase. She was moving fast for someone in skin-tight leather and four-inch heels.

"Hey, wait up!" Morrow hollered.

Following after the Countess, he made his way over to the candle-lit staircase and started up the wide steps. He could hear the sound of the woman's high heels clicking faintly up above and knew she had a good lead on him.

Hell, she was getting away.

Morrow increased his speed, throwing caution to the wind. He was practically running the steps, and there were a lot of them. The winding staircase had him out of breath by the time he reached the top a few minutes later.

"Goddamn," he said, breathing hard. "I have to start running more often."

He stepped out into a dark, empty room. A little light from the staircase below helped him to see his way around. The place was as empty as a poor man's bank account. It looked abandoned. He was standing in what appeared to be a bedroom. Turning around, Morrow saw he'd come out of a walk-in closet.

"Where the fuck am I?"

Seeing an opened door leading out into another room, he walked over to it and stuck his head cautiously around the doorjamb. He saw an empty living room with a window. Morrow went over to the window and looked out into the night. He could see West Tropicana below and the corner of Valley View to the right. The trestle for trains over Tropicana was to the immediate left. Further on the right side was a rundown shopping center on the northeast corner where a person could buy an inexpensive Italian suit for a hundred bucks. It finally dawned on him that he was standing in an apartment belonging to the decrepit Bel-Aire Suites, which had been closed for six years. The Countess must have purchased the property above the concrete walls that enclosed this area of Tropicana and built a connecting tunnel underneath it to the cavern.

Morrow needed to get busy finding her. As he turned back the way he'd come, his eyes widened as he suddenly saw her standing there in his face.

"You should have let me escape," she said.

"I would have if you hadn't told Alexei and Sergey to kill me. Why did you do something crazy like that?"

"Because I'm more than what you see, Frank."

"You are?"

"Yes."

The face of Countess Antonova began to change into a hideous shape that wasn't as beautiful as the original. In fact, it was the most horrifying creature Morrow had ever seen in his life. Her mouth seemed to elongate with dozens of sharp, pointed teeth exposed. Her jaws and cheekbones grew in size as if she had something alive underneath her skin, trying to get out. The skin texture on her face morphed into a type of leathery and scaly piece of flesh, reminiscent of a giant reptile. The Countess's eyes became a greenish yellow and now appeared to glow with what struck him as pure goddamn evil. Her nostrils even flared outward like the snout of a short-nosed pit bull.

She was now one ugly broad.

"*What the fuck!*" Morrow said with disbelieving eyes. "Hey, listen, if you want to leave, go ahead and be my guest. I won't stop you."

It was too late for humor as he watched her take hold of his leather bomber jacket and lift him right up in the air like he was a two-year-old about to be playfully tossed up and down. He dropped the branding iron in shock. The Countess then started moving toward the glass window that overlooked Tropicana. It didn't take a rocket scientist to guess her intention, and Morrow had no desire to go flying down the concrete embankment like a garbage bag filled with left-over debris. He did the only thing he could think of which was to poke his right forefinger into her left eye. His finger went down all the way to the first knuckle inside the squishy orb.

The Countess immediately dropped him.

She didn't scream out in pain, but rather roared like a demon from hell as she reached up to her gouged eye. The terrifying sound caused goose bumps to break out over Morrow's body. Crawling frantically around her, he grabbed the metal branding iron, sat up, and smacked her good and hard on the side of the kneecap. She went down just like Sergey had done in the cavern. She now had one hand over her bleeding eye and one hand on the side of her banged up knee.

While Morrow was there on the floor, he threw a kick at her face and hit pay dirt. The kick pissed her off to no end, and she glared angrily at Morrow with her good eye. He quickly scrambled to his feet and then struck her across the forehead with the iron. The Countess, however, didn't go down like he thought she would. Instead, she slapped the branding iron from his hand and hissed like a cornered possum. He delivered another fast kick to her grotesque face and then ran out of the living room. He could hear her bitching in some strange language as he hurried from room to room, searching for anything that could be used as a weapon.

He couldn't see anything that would be useful in helping him to stay alive.

"Shit," he said.

Rushing back to the living room, he darted around the Countess as she staggered to her feet and reached out haphazardly for his arm.

"*I'm going to rip your heart out,*" she said.

"Too late," Morrow said as he ran out the opened front door and into the enclosed hallway. "My first wife already beat you to it."

He stopped and looked swiftly in both directions, not knowing which way to go. He heard the Countess shuffling behind him in the apartment and knew what would happen if she got her hands on him.

Morrow took off to the right.

There was a dank, moldy, rotten smell in the hallway that reminded him of a fetid swamp. He also caught a faint whiff of something slightly sweet and sickly in the air. It caused images of the downtown morgue to flash through his mind. He didn't think he was headed in the right direction. When he got to the end of the hallway, he attempted to open the Exit Door, but it was jammed shut. He swiveled around and saw the Countess approaching him like some kind of bizarre specter of death. Her left eye was hanging half out of its socket. The smile on her face was anything but pleasant. The exposed teeth looked razor sharp. Sticking out between them was a long, forked tongue that reminded him of a hungry snake in search of nourishment.

He was glad he hadn't kissed her back in the cavern.

Morrow saw a closed door to his immediate right. Stepping over to it, he tried the doorknob and it turned. As he pushed open the door, he was hit by a wave of pungent gases and foul odors like a hard brick in the face. He entered further into the apartment and saw the shapes of bodies stacked up in the living room. They were in various degrees of decomposition. Some of the bodies were fresh, while others had been there for weeks and months. Morrow knew he only had seconds left and forced himself to walk past the corpses and down a short hall to the rear bedrooms. He was trapped like a rat and knew it. There was nowhere to go and soon his body would join the pile in the living room.

He could hear the Countess as she stepped into the rundown apartment. She wasn't trying to be quiet. The bitch wanted him to hear her coming so he'd tremble in fear. Well, he wasn't trembling in fear, but he was scared. In fact, the fear made him more concerned with finding anything to defend himself with. His eyes searched the empty bedroom and saw nothing. He quickly made his way over to the closet and slid open a sliding door. There was nothing in there but a thick, wooden rod stretching across the length of the enclosure and clothes hangers dangling from it.

Having nothing to lose, he jerked the rod off its holders and then stomped down on the end of it. The last quarter of the rod broke off, leaving a sharp, pointed tip on the longer part. Morrow raised it just as the Countess blocked the doorway of the bedroom. He lunged forward with the rod, driving the spear-like weapon straight into her heart, burying several inches of it within her flesh. She stared at him in startled amazement and then glanced down at the long piece of wood sticking out of her chest.

"*You bastard*," she said.

"You sound like my ex-wife," Morrow said.

He watched her back out into the short hallway and collapse to the floor. Her left hand reached up to grab the rod, but she didn't seem to have the strength to pull it out. He stood there for a moment, not knowing what to do. Finally, he scooted around her and got the hell out of there while he was still breathing and in one piece.

The walk back to the Adult Entertainment complex took fifteen minutes.

Identifying himself to one of the patrolmen out front, Morrow had him call Lieutenant Robinson on the police radio. He met his boss out in the parking lot five minutes later and told him what had happened. Together, along with four other patrolmen, they drove over to the Bel-Aire Suites. Morrow led them into the apartment complex and showed them the room with the bodies in it. The Countess had disappeared. All that was left of her presence was the bloodied clothes rod.

If it hadn't been for the nineteen bodies, Lieutenant Robinson wouldn't have believed him, but as it was, the only thing the police officer could do was shake his head in bewilderment. The story was right out of *The Twilight Zone*, but so were the bodies. This certainly wasn't a story he'd be telling his fellow officers.

Both Alexei and Sergey claimed to have no knowledge of the murders and that they only acted as bodyguards whenever the Countess was inside the cavern. In time they were released on bond and then vanished without a trace from Las Vegas.

The Countess was never found.

Frank Morrow was given a medal for heroism and a pay-rate increase for what transpired that night below ground and above. It meant nothing to him, though it was nice to have a few extra bucks to spend. No, from the night of the raid and on, Morrow had been constantly looking over his shoulder during the darkened hours of the evening. He had an acute sense of being watched and was afraid the Countess would seek revenge against him for destroying her operation. He knew that hell hath no fury like a pissed-off woman.

The one thing Morrow did do was contact a friend of his in the San Francisco Police Department. He and Sergeant Ricky Childress had served in the Army together and had then been stationed in Iraq for two tours. He'd told Childress about the sister and warned him to be careful if he went after her.

That had been back at the end of February.

It wasn't until November that Childress finally called him one night and said he was onto something. Childress had then disappeared from the face of the earth. No one in the San Francisco PD ever saw or heard from him again.

If Morrow hadn't been so afraid, he would've gone to San Francisco and searched for his friend, but he didn't want to chance an encounter with the sister. One sibling was enough, and he'd been damn lucky to escape with his life.

You never tempted fate a second time.

For the Love of Death

Deb Eskie

Emily and David had a good marriage. David worked in marketing, while Emily was a homemaker. She cleaned, cooked, and tended to their young one, Paul. Emily's life was perfect, for the wedding vows David gave promised to provide her with everything she ever wanted. They lived in a quaint, comfortable, white hinged house, surrounded by a picket fence that was covered in pink roses, matching the pink curtains that decorated the windows. Out back was a swing set for Paul, and often times the family would eat dinner at the picnic table, and David would play games with their child under the lush Oak tree. Emily was fond of her blessings, and would thank the Lord for sending her a man that she knew loved her so completely. But just beyond Emily's perfect home, at the end of Willows St., was an old cemetery upon a massive hill. It was chilling in its appearance, with its twisted branches and black clouds that always seemed to hover above it. The stench of death exuded from within its gates, and children and adults alike took caution to avoid the unsettling part of town, all but Emily.

Some afternoons, while David was at work and Paul was at school, Emily would take a walk through the neighborhood and down to the cemetery. It began as a peaceful escape from her daily chores, but it became much more than that. Now when Emily would enter the gates, she would lie upon a grave spot and stare up at the sky, letting the heavy wind sweep over her. Then slowly her hands would glide up her thighs and beneath her skirt, touching herself and becoming engorged and wet. Many times when she did this, she could almost feel the spirit of whoever was beneath her, join in and make love to her. She could feel the power of its presence throughout her body, and she would explode with thrill as fluids poured out of her and absorbed into the graveyard soil.

Late at night David and his wife would be in bed reading quietly to themselves. David would ask her how her day was and she would tell him about the infomercial she saw on television, or the latest town gossip she heard from her best friend, Bessy. She would not mention the cemetery. Then David would kiss her, and place a hand upon her breast. He would grow hard between her legs and softly hump her until he came. To inspire an orgasm, Emily would close her eyes and envision, not only the cemetery, but the coffins buried within. The foul, gruesome, rotting flesh that she could only imagine was kept inside those coffins. The various diseases, accidents, and murders that caused their deaths, and it was then that she would feel passion. But David knew it was not genuine. He knew all along. It hadn't always been like this. Together, they used to have a wonderful sex life, but ever since Paul was born, and David's career managed to steal all his time and energy, Emily's responses in bed were not as they once were. "Is it me?" David finally asked one night, when her bored expression and unimpressive moans became far too unavoidable.

"No, Sweety! You're great!"

"Then what is it?" Emily didn't know how to approach

the topic. She loved David, she really did. He was a kind and sensitive man, a good person. She was more than lucky to have him, and did not want to lose him. However, she was not so sure he'd be open-minded enough to consider her desires. "Perhaps if we spiced things up a bit," Emily then suggested, "what if we watched some pornography together to help the mood?"

"That sounds fine!" David replied, "I'll pick some up after work tomorrow."

"That's all right," Emily said. "Let me pick it out."

The next night, Emily and David got under the sheets and Emily pressed play on the VCR. They watched as a young woman was beaten with a crowbar, and then fucked in the ass, as her bleeding body went limp. The audio was difficult to make out and the filming was unsteady and amateur. Emily removed her bra and began to kiss David's naked chest, but he pushed away.

"What the hell is this, Emily?"

"What do you mean?"

"This isn't porn, it's snuff! Where did you get this?"

"I had it!"

"Since when?"

"I don't know. I just had it." David jumped out of bed and put his pants on. "You've had this tape for a while, and I didn't know about it? Who are you?" He grabbed his coat and keys.

"Where are you going?" Emily wanted to know.

"I'm going out for a drink!" he snapped.

"Are you coming back?" David left and slammed the door behind him. "Are you coming back?" Emily called once more, but she could hear the engine of his car speed away. She removed the tape from the VCR and went down to the basement where she placed it in her secret box filled with other tapes just like it. She checked on Paul in his bedroom, who rested peacefully, and kissed the top of his little head. Then she stayed up all night chain-smoking her cigarettes and contemplating suicide until the sound of David's car pulling into the driveway perked her up and had her running to the front door.

"I was afraid you'd left me," Emily cried. David shook his head and Emily rushed into his arms and held him desperately.

"I would never leave you," he assured her. "I've given it some thought. Everyone has their thing. Everyone has their fetish, and if this is yours, then I can accept that. I love you, and if this is the only way to make you happy, so be it." Emily kissed him. She loved him so very much and felt undeserving of his loyalty and forgiveness.

In the most soothing manner possible, Emily told her husband for the first time in eight years of marriage about her visits to the cemetery. About the times she'd walk there by herself, with the echoes of a thunder storm brewing in the distance. If Paul was at a friend's and David was working late, Emily would go during the night to lie upon the wet, cold grass and listen to the hoots of owls and the howling of wolves. The scenery only added to her beautiful necrorgy in which she felt most alive. Surely David would be disgusted with her now, but he heard her fantasies with control over his judgments. He even managed to participate in graphic scenarios Emily created for the two to role play in. And he humored her when she requested that they engage in torturous bondage and sadomasochistic activities. In a way David found these games to be sort of hot and did consider them an improvement in the bedroom. But the games became more and more disturbing, as Emily would bring in small dead animals to tease each other with and also cut herself for David to feed from. "Punch me," Emily asked of him one night.

"What? No!" he protested.

"Come on! Do it!" insisted Emily, her body sprawled on the bed for David to have his way with her. "Make me bleed! Punch me! Punch me! Punch me!"

"No!" David shouted and he started to sob. "I can't do this anymore, Em. I can't hurt you anymore."

"But you love me?"

"I do. I do love you. I can't do this." For David and Emily the sex between them stopped all together and so did the communication. Now Emily was sure David would leave her and everything she knew and loved would be taken from her. What would the courts think of a mother who liked masturbating in cemeteries and being fist fucked? No doubt they would keep Paul far away from her.

"My mother's dead," David told his wife as he lay next to her in bed, facing away from her. It was the first time David had spoken to Emily in weeks. "My brother called me at work today. The cancer won."

"Oh David, I'm so sorry!" she said. She'd been close to David's mother. In fact, since her own mother was killed, David's parents were all she had. His mother was a dear, affectionate woman that had taken Emily under her wing. When the couple married, Emily detached herself from her father, whom she despised, and with a new family, she rebuilt a new life. Emily comforted her distraught husband, squeezing him and kissing his lips tenderly. This was the woman he remembered, beautiful, caring, and good. Their kissing grew heavier and they began to make love the way they used to. Emily was surprised, for she was very much into it, and as she rode on top of him, she could feel herself reach orgasm. But just as she began to cum, Emily grabbed a pillow and smothered David's face with it. He kicked and screamed and threw her off, and onto the floor.

"What the fuck is wrong with you?" he yelled; his face red with rage and loss of breath.

"Asphyxiation! I read that it's supposed to increase pleasure!" Emily told him, but she could see he was not amused. "Oh god! You're gonna leave me now, aren't you?" she cried, wrapping her arms around his legs and weeping. "I'm crazy! I know! I need help! Just please don't leave me!" David cried with her.

"I'm not going to leave you," he said. "You're sick. You

need help. I want to help you." He picked her up off the floor and carried her to bed. They held each other all night.

It was cloudy out and bitter cold. Emily could sense the various ghosts of the Willow St. Cemetery, her illicit lovers.

One by one, family members approached the open casket to pay their respects. David brought Paul up to the coffin, but with one look at his dead grandmother, the young boy shut his eyes and whimpered, clinging onto his father. As they sat down in their seats, Emily ran her dainty fingers through her son's hair, calming him. She then slowly made her way down the aisle to view the body of her mother-in-law. The old woman lay still and stiff in her blue Sunday church dress. Her face was wrinkled and gray, almost as gray as the tangled mess of hair upon her head. Emily had not seen death this close up since she found her mother's body hacked to pieces on the kitchen floor. She remembered the blood splatters everywhere and the stench of her corpse rotting away. The terror permanently stained on her face. She was gorgeous.

Now as Emily looked at her mother-in-law she felt similarly. She considered it a privilege to view such a remarkable event, to be a part of it, like the day she gave birth to Paul. A tingling sensation overcame her and she realized she had to touch her, to know what death felt like, and she caressed her mother-in-law's flesh, rubbing along the curve of the body's large breast. Emily then sat down beside David and carefully undid his zipper and began to jerk him. David's aunt noticed and stared with horror. Firmly he snatched his wife's hand away, and grabbed her by the arm, bringing her away from the crowd. "You're disgusting!" he hissed shaking her aggressively. "I will not subject our son to this illness of yours!"

"Oh god, David, please don't leave me!" Emily could only say.

"That's not gonna work this time, Em!"

"Please don't leave me! I love you! Without you, I have

nothing!"

"Then you have nothing!" David's family turned toward the couple and noticed the quarrelling. David then rejoined his son at the service, but Emily stood very still and quiet.

Bessy Botwitz, the town gossip, called Emily after hearing about the feud that occurred at David's mother's funeral. Emily assured her friend that all was well in the marriage and that the little tiff had been resolved. "I saw David's car parked out front yesterday. Has he been home from work?" Bessy asked.

"He's on vacation. We've been getting reacquainted with each other all week if you know what I mean. In fact, Bessy, do you mind if Paul stays with you and your boy this week? David and I just need some time to ourselves."

"Oh boy, you two still have that spark, don't you?" Bessy giggled.

"Always and forever," Emily replied and she hung up the phone. Then she removed her silk robe to reveal black laced bra and panties, and wandered into the bedroom where candles were lit and a romantic melody played on the stereo. David sat up naked in bed. His lifeless eyes stared ahead as he leaned on a mound of pillows. Emily crawled on top of him and snuggled against his chest which was covered in bloody stab wounds. "I'm so lucky to have you," she told him, aroused by the silence of his heart, "I'll never let you go."

A Head Full of Hell

Mark Zirbel

Rubber Nurse Woman secures me to the bed, meticulously attending to each strap, fastening each buckle with great care and precision. It's like watching a pilot go through a pre-flight checklist, preparing me for takeoff for my nightly trip to Hell.

I used to resist Rubber Nurse Woman, fighting her every step of the way, especially when she tried to put the ball gag in my mouth. But not since the night I almost bit off my tongue in my sleep. Now I understand that everything Rubber Nurse Woman does, she does for my own protection.

And I love her for it.

At first, I thought my love for Rubber Nurse Woman was purely a physical attraction. She *is* gorgeous, after all—white latex bodysuit clinging to her slender frame, the holes in her bondage mask revealing dark, exotic eyes and full, red lips. But it's so much more than that. It's the way she gently tucks me in each night; it's all the little reassurances she gives me.

"Remember, I'll be right here when you get back," she

says, standing beside my bed. "Listen for my voice. I'll talk you out of it."

I try to respond, but it comes out as a slobbery garble against my ball gag. I nod my head instead.

"And do your best to bring back something better than last night, okay?"

She's talking about the pelvis—the female pelvis that was flopping around like a fish out of water on the floor of my sleep chamber. Without a torso above or legs below, the hunk of flesh didn't even look like a part of the human anatomy. By the time I woke up, a couple of lab technicians had already come inside my chamber to collect the thing. They wore identical black PVC bodysuits and gas masks, so the only way to tell them apart was by noting that one was a little taller than the other.

"What the heck is it?" Taller Lab Tech asked.

"My guess would be a low-level power," Shorter Lab Tech said. He reached down and snatched the pelvis with a rubber-gloved hand, four fingers gripping a buttock and his thumb jammed up the anus. "Probably a worthless little imp."

"Coochy-coochy-coo. Coochy-coochy-coo," Taller Lab Tech said as he reached out to tickle the thing's clitoris. The pelvis's vaginal lips curled into a smile, and then parted to reveal two rows of razor-sharp teeth.

"Aw, ain't it adorable!" Shorter Lab Tech laughed.

And all the while, Rubber Nurse Woman knelt beside my bed, stroking my sweat-drenched forehead. "Don't let them get to you," she said. "You'll do better tomorrow night. I know you will."

Well, tomorrow night is here, and I'm not feeling particularly confident. As if she's just read my mind, Rubber Nurse Woman says, "You seem tense."

I nod.

"Do you think it could be a build-up of sexual tension? Going to sleep while craving gratification can significantly impede your astral projections. We'd best take care of this."

Rubber Nurse Woman unzips a small compartment on the side of one of her thigh-high, white boots. She reaches inside a pulls out a green plastic tube—the kind like hair gel comes in. But this one says SUPERGLIDE PERSONAL LUBRICANT. Sitting next to me on my bed, Rubber Nurse Woman unsnaps the crotch of my bodysuit. My constrained erection suddenly leaps free, causing it to bounce back and forth a few times before stopping and standing at attention. Rubber Nurse Woman squeezes a glob of lube onto my cock head and lets it slowly overflow down my shaft.

I can't believe this is happening. I've dreamt of a moment like this—figuratively speaking, of course. In actuality, I rarely dream when I sleep—instead, my astral body leaves our plane of existence and travels to Hell. I become so deeply immersed that when I wake up, I can bring back pieces of the Underworld with me. My unconscious mind has clutched onto countless atrocities and released them into my sleep chamber, but still the Company wants more. Rubber Nurse Woman does what she can to help me comply. Tonight, it appears that she's trying out a new method.

Rubber Nurse Woman wraps her fist around my cock and begins to stroke me. The sensation of her slick rubber glove pumping my dick reminds me of having sex while wearing an internally lubricated condom. It's not the same as going bareback, but it's still pretty damn good! With her free hand, Rubber Nurse Woman begins caressing her massive, latex-enshrouded breasts. She lavishes each tit with attention, sliding her hand all over one shiny mound before moving on to the other. Despite her vigorous self-massage, Rubber Nurse Woman's breasts don't budge. Her ultra-tight bodysuit gives her double D's the gravity-defying firmness that's usually only seen in the pages of a comic book. But there they are, just inches away from me. I'd give anything to be free of my restraints, to be able to join Rubber Nurse Woman as she fondles herself. The thought of this brings me right to the edge of ejaculation.

Perhaps sensing how close I am, Rubber Nurse Woman picks up the pace of her handjob. Within seconds my cock explodes, the come shooting out of me in three rapid bursts. I buck and wrench against my straps, but Rubber Nurse Woman doesn't let up. Instead, she concentrates her efforts on the ultra-sensitive tip of my penis, making sure she milks every last drop out of me.

"There," she says, "no more sex on the brain." Rubber Nurse Woman stands up and removes a small package of tissues from her boot. She wipes me off and tucks my spent penis back inside my bodysuit. "With your mind no longer preoccupied by such trivial matters, perhaps it can better concentrate on more important things tonight. Yes?"

God, she's so wonderful!

Rubber Nurse Woman straps on my full-face oxygen mask and checks the bedside monitor to make sure all my vital signs are normal. Then she walks to the door, pressing a button on her way out to dim the lights in my sleep chamber. I hate it when Rubber Nurse Woman leaves, but at least I know she'll be right next door in the control room. I take a deep breath and close my eyes, apprehensive about returning to Hell, but confident that my loving protector is watching over me.

My journey through Hell usually begins at the Torture Playground, where the souls of evil children are ensnared in barbed-wire jump ropes and buried in lye-filled sandboxes. So when I find myself in my apartment, sitting on the couch with Mary, it's clear I'm having a dream rather than experiencing an astral projection. Strange, though . . . my dreams are never this lucid. I see the closing credits of *The Godfather* scrolling up the television screen, and I suddenly realize that this is a flashback to the last evening Mary and I ever spent together.

"Wow, what an awesome movie," Mary says.

"Very long but very good," I respond, right on cue. Apparently I'm powerless to prevent this night from unfolding exactly the way it happened. I'm going to have to live the nightmare all over again.

"Holy cow—it's past midnight," Mary says as she checks her watch. "Would it be okay if I slept over?" She gives me a sly smile and rubs her bare foot against my crotch.

"Mary, what are you . . . ?" I cut myself off as she curls her pedicured toes to give the bulge in my jeans a little squeeze.

Mary pulls her sweater over her head. What was obvious all evening is officially confirmed: she isn't wearing a bra. I felt lightheaded throughout the movie with Mary nestled up to me, her large breasts sprawling softly against my chest, her nipples protruding through pink cashmere. Now, seeing her topless for the first time, I feel like I might pass out. I've never seen such perfectly round and firm globes outside the pages of *Playboy*. "Mary, we've already talked about this," I say, trying to compose myself. "I don't think it's a good idea for us to sleep together."

"I know . . . I know . . . because of your night terrors. Listen, if you wake me up during the night with your screaming, so be it. But I'm such a sound sleeper, I probably won't even hear you."

"It's not just the screaming. I thrash around a lot too. I'm afraid I would hurt you."

"I'll tell you what—let's go into the bedroom and have a little fun, and then I'll come back out here and spend the rest of the night on the couch."

"I'm still not sure you'd be safe. Last month I . . . I . . ."

"You *what*?" Mary asks, a bit of annoyance creeping into her voice as her easygoing personality is pushed to its limits.

I sit there in silence, looking deeply into Mary's sad, confused eyes, contemplating how to explain this to her. Anything I say will make me sound insane. She needs to see for herself. "Wait here a minute," I tell her.

As I hop off the couch and head to the hall closet, part of me wonders if I'm doing the right thing. I've never shown anyone what I'm about to show Mary. But I love her, damn it—enough to be honest with her about my condition, enough to let her know what she'll be getting herself into if she stays with me.

After rummaging through a large storage tub in the closet, I return to the couch holding a Mason jar with air holes poked into the lid. A gray, lumpy, slug-like thing, about the size of a person's fist, is moving around inside. It looks like a huge, undulating tumor, as if some mad scientist has brought a nasty chunk of cancer to life.

"My god, what is that?" Mary asks.

"I have no idea. I woke up screaming one night, and there it was on my bed sheet. I've kept it in this jar ever since. Whatever the hell it is, it's got me wondering if what I've experienced for all these years is really night terrors at all. I'm starting to think that I've been having out-of-body experiences, like my consciousness is traveling someplace. Someplace *terrible,* where my mind can grab a hold of things. What if I bring back something even worse next time? It kills me not to be able to sleep with you, Mary, but I can't put you in that kind of danger."

She takes the jar from me and examines the creature inside more closely. It starts to hiss and spit, fogging the inside of the glass and speckling it with a milky residue. Suddenly, Mary begins shouting. "I have a sample! All units move in! All units move in *now!*"

The room explodes in chaos.

Men wearing black PVC bodysuits crash through the living room window. The front door flies off its hinges as more latex commandos storm their way in. All of them are armed with M16s. Within seconds, my body is dotted from head to toe with their laser sights.

"Mary . . . what the hell is happening?" I ask in a panic.

"My name isn't Mary," she replies coldly. "I'm a field op with the CIA, Metaphysical Weapons Division."

"But we've been friends for more than a year!"

"Shit, that's nothing. The Company's been watching you ever since you were a child—monitoring your abilities, waiting for them to develop to a point that would warrant bringing you in."

"Bringing me in? What are you talking about?"

One of the commandos holsters his M16 and pulls out a stun gun. I close my eyes and begin to scream. Over and over and over again. My cries fill the room and reverberate inside my head. The effort scours my throat raw but I don't stop. I just keep letting loose all of the fear, anger, and confusion within me. It isn't until I open my eyes that I realize I'm back in my sleep chamber, howling against my ball gag, forcing my own screams back down my gullet.

Huge, red flames engulf the room, darting and snapping like a den of vicious serpents. The overhead sprinkler system has been activated. Torrents of water pour down, but the inferno isn't the least bit affected. Suddenly all of the gas masks and rubber clothing seem less like a fetishistic fashion statement and more like the fire safety measures they really are.

Outside my sleep chamber door, I hear someone shouting. "He brought back Hellfire! It's spreading throughout the compound! We can't contain it!"

Well I'll be damned. I wasn't having a dream after all. I was in Hell all along—my own private corner of it. And I brought back something more than just the flames. A creature is lurching toward me, its bulbous, misshapen torso perched high atop a pair of spindle-shank legs. It's hard to get a clear picture of the thing through all the smoke, but I can see dreadful bits and pieces. Like the gooey trail of blood it's leaving behind as it drags its head across the ceiling. And the sparks that are flying into the air as the tips of its razor blade claws scrape the floor.

But I'm not afraid.

Soon, Rubber Nurse Woman will come and undo my straps. She's going to be so proud of me! Maybe as a reward, she'll take me home with her tonight. Maybe she'll peel off her latex bodysuit, finally revealing the soft, talcum-dusted skin beneath. Maybe she'll hold me in that softness, hold me all night long—never leaving me, never betraying me.

And then, it'll be just me and my beautiful Rubber Nurse Woman. Forever.

Imitation is the Sincerest Form of Flattery

Vi Reaper

Carl heard the car coming from miles away. The engine rattled and squealed with age; its harsh complaints echoing off the bricked-up store fronts that lined the street. With the winter wind playing its part, it was difficult to tell from which direction the car was coming. Carl stood still, hands in pockets, he knew he was alone on the street, he had been alone all night, the freezing temperate and biting winds kept people indoors, hugging their drinks in the café's and bars that were the only businesses remaining in this town; plus there was some game on. Carl did his best hunting when people were distracted by television. No witnesses.

It was a small car, not a truck or some four-wheel drive metal monster, an economy sedan maybe; Carl could recognize cars by their engines. Police cars were very easy to distinguish if you knew how to listen. This wasn't a police car, he knew that, but something was different about this car, something that made Carl step back into a black shadow cast by one of the derelict stores. Disappearing from sight, the only clue anyone was there was the occasional white mist puff as Carl breathed and as the car turned the corner onto the street, even that little clue vanished.

It was a Volkswagen Beetle, dysentery beige in colour. It weaved across the road occasionally burping out blue smoke and all the time rattling like metal teeth chewing a spanner. The driver was just a black mass behind the wheel, but as the car sped up on the straight road the passenger door was flung open with a caterwaul scream and a moment later a body was violently pushed out. Rolling along the frost speckled ground, a tangle of arms and legs that made sick thuds as they crumpled and flexed until the body finally rolled to a stop clattering into a metal sign post that stated, NO DUMPING. The car turned left at the end of the street, as it disappeared from sight the passenger door slammed shut with another rusty hinge yowl. The engine's rumble soon dissipated into the distance allowing the silence to return.

Carl remained still, remained hidden, not breathing, controlling his heartbeat, and knowing that if there were any witnesses now would be the time they would show themselves. Maybe they wouldn't yell for help, people didn't seem to do that unless they themselves were in trouble, but Carl knew people loved a scene, a good gawk at someone's misery and if that was going to happen Carl wanted no part of it. He hadn't seen a thing, nothing at all and if someone said he had then he'd poke their eyes out with his fingers and swallow them whole.

Steam rose from the body. It was unmoving, wrapped inside a grey woolen blanket. As the breeze blew, Carl picked up the scent of fresh blood, piss and perfume. A woman. He stayed still and silent. Carl knew he should just walk away, he'd seen things worse than this and hadn't blinked any eye, hell, he'd done things worse than that and slept like a baby, but much to the chagrin of his little inner voice, Carl was curious. If this area was already inhabited by someone like him, Carl would have some decisions to make and it was best to be informed.

With a decision made, he checked the street again to be sure of no witnesses and approached the human cast off. The blanket covered most of her body with just a tuft of blood-caked dark hair sticking out from one end, and a pair of bruised and scrapped-up legs protruding from the other. She had on one black sock. Carl nudged the woman with his foot. Steam still trailed up from her and he guessed it was the blood cooling in the frosty night air. Leaning over, he pinched a corner of the blanket with his black leather gloved hand and peeled it back. Quite a mess. Her face was a mask of blood that looked as black as tar. Her eyes were closed and swollen, her nose had a strange angle and her top lip had a thick gash in it. Whoever done this had been mighty pissed and used her as a flesh punching bag. He revealed more of her. She was naked. Someone had bitten a good chunk out of both her small moon-white breasts. Her dark nipples had also been chewed on and her torso and arms were a maze of scratch marks, bruises and cuts that had crusted over with dried blood. Between her legs, amidst the dark patch of pubic hair, her attacker had carved the initial T into her skin. Carl savoured her for a moment longer, a wonderful work of art but done by a novice of the game. The guy who had done this would be caught in an instant. Carl was just about to let the blanket drop when something caught his eye. In the space between her nostrils and her lips a large glistening blood bubble formed, as it popped, the woman let out a thin wheeze and her left eyelid opened to reveal a pale blue, bloodshot eye. She looked at Carl and again wheezed, her left arm twitched in his direction. Carl dropped the blanket and stepped back, she was silent once more but now he could see steam rising from where her mouth was and she began to shiver violently.

She had seen him now. Just a glimpse, yes, but still and in her state she could have pointed to Carl as her attacker. This could all be fixed with a swift boot to her head. She was barely alive as it was, where was the harm. Carl had to protect himself.

He took a step towards her again and raised one steel-toe capped work boot and aimed it at the bulge in the blanket where her face was. He stayed in that pose for a moment, foot wavering, arms out to keep his balance and add some force to the kick and then he dropped his foot, bent down, gathered the woman up still wrapped in the blanket, hung her over his shoulder into a fireman's carry and set off for home.

Carl smiled as he walked. Sometimes, he even surprised himself.

During the six days and nights the woman had been with Carl, she had only opened her eyes for a few moments. Occasionally she would moan and try to move but he kept her still, applying pressure to her shoulders until she once again floated away into unconsciousness. Carl had spent most of the first night and day cleaning her up, disinfecting and dressing her many wounds. He had inserted a drip into her arm and gave her regular shots of antibiotics to keep away infection, he'd also set her nose so it was at least a little straighter than it had been. Carl kept a close eye on the bite wounds in particular as they were the ones that were the most likely to fester. He had enjoyed washing her, wiping at her pale skin with soft towels, lathering up sweetly scented anti-bacterial soap and massaging it into her pores, rubbing it over the raised rough edges of the scratches and scrapes, pressing on the many bruises that tattooed her body and watching as her skin kaleidoscoped in colour under his fingers. He skimmed his fingertips over the finger marks around her throat. If she had been awake it would have hurt her, he was sure, but she made no sound in her slumber and never flinched from his touch. Carl liked that. He liked that a lot.

She awoke on Friday. At the time Carl was eating noodles and reading the local newspaper. He felt her eyes on him and swiveled on his stool to face her and smiled. The deep black bruises that puffed out each eye gave her a natural hooded glare.

Her first reaction was to move, to jump up and run away but with just the slightest shift of her body, Carl watched her eyes bulge and her face flush as red-hot pain raced through her. She hissed through her teeth to vent the hurt, never taking her eyes off Carl and despite the agony, she tried to get up once more.

"Please miss, you should really stay still," Carl said as he rose from the stool. He tried to advance on her in the most non-threatening way he could think of, with his hands up (still holding the pot of noodles) and then realized that at that moment a fart would be judged as a threat by this woman. Carl stopped. Trembling, she opened her mouth to speak and all that came out was a dry sounding croak. She tried to swallow and began to cough. A violent sound like something deep down inside her was tearing loose. Carl took his lukewarm milky coffee he had been drinking and held it out to her. She viewed the cup with suspicion. Understanding, Carl took a large swig from the cup himself, proving to her that the liquid was fine before offering it once more. She snatched it from him and gulped the contents, some of which dribbled down her chin and splashed on the sheets, all the time she kept her bruised red-rimmed eyes focused on him. To Carl's surprise she now seemed more furious than afraid.

The last of the coffee gulped, she made a fist round the heavy ceramic mug, ready to use it as a weapon.

"Who are you?" Her voice was still crackly.

"How are you feeling?"

"Who are you?" She was near shouting now.

"You should try and—"

"You're a friend of his, aren't you, you fucking cocksucker?" She glared at Carl who in turn wondered what she was talking about. During these last few days, he had rehearsed possible outcomes of this first conversation. He was nervous about it and wanted to make sure he had every angle covered, but to be truthful, he was still unsure why he had brought her here in the first place. Keeping her alive was dangerous to him. He had a frozen head in his fridge, for Christ's sake and now there was a hysterically pissed off woman in his bed. Why had he brought her here? This was obviously a question she wanted answering too, because now she was making a more determined effort to get out of bed. She ripped the drip from her arm and staggered to her feet, wavering like a drunkard. She glanced down at her body. Carl had put her in one of his old midnight blue shirts and a pair of his black cotton boxers, the majority of her body that was visible was either tinged green with bruise or swathed in bandage. Carl moved towards her.

"Please, I mean you no harm, Miss, I swear. You must . . . What's your name?" Be pleasant, he thought.

She ignored his question, eyes darting around for the exit. "Where are my clothes?"

"You didn't have any."

"Yes, I did." She said this like Carl had just told her that she didn't have a nose on her face.

"No you didn't."

He watched her take in this information. Her body still trembling, seemed to deflate, her shoulders dropped, her head hung. He wanted to reach out to her but noticed she still had the mug clasped in her hand like a rock ready to bludgeon.

"Can I go to the bathroom, please?"

"Of course. It's behind you." She turned, steadying herself by gripping the wall and limped into the bathroom. It was the only place in Carl's flat where he couldn't see her. The bedroom, living room and kitchen were all in one. There was no carpet on the floor. No curtains at the windows. A suitcase was Carl's wardrobe. A small fridge-freezer (with head), a deep stainless-steel sink and a microwave was his kitchen. Carl's only neighbours in the block of flats were a couple of squatters come drug-dealers that hung around ten stories below and Carl's only entertainment was books, newspapers and the occasional killing, dismemberment and cannibalism of people he took a disliking to. He moved around a lot and up until now, thought he had the perfect existence.

Sitting on the edge of the bed, Carl heard her soft sobs. Pressing his ear to the flaking paint of the bathroom door, he listened. Crying, along with begging and pleading, usually turned him on. The more desperate the better. But her sounds were different. He didn't know why.

Carl tapped on the door gently before pushing it open. The bathroom smelt heavily of damp rot. Dark water stains decorated the walls where the wallpaper had blistered and peeled off in long thin strips that hung down like dead brown leaves of a diseased tree. The toilet, sink and bathtub were a hideous avocado colour with the taps peppered with rust. Once again the floor was bare, grey concrete. The first thing he noticed was a small trail of watery blood on the toilet seat, then as he pushed the door wider he saw her on the floor in the corner under the sink. She was balled up, her knees under her chin, her hands and face hidden. He knelt before her and reached for her hands. She gave up the mug without effort, her scabby red knuckles and split fingernails oozed fresh blood in places where she had gripped the mug so tightly. Carl thought her hands were nice despite the damage, "piano hands" his mother would have said, long and delicate. He'd had piano hands before, usually with peas, carrots, mashed potatoes and vegetable gravy.

"Who are you?" she mumbled.

"I'm Carl." He had been born Harry. Last year he was Mike. A month ago he had been John. Now he was Carl.

"I found you, Miss."

"Found me?" She was still hiding her face, her voice dull with emotion. Carl liked her better when she was pissed off and vicious looking, but he decided to let it go for a while. He had seen the state of her pussy. It wasn't just the initial T that had been carved into her pubic area, whoever had done this had very literally ripped her a new one and Carl had done his best to sew it all back together with about as much success as Dr. Frankenstein.

"Someone tossed you out a car . . . naked . . . and I found you and brought you here." He wanted to touch her hair. He had been careful to wash it every day while she was unconscious using dish-washing liquid, but it still smelled nice.

"So, you aren't one of his friends?"

"I'm friends with no-one." Finally, he let himself touch her hair, rubbing a few strands between his fingers. He expected her to flinch, to her credit she didn't.

"You know who did this to you then?" he inquired. That did it. She raised her face to within an inch of Carl's with a look of complete hatred and rage plastered all over it. She had torn off the brace that Carl had placed across her smashed nose.

"Yeah, I fucking know," she seethed. "Dennis did this. I remember that he was looking at me weird all day, but he's weird anyway so I didn't think much of it and now this. Bastard." She tried to stand and winced at the pain; Carl hooked her around the waist and pulled her up.

"Dennis, you say?"

"Yes. Dennis. Why?" She was looking at the blood on the toilet seat as though she had discovered some new life-form that was grotesque of appearance.

"It's just, well, I don't think it was him," Carl said. She located the toilet roll, tugged off a couple of sheets and cleaned her mess.

"Why not?"

How to put this, Carl considered. Just say it, the answer.

"You have the letter T carved into your . . . bits." Why hadn't she noticed that? Carl thought.

"That's how I know." She tried to flush the soiled tissue and failed, the pipes making hoarse barking noises in protest of being used without water lubrication, shrugging she moved to the avocado coloured sink to wash her hands.

"There's only water in the kitchen. How do you mean, that's how you know?" She limped out the bathroom. Carl followed behind. She was still unbalanced so he held out his hands ready to catch her if she fell, like a proud dad watching his rug-rat take its first steps.

"He was driving a Beetle, right? A beige-y coloured thing, right?"

"Yes, he was. But the T?"

"Ted Bundy?" Having washed her hands, she looked around for a towel; found none so she wiped her hands on the shirt tails grimacing as she knocked off more scabs. "Ted Bundy, the serial killer?"

"That's right. Dennis likes him. Always talks about him. Even brought the same kind of car Bundy used to have. Same colour and everything. Dennis likes to say how Bundy was some misunderstood Romeo and how he used get loads of sex with women, even in jail. He told me how Bundy used to bite his women." At this she pulled down the collar of her shirt and showed Carl the half moon, angry red bite marks on her chest. Obviously she had examined herself in the bathroom. No wonder she had cried.

"I didn't think he'd take it this far though. Jesus. I was coming out of work; he pulled over and offered me a lift. I said no. Then, he gets out and opens the passenger door for me like he's trying to be sweet. I still say no. Then I remember a pain in my head, so he must have hit me and . . . Well, I guess you know the rest."

Taking in her words, Carl walked in slow, small circles around the room, his head down. The reoccurring thought of having competition in the sport he considered himself to be an all-conquering champion in gave him trouble and the idea that this fucker was aping Bundy pissed him off to the extreme.

Ted Bundy was a master at his art. Intelligent and handsome, Bundy had known how to use his gifts to his advantage, to entice women to their grisly deaths. In the movie *The Silence of the Lambs* they had based the killer Buffalo Bill partially on Bundy. The trick of faking an injury and asking girls to help him had been Bundy's idea. He had even represented himself at his murder trial just so he could intimidate and terrorize the witnesses in court, still playing his games. And Dennis had been right; Bundy had even charmed women reporters and received up to two hundred letters from women a day while he was sitting on death row. He'd even got married in jail. And although many people had cheered when Bundy had fried in the electric chair, many other people had wept.

The pseudo-psychological idea was that serial killers wanted to get caught. To get famous they had to get caught. Carl didn't want to get caught, not in the slightest. The idea of jail didn't appeal to him anymore than seeing his mug shot in the paper. What did bother him however was the purity of his art. To kill someone you didn't like, was one of the purest, most honest thing Carl thought a person could do. There was no lying or deceiving, pretending that you liked someone when you didn't. Smiling at their jokes or making nice at parties and complementing their choice of hairstyles. For Carl to kill was to be true to the human soul. Many would scoff, but that's just what he believed and, as he had discovered, the people who laughed at his theory had never killed anyone so how the hell would they know anyway. But it was true that most serial killers have a pattern they can't help but repeat. Bundy had invented his own way of doing things and for this Dennis fucker to just copy and paste was as blasphemous as re-recording Elvis's "Suspicious Minds" using only tuneless, wet farts.

"Do you think he's done this before? That he's killed someone?" Carl asked.

"I don't know. Probably not."

"What makes you think that?"

"Well, he fucked up didn't he? I suppose he thinks he killed me. I mean, I work with him, he'd have to kill me because otherwise I could identify him and if he'd done it before he would have had some practice at it, then he would have done the job properly and finished me off. Plus, don't they say that most serial killers kill someone they know the first time they do it?"

It was a good job that the woman wasn't looking at Carl the moment she said that last sentence because a shiver passed visibly through his body.

Memories.

"Hey, Carl do you have anything to eat?" The woman had the fridge freezer door halfway open before Carl could slam it shut and block her path to it. She stepped back, her hands balled into fists, past experience had made her wary.

"Sorry, I just, I don't have anything. But I can order something." Carl pulled out his mobile phone from his pocket and smiled.

They ordered Chinese food and the woman ate hungrily, for his part, Carl picked at his mushroom chow mein, thoughts weighing heavy on his mind. When there was nothing left but soy sauce blobs congealing at the bottom of the silver take-out trays Carl spoke out.

"Can I ask you something?"

"Sure."

"If you could get back at Dennis. If you could do anything to him to make him pay for what he did, what would you do?"

Carl expected the first words out of her mouth to be something along the lines of "jail" and "make sure he can't do anything like that again". Instead, she thought, absently rubbing at the bruises around her throat. Then a small smile creased her lips, it cracked the scab there and blood trickled out making the grin look garish.

"I'd want him to go through what I went through. Exactly what I went through."

"Exactly?"

"Raped, cut, bitten, choked . . . everything."

Carl and the woman stared at each other in silence. He wanted to show his hand here, but he knew to do so and gamble wrong would end with him losing more than a stack of chips.

He reminded himself of that look she had first given him. There was also the fact she was here and that he had brought her here. During those days she was out cold, Carl could have messed with her, fucked her, took her skin and made a belt, boiled her bones and sucked the marrow from them, shaved her hair and pushed those shiny dark strands into a sock and then used it to masturbate, he could have scooped out her entrails and decorated the walls with her half-digested last meal, made her skull into a plate, he'd done it all before but he hadn't, he hadn't and as for this woman's part, since she had awoke she hadn't screamed blue murder at the top of her lungs, she hadn't even asked him why he hadn't taken her to the hospital or the police. He knew she wasn't dumb, a victim with legs. Maybe there was something in her, something that had been jolted into life by her brutal attack that recognized the darkness within Carl and was drawn to it, even if she would refuse to acknowledge its presence.

"I can make that happen."

"What do you mean, Carl? Make what happen?"

"Everything you just said you wanted to happen to Dennis, I can do those things to him."

If she laughed at him now, Carl decided to laugh along. Yeah, he was a funny guy.

She didn't laugh.

"You shouldn't say stuff like that unless it's true, Carl. Get girls' hopes up just to make a joke."

"I'm serious." She looked at him funny. Her pale blue eyes spider-webbed with broken blood vessels searching for some clue from him that he was truly serious.

"Where do you work? Will he be there now?"

"Carl, please."

"What's your name?"

"Emily."

"Emily. Look in the fridge."

*

Dennis didn't look like Ted Bundy. Whereas Bundy had dark, wavy hair and brown eyes set into a smooth handsome face, Dennis had straw-coloured greasy hair, grey eyes that seemed to be looking in two directions at once and pock-marked skin. Emily had told Carl that Dennis was the same age as her, twenty-eight, but he walked like a sulky teenager. Moving between tables at the café, taking orders and serving plates of food he shuffled with rounded shoulders and a general look of boredom.

Maybe it was wearing off, Carl thought; maybe Dennis had practically danced around this place a week ago when he thought he killed someone for the first time. Carl knew both feelings well. The high of the blood rush, knowing you had stepped over an invisible line that most people ran from. Then, you had the down that soon followed, the paranoia, the agitation.

Emily had told Carl where to sit in the late-night café so that he wouldn't be served by Dennis, which then afforded Carl time to watch his prey from a distance. A young blonde waitress took his order, telling him that alcohol wasn't served before six o'clock and that if he wanted to stay at a table he had to order food. Carl already knew all this from Emily, but played along anyway after all if anyone asked he was just another faceless traveler passing through this dead town on his way to the excitement of the major city that lay just a couple of miles away.

As the hours passed the crowded café became increasingly empty until there were just a handful of men hanging on the bar doing their level best to stay upright. Carl had joined them, sitting on a bar stool he was ordering pints of lager with a shot of whiskey. Dennis was serving, lazily walking up and down filling empty glasses and ringing up the bills but paying most of his attention to the TV that was bracketed to the wall up one corner that was showing highlights of a football match. One of the other drinkers belched loudly as Carl checked his watch. There was just over an hour left on Dennis's shift as Emily had told him. Time for the plan.

Carl turned on his stool; the young blonde waitress was now wiping down tables. Emily had guessed that the café would have replaced her with another attractive female. On any given shift there was a man to deter trouble and a woman to keep 'em drinking. Carl called the blonde over with a wave of his hand. She approached him with a false smile cracking her face.

"Can I help you?"

"I hope so," Carl said. "I was just wondering how much it would cost?"

Carl had raised his voice making sure he had everyone's attention especially Dennis's.

"How much would what cost?" the blonde answered.

"How much it would cost to get you to suck my balls?"

Dennis was the first one to burst out laughing. A great braying sound that reminded Carl of Pinocchio when he was half donkey. A few of the other patrons giggled but soon lost interest. A couple of others showed no emotion at all and one big, bearded guy at the far end of the bar looked at Carl like he would happily turn Carl inside out through his arse. The blonde's smile fell, a redness rose in her cheeks and she turned around stiffly and resumed her work at the tables.

"Well, what of it?" Carl yelled. "Okay then, fuck it, I was only asking."

Carl swiveled back around to face the bar. Dennis was still roaring with laughter. This act had served two purposes. One, it had gotten the attention of Dennis. Two, if someone did remember Carl it would be for being a sexist twat that was only interested in women and therefore couldn't possibly have anything to do with what was going to happen to Dennis.

Having claimed some control over himself Dennis picked up a glass filled it with lager and put in down in front of Carl.

"It's on me. That was the funniest thing."

"Cheers. What's up with that bitch anyway? I was only kidding with her?"

"Ah, she's a whore, is all. New here and already thinks she's hot shit."

"New?"

"Yeah, started a couple of days ago. If you think she's a cow, you should have seen the bitch that was here before her . . . now there was a cunt of epic proportions."

If Dennis had been paying attention he would have noticed Carl's grip on his pint glass turn his knuckles white. Carl wondered why some younger men talked like this. Did they really think this way or did they want to seem like they did so they would fit in? Like being insulting made them more attractive. Carl didn't know, but he did have Dennis on the hook.

"What happened to her? She get sacked for pissing in the beer?"

"Yeah, something like that, man. Let's just say she got what was comin' to her." Dennis grinned, showing what seemed to be his best feature, his perfect white teeth. Then Carl thought of the damage those munchers had done and had to swallow hard to keep the alcohol down. Up close Dennis was nasty. The once white collar of his waiters' uniform was now stained brown with dried sweat. His fingernails were long and mucky and his breath had the odour of three week old haddock. Carl wondered how the man kept his job.

"Hey, you wanna 'nother whiskey. You're dry?" Dennis picked up the empty shot glass.

"Sure, why not . . . errrmmm. . . ."

"Dennis."

"Okay, Dennis." Carl handed him a twenty pound note. "Keep the change."

What had finally convinced Dennis was the mention of drugs. Emily had gifted Carl with that tidbit of information too. If all else fails mention free drugs and Dennis will follow.

The two men had continued to chat until the café bar had

closed but by this time Carl had tempted Dennis into having a drink, even though it was against the rules for the staff to drink. He hadn't taken much convincing. Distracting Dennis for a moment Carl had dropped a little liquid ecstasy into the younger man's drink. Just enough to knock any strength out of him. Clinging to each other, the two men now wobbled across the café car-park towards Dennis's beige Beetle. There was spitting rain in the freezing wind. Tomorrow morning this little part of the world would be crisp and clean with frost.

"You know who used to own this car?" Dennis slurred.

"Who?" Carl asked, digging his hands into Dennis's trouser pockets for the car keys.

"Bundy. Ted Bundy. You know him? He was a great fuckin' guy."

The passenger side door squealed as it opened and Carl pushed Dennis into the seat and buckled him up. Only a few seconds ago, anyone would have looked at Carl and swore up and down that he would be spending the rest of his evening paralytic, rendered unconscious from the drink and possibly chocking to death on his own vomit but now Carl moved as steady as panther. Opening the driver's side, Carl climbed behind the wheel. Dennis was still mumbling about Ted Bundy but was abruptly silenced when Carl elbowed him in the forehead. Opening a window to dispel Dennis's foul stench, Carl started the engine and set off back to the flat. The notion that Emily might not be there when he returned had crossed his mind. Right now she could be telling the police about him, about the contents of his fridge, leading them back to his flat and forever branding herself, "The lucky one that got away." A picture flashed through his mind. It was Emily's face on a book cover underneath the title; *Emily: The Survivor*. Her story was amazing. To be brutally attacked by one maniac only to be left for dead and end up in the clutches of a serial killer. She'd sell the story for millions. The movie of her life would win an Oscar. Carl tried to shake those ideas from his head; after all it was she that had told him how to get Dennis. But still, to a man like Carl who couldn't afford to take risks, Emily had become a huge wild card. Maybe too huge to be ignored.

Dennis wasn't given the luxury of the bed. As he regained consciousness he was tightly hog-tied and face down on the concrete floor. His hands and feet were bound tightly together out in front of his body forcing him into a fetal position from which he could not straighten out. Dennis murmured something, so Carl rolled him over with his foot.

"What did you say? Speak up?"

Dennis blinked rapidly as though trying to focus. The only light in the room was the bare bulb that was fixed on the kitchen wall behind Carl making the serial killer appear only as a looming shadow.

"What's going on?" Dennis mumbled. He began to struggle against his bonds. The look on his face amused Carl, it was the look of someone who simply couldn't for the life of them figure out why they couldn't just stand up.

"Do you know who I am, Dennis? Do you remember?"

Dennis began to fight. He made small grunting sounds as he wriggled frantically, rolling himself in useless tiny circles. He had also found his voice.

"What the fuck. Let me up you bastard. You fucking cocksucker. Let me up. You know who I am, you wanker. I'll fuckin' kill you." For all Dennis's outraged fury, it was silenced as Carl booted him in the stomach. Dennis wheezed like an emphysema sufferer and spat up a mouthful of vomit.

Carl leaned over him.

"From now on you must only answer with a yes or a no. You can cry and moan but if you make a word that isn't yes or no there will be a punishment. Do you understand?"

A tear rolled across Dennis's pale, sweaty face but he still had the look of someone who didn't quite believe this was happening.

"Yes, I—" Carl kicked him again, this time in his thigh. Dennis moaned and shuddered.

"Yes or no, remember?"

"Yes," Dennis hissed.

"You know who I am?"

"Yes."

"You know who you are?"

"Yes."

The shadow moved away from Dennis. A moment late there was the audible click of a light switch and the place was thrown into brightness. Dennis turned his head from the sudden glare, squinting his eyes.

"Now, do you know who this is, Dennis?"

Dennis tried to focus through watery vision. The light was too bright but slowly he gained clarity. Someone stood behind Carl. A small, dark haired person with a strange coloured face.

It was a ghost.

Emily, her face marked by his knuckles and fingers.

"Do you know who this is, Dennis?" Carl inquired again leaning close over his victim. He enjoyed the scatter-shot flow of emotions and questions that rippled over Dennis's face. He watched as sweat bubbled on the younger man's brow. How his red face paled to off-milk white and how the almost cartoonish way in which Dennis's jaw dropped, the tongue within a chunk of useless meat that failed to respond to its master's calling.

Emily stepped forward. Carl had given her some of his trousers to wear. They were too long, so she had rolled them up to mid-calf. She reached out to Carl, but kept her eyes on Dennis. Carl took her hand, it was cold and slightly damp but there was no tremble or quake in her fingers.

"It's okay, Emily," Carl said. "He can't do anything now."

Dennis still stared at her like she was a vengeful spirit visiting him in a nightmare. It was only when she spat in his face and he felt the warm saliva dribble down his cheek that he knew she was flesh and blood real and then he began to cry.

*

"Everything," she had said. *"Do everything to him that he did to me."*

"It's funny you like Ted Bundy. And that your name is Dennis," Carl said. "You ever hear of someone called Dennis Nilsen? Well, I'll tell you about him. He was a serial killer too, like Bundy. The difference was that Dennis Nilsen liked guys instead of women. He would pick them up at bars, take them home so he could kill them, then he would cut them up into little pieces and either burn them up or flush them down the toilet. But before all that, the first thing he'd do to them was fuck them."

Dennis, now gagged with masking tape, was bent over the bed. His arse sticking out and up. Carl popped the button and undid the zipper and pulled Dennis's trousers down. He wasn't wearing any underwear. Dennis moaned and squirmed as Carl touched his buttocks. The skin was smooth and unblemished making Carl reconsider his opinion that Dennis's teeth were his best feature. Carl moved his fingers into the crack where it was warm then dipped his middle finger into the hole. Dennis screamed with outrage and sobbed, so Carl brushed his greasy hair lightly and hushed him as he moved the other hand to Dennis's crotch. He cupped the balls and gently squeezed them then began to try and masturbate him. After a few moments, with the dick still flaccid, Carl returned his attention to Dennis's arse. He unzipped his own trousers and pulled them down, exposing his erect penis, then he lent over Dennis so he could whisper in his ear.

"You ever wondered what it's like to be a woman?" As Carl said it, he thrust his dick into Dennis who squealed with pain, snot flying from his nose, his eyes streaming with sharp tears. Dennis banged his head against the bed as if trying to knock himself out so he wouldn't have to participate in his rape but Carl grab a handful of his hair and bent him back, all the time pumping him with hard thrusts. He bit down on Dennis's shoulder and sucked at the blood that flowed into his mouth. Carl felt something tear inside Dennis and then there was a warm, wet trickling sensation. Carl looked down to see blood flowing from Dennis's hole—it made it better. The squelching sound. The flat slaps as skin smacked against skin. Carl could keep this up for hours, never climaxing, just fucking, until Dennis's arse would be nothing but chewed-up ravaged flesh.

Emily had been watching from the corner, her arms wrapped around herself. Carl turned his head to look at her, his body moving. He smiled at her, a strange glazed look in his eyes. He flicked his head, calling her closer. She hesitated for a second before approaching.

"Get on the bed and watch his face it's the best part," Carl huffed. His gaze followed her as she stepped up onto the bed, keeping her distance from Dennis, she then sat down legs crossed and stared at Dennis's face as he screamed through the gag and wept in agony. After a moment that little creased smile returned to her lips.

Eventually, after many minutes Dennis became limp, offering no resistance to what was happening to him.

"Is he awake?" Carl asked Emily, out of breath.

"Yes, he's looking at me . . . and crying." She felt no pity for Dennis.

Carl withdrew and then stripped off, discarding his clothes into a pile. His body sparkled with sweat, in places his skin was so pale maps of blue veins could be seen beneath. His penis still hard, stuck out in front of him, covered in slimy, dark blood.

He felt Emily's eyes on him as he went to the stack of suitcases. Pushing aside clothes and shoes, Carl grabbed a small black leather briefcase and then set it on the bed near Dennis who had now closed his eyes but was panting heavily.

"What now, Carl?"

"I'm going to cut him."

"You mean, cut him into bits." This was usually the conversation Carl was having with himself while he was torturing and killing. To be having these words spoken aloud to a living human being was, to him both absurd and comforting. He popped open the briefcase, revealing his collection of razors, pliers, shears, long matches, latex gloves, clamps, screwdrivers, assorted nails and screws, a small hammer and a hacksaw with the shiny, red plastic handle with a selection of blades.

"No, not that. Not yet. Just cut him. Get his attention. Make him bleed. You want to watch?"

"No," she said then paused looking at the contents of the briefcase. "I want to help."

A cut anywhere on the human body is painful but with a little knowledge of human anatomy, you can cut in places where the bleeding is minimal but the pain exquisite. Carl and Emily worked on Dennis for the next two hours. He taught her about the tender spots, between the fingers and toes, just inside the bottom lip, the groin, the inside of the upper arm, the soles of the feet, the sides of the neck, behind the ears and the eyelids. Although none of the cuts they made were as deep to be life threatening, Carl had once lost someone by sheer shock of the pain inflicted. Watching Emily get into the violence was exciting for Carl. At first she had been hesitant, but with gentle direction the fine blade of the razor became an extension of her and now they both stood back and admired their handiwork.

Back on the floor, Dennis was also naked now, stripped of his clothes, his wiry framed body and sallow skin that was plagued with freckles was raw with thin slices of the skin and bite marks that dripped blood which splattered and smeared on the ground around him. He shivered uncontrollably. Through it all he had swam in and out of consciousness, his scratched eyelids fluttering. Carl pulled him up to a sitting position and slapped him hard around the face until he was sure he was alert. Dennis's eyes darted back and forth between his two tormentors, trying to guess what was coming next. With a flick of his wrist, Carl pulled the tape from Dennis's mouth allowing the younger man to gulp in air.

"Is there something you would like to say at this point?"

Dennis nodded.

"Go ahead, but if I find what you have to say rude or upsetting I'm going to have to hurt you again."

Dennis sniffed, took a deep breath and looked at Emily.

"I'm . . . sorry." His voice wobbled with emotion and pain.

Emily seemed to take in his words. Her eyes scanned his broken body and she blinked once very slowly.

"Of course you are, Dennis, but only because all this has happened to you otherwise you wouldn't regret a thing."

As Emily watched, Carl wrapped his hands around Dennis's neck and squeezed. Spit sizzled from between the choking man's teeth as his face turned bright red. His eyes bulged in their sockets and he pissed himself and farted loudly at the same time. Carl applied his full body weight to the pressure as Dennis's body writhed and jumped like it was being randomly shocked with high voltage electricity. Just like in Emily's, the blood vessels in Dennis's eyes burst giving him the glare of a vampire as his face soon turned dark blue, almost black. His feet and hands continued to twitch for many minutes and his nose and ears dribbled out blood. In the final seconds of Dennis's life, Carl ejaculated all over him.

"You know, Emily while you were unconscious, I checked the newspapers every day to see if anyone had reported you missing."

"And what did you find?" They were sitting in Dennis's car. Carl was going to get rid of it along with Dennis's body which was in the back seat in a black plastic bag, dismembered with each individual chunk of meat wrapped in newspaper. Wrapping body parts in newspaper was Carl's thing. They wouldn't find all of him however because Carl had kept some of the juicier bits for his Sunday lunch. By that time, he would be untraceable in another city or town miles away from here.

"I didn't find anything. No one seemed to care that you had disappeared."

Outside, the world around them was white, not only had there been a frost last night but it must have snowed a little too. Ice caught the weak early morning sun and shattered it into rainbow shards of colour. It would all soon melt away without the help of a winter wind to keep the temperatures down.

"There's no-one to care, Carl. Hasn't been in a long time."

Again they were quiet for a while.

"Why didn't you kill me, Carl?" She looked at him. The bruises would be faded soon and even though little silver scars would remain she could pass for normal without the use of too much make-up. The rest of her body was another thing entirely, but Carl knew she'd deal with it.

"Honestly . . . I don't know why I didn't kill you. You could ask me every day for a decade and I still wouldn't have an answer."

She brushed the back of his hand with a finger then got out of the car. Added to her outfit, he had given her one of his old leather jackets and pair of trainers that she'd stuffed socks into the toes to make them fit. He had also given her Dennis's money.

Carl had no clue where she was going or what she was going to do, just as she didn't know anything about his future.

Leaving her on the street, Carl drove away watching her fade into the distance in the wing mirror until it seemed like she wasn't there at all.

Biographies

Alan M. Clark

Alan M. Clark grew up in Tennessee in a house full of bones and old medical books. His illustrations have appeared in books of fiction, non-fiction, textbooks, young adult fiction and children's books. Awards for his illustration work include the World Fantasy Award and four Chesley Awards. His short fiction has appeared in magazines and anthologies and five of his novels have been published. Lazy Fascist Press will release his sixth novel, *A Parliament of Crows*, in the Fall of 2012. Mr. Clark's publishing company, IFD Publishing, has released six traditional books and sixteen eBooks. He and his wife, Melody, live in Oregon. www.alanmclark.com.

Jeremy Terry

Jeremy Terry is the author of *Dreams of the Dead*, an apocalyptic horror novel available from Damnation Books as well as the author of short stories appearing in anthologies from Wicked East Press, Pill Hill Press, and Nightscape Press. He lives in the Florida Panhandle with his wife, three sons, and Great Dane named Max. You can follow him on the web at www.facebook.com/jeremyterrywrites and http://sites.google.com/site/jterrywrites/.

Gene O'Neill

Gene O'Neill lives in the Napa Valley with his wife, Kay, a

retired primary grade teacher at St. Helena Elementary School. They have been married for 40 plus years; their grown children, Gavin and Kay Dee, live in Oakland and Solana Beach. Gene has two degrees, neither having anything to do with writing (or much of anything else). At one time or another he has been a college basketball player, an amateur boxer, a Marine, carried mail, worked on seismic crews exploring for oil, been a Right-of-Way Agent (appraised, acquired, condemned, and managed real property to build the interstate highway system around Sacramento), been a contract specialist for AAFES (contracting to bring private services like barbers, cleaners, and beauty parlors onto military bases), and vice president of a small manufacturing plant. Gene describes his employment background as "rich, varied, and colorful." His brother-in-law, the president of the above manufacturing plant, describes Gene as more of a "disgruntled ne'er-do-well."

Since surviving the Clarion Writers' Workshop in 1979, Gene has seen over 120 of his stories published, perhaps most notably: two in the *Twilight Zone Magazine*, six in *The Magazine of Fantasy & Science Fiction*, two in *Pulpsmith*, four in *Science Fiction Age*, three in *Cemetery Dance*, and many in specialized publications like *Dragon* and *Starshore*, with numerous anthology placements, including *Borderlands 5* and *Dead End: City Limits*. Stories have been reprinted in France, Spain, and Russia. A few of his past stories have garnered Nebula and Stoker recommendations, including "Balance," a short story Stoker finalist in 2007, and *The Confessions of St. Zach*, a Stoker finalist in the long fiction category in 2009. *Doc Good's Traveling Show* was a long fiction Stoker finalist in 2010 and *Taste of Tenderloin* won that year for collection. Some of these stories have been collected in *Ghosts, Spirits, Computers and World Machines*, *The Grand Struggle*, and *Taste of Tenderloin*, which also garnered a 2009 starred review in Publishers Weekly. Upcoming are two collections in 2011/2012: *Dance of the Blue Lady and Other Stories* and *In Dark Corners*.

His novels include, *The Burden of Indigo*, *Collected Tales of the Baja Express*, *Shadow of the Dark Angel*, *Deathflash*, *Lost Tribe*, and the recently completed *Not Fade Away*. All of these novels and the two forthcoming collections have been/will be released as s/l HBs in, 2011 and 2012 along with the Cal Wild series in 2012/13. Also just released are two novellas, *Rusting Chickens* from Dark Regions Press and *Double Jack* from Sideshow Press. SSP will also release a Cal Wild chapbook, *Chronicles of the Double Sparrow* in 2012 sometime. Thunderstorm Books will release a novella, *Operation Rhinoceros Hornbill*, in October 2012.

Gene writes full time now, currently putting the finishes touches on the Cal Wild trilogy and beginning a series of promised short stories (novelettes).

Savannah

Carol MacAllister is widely published in trade paperbacks, small press and online for over twenty years in short story horror, dark fantasy, non-fiction and poetry. Mostly recently, *The Call of Lovecraft*. She is past officer of the GSHW, member of SIC-CNJ, AWP, HWA, and holds an MFA in Creative Writing and an MFA in Fine Arts. Her work has won numerous awards and competitions. She recently completed an historical novel, *God Only Watches*, a sci-fi UFO novella, *Mayan Calendar Reveal*, and is finishing a collection of threaded dark fantasy stories—*Blackmoor Tales*. She has successfully edited and published four collections of others' works.

Allen Dusk

Allen Dusk is the author of the gritty, urban horror novel

Shady Palms and numerous other short stories. He lives in San Diego, CA with his wife and daughter. Other than writing, his favorite pastimes include photography, geocaching, watching old horror movies, and researching supernatural folklore. Curious readers may visit www.allendusk.com for more information.

John Claude Smith

John Claude Smith has published over 60 short stories, 8 poems and 1,100 music journalism pieces. His first collection, released late 2011, is entitled, *The Dark is Light Enough for Me*. He is currently working on a second collection while shopping around his novel, *The Wilderness Within*. Under a former pseudonym—John Kiel Alexander—his story, "The Sunglasses Girl", was published in the first *Peep Show* anthology. He splits time between the San Francisco Bay Area and Rome, Italy.

Eric Red

Eric Red is a Los Angeles based motion picture screenwriter, director and author. His original scripts include *The Hitcher* for TriStar, *Near Dark* for De Laurentiis Entertainment Group, *Blue Steel* for MGM and the western *The Last Outlaw* for HBO. He directed and wrote the crime film *Cohen and Tate* for Hemdale, *Body Parts* for Paramount, *Undertow* for Showtime, *Bad Moon* for Warner Bros. and the ghost story *100 Feet* for Grand Illusions Entertainment. He created and wrote the Sci-Fi/Horror comic series and graphic novel *Containment* for IDW Publishing. Eric's recent published horror and suspense short stories include "The Buzzard" in *Weird Tales* magazine, "Little Nasties" in *Shroud* magazine, "In the Mix" in *Dark Delicacies III: Haunted* anthology and "Past Due" in

Mulholland Books' Popcorn Fiction. His first novel, a dark coming-of-age tale about teenagers called *Don't Stand So Close*, is published by SST Publications.

Florence Ann Marlowe

Florence Ann Marlowe is a former news anchor for WRNJ in Hackettstown, New Jersey. After years of writing as a news reporter, she published her first short Horror Fiction story in 2008. Florence has been published by *Macabre Cadaver*, *Demon Minds*, *Pseudopod*, *69 Flavors of Paranoia*, *Fantastic Horror*, *Death Head Grin* and *Wiley Writers* ezine. Her short story "Peanuts Inside" was published in the anthology, *Reflux* last year. She's currently working on her first novel, a combination of *Ghost Hunters*, *Ghost Whisperer* and *Harry Potter*. Florence lives in the Pine Barrens of southern New Jersey in the same neighborhood where the Jersey Devil was born. Rumor has it, he lives next door.

Terry "Horns" Erwin

HORNS writes from his birthplace haunt on the urban outskirts of downtown Cincinnati, Ohio. He slithered into the world of literary horror in 1999. From this genre of darkness, he's written the slasher novel *Chophouse*, which celebrated scream queen Linnea Quigley (*The Return of the Living Dead*) declared: "CHOPHOUSE makes me scream!" His first published work is featured in the anthology *Cold Storage*, and includes an introduction by famed horror writer Graham Masterton. His many short stories over the years have appeared both online and in print. His next slasher novels, *Stationhouse No. 1* and *Chophouse 2* are set to be released. In his real life, he's a busy writer. And in his pretend life, he's a certified personal trainer, a security officer, and a down-to-earth higher animal. ~ http://trryerwin.wix.com/horns.

Walter Jarvis

Walter Jarvis lives in Los Angeles, California but grew up in Central Texas which is the setting for his story. He has been a publisher, editor, teacher and now sells health insurance over the Internet. He is married and has two adult children. His first novel, *The Fleshing*, will be published later this year by Post Mortem Press.

Walt Hicks

Walt is author of *DeathGrip: the Collection*, co-author of *Exit the Light* with Horns, and numerous small press-published short stories, including the recent short "Coda" in the *Dark Light* anthology. Owner/operator of the now-defunct small press HellBound Books Publishing, Walt edited and published several anthologies, along with well-received novels by Randy Chandler and Tim Curran, as well as a screenplay and limited edition collection of stories, poetry and artwork by the legendary William F. Nolan. Walt is a veteran of the United States Navy and now resides in Florida.

Owen Z. Burnett

Owen Z. Burnett is some asshole who lives in Pennsylvania. He is in his final year of college where he is obtaining a writing degree. His work has been featured in a slew of online and print magazines, including *MicroHorror*, *Flashes in the Dark*, *Dark Eclipse*, *Broken Teeth of the Counterculture*, *Eclectic Flash* and others. He normally has his work published under an alternative name. He is currently working on a novel entitled *Plush* and spends his free time avoiding girls named Tina and absorbing schlock.

Wayne C. Rogers

Wayne C. Rogers, a casino worker in Las Vegas, is the author of the erotic/horror novel, *The House of Blood.* He has written dozens of horror and suspense short stories, some of which have recently appeared in the paperback anthologies, *I'll Never Go Away* and *Grindhouse.* Mr. Rogers is also the writer of four screenplays and is currently at work on two others. As he's fond of saying, "Too much to write and not enough time to do it."

Deb Eskie

Deb Eskie is a resident of Somerville, MA and has a M.Ed. in creative arts education. With a background in women's studies, her focus as a writer is to expose the woman's experience through unsettling tales that highlight the dilemma of sexual repression and oppression. By combining the genres of feminist and horror fiction she aims to not only disturb readers, but deliver a message that is informative and thought provoking.

In 2005 Deb's play, *Tell Me About Love*, was featured in the Provincetown Playwrights' Festival. She has been featured in online magazines such as *Deadman's Tome, Bad Moon Rising, Death Head Grin,* and *69 Flavors of Paranoia.* Deb has also had a number of short stories published through Pill Hill Press, Post Mortem Press, and Cruentus Libri Press.

Mark Zirbel

Mark Zirbel lives and writes in Milwaukee, Wisconsin. His horror fiction has appeared in numerous magazines and anthologies, such as *Redsine #9; Peep Show #4; Bare Bone #10; Chimeraworld #4; Cthulhu Sex Magazine; Peep Show, Volume 1; Book of Shadows, Volume 1; DeathGrip: Exit Laughing; Cthulhu Unbound, Volume 2; Dead Bait;* and *Morpheus Tales: The Best Weird Fiction, Volume 1.* Mark's story "Bags" received an honorable mention in the 20th edition of *The Year's Best Fantasy and Horror,* published by St. Martin's Press.

Vi Reaper

Vi Reaper first got interested in all things horror through her father who always told her about the classic horror films and how they used to scare him as a kid. As she was too young to be allowed into the cinema to watch horror films, her father would instead rent them and let her watch them that way. Add to that her late grandmother who would provide Vi with as many books as she could afford and never complained that the books Vi always wanted to read were either horror or true crime. Vi's main influences are Edward Lee and Wrath James White, both writers who never shy from the nasty and make horror what it should be; horrific. This is her first published story. This is for her grandmother.

Paul Fry

Paul Fry was born in Birmingham, England in 1971. Ever since he read *The Cellar* by Richard Laymon he has always loved horror stories. It was because of his love of Richard Laymon's books that he got into writing and editing. The first book he edited was an anthology based on the undead called *Cold Storage*, back in 2000, which included an introduction written by the legendary Graham Masterton. Then in 2001 he created, edited and published *Peep Show* erotic horror magazine, which ran until 2003. In 2004 he edited and published *Peep Show, Volume 1*, the first erotic horror anthology which took over from the magazine. He then edited a zombie anthology called *Cold Flesh*, which was published in 2005 by US publisher, HellBound Books. He has recently published the debut thriller novel, *Don't Stand So Close* from motion picture screenwriter (*The Hitcher* and *Near Dark*) and director, Eric Red. Paul is currently working on the first issue of his new horror magazine, *Tales of Obscenity*, which is due to be published March/April 2013. Please visit talesofobscenity.sstpublications.co.uk for more information about the magazine and to subscribe.

ThrillerFest VIII

july 10-13, 2013
grand hyatt - nyc

ANNE RICE
2013 ThrillerMaster

Spotlight Authors include:
MICHAEL CONNELLY - T. JEFFERSON PARKER - MICHAEL PALMER

Events include:

ThrillerFest - CraftFest
AgentFest

Register for ThrillerFest VIII at:
www.thrillerfest.com

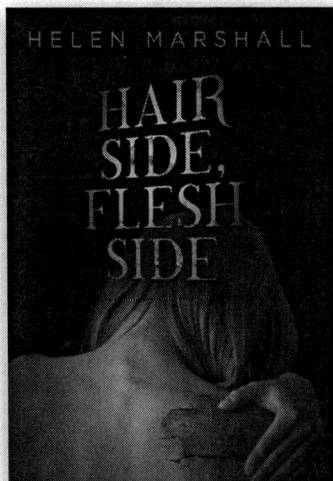

"A master of the macabre!"
—Stephen King

the circle

the circle the circle the circle the circle the circle the circle the circle

Bentley Little

PAPERBACK PARADE

THE DARKEST PART OF THE WOODS

THE INHABITANT OF THE LAKE & other unwelcome tenants

JUST BEHIND YOU

CREATURES OF THE POOL

RAMSEY CAMPBELL

RAMSEY CAMPBELL

RAMSEY CAMPBELL

CAMPBELL

SECRET STORY

THE SEVEN DAYS OF CAIN

THE OVERNIGHT

TOLD BY THE DEAD

RAMSEY CAMPBELL

RAMSEY CAMPBELL

CAMPBELL

DIP

RAMSEY CAMPBELL

www.pspublishing.co.uk

www.hufkens2000.be

MARCH / APRIL 2013

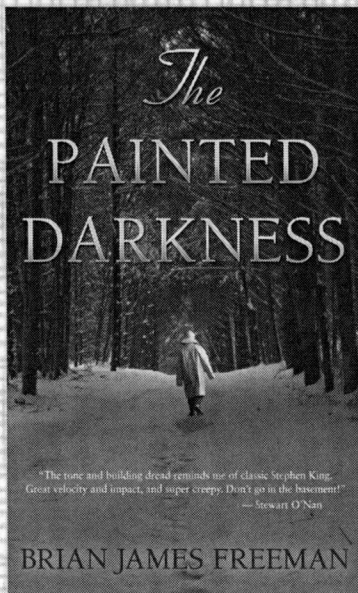

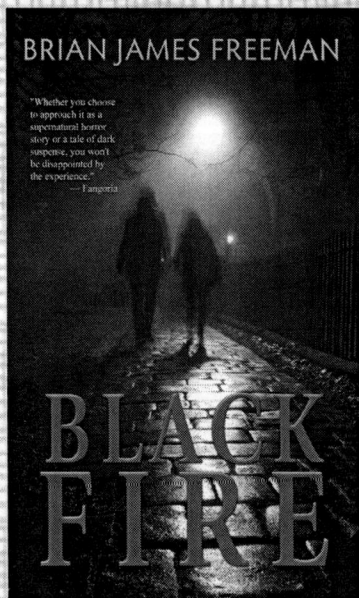

Imagination Fully Dilated Publishing
is dedicated to presenting works
of fiction that reflect the glorious
and terrifying nature of life itself.
Our ebooks bend the mind, tickle
the heart, revive the child within,
or engage the inner sleuth. Our
authors include award-winning
writers like Elizabeth Engstrom,
Alan M Clark, Eric M. Witchey,
Mitch Luckett and F. Paul Wilson.

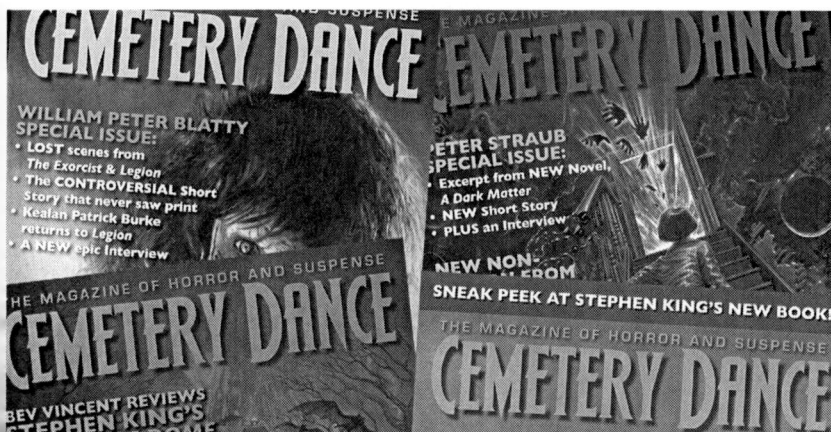